Captain of the Tides
Gunner Morgan

Captain of the Tides
Gunner Morgan

Charles D. Morgan
With Jacque Hillman

High Praise for

Captain of the Tides Gunner Morgan

As a Marine and avid reader of all things military, it was a real thrill for me to discover a real-life US Navy hero, "Gunner" Morgan, in the historic novel *Captain of the Tides Gunner Morgan.* Enlisting on the New Orleans docks in 1882, his first ship was the USS *Kearsarge,* famous for sinking the CSS *Alabama* off Cherbourg, a fitting start to a stellar career spanning four wars. Working his way from the galley to the gun deck, he became an expert on naval gunnery, earning the title of "The Man Behind the Gun." Gunner found additional fame as the lead diver during recovery operations after the explosion on the USS *Maine* in Havana harbor. From his reports on the likely cause of the sinking, he was called "The Man Who Started the Spanish-American War."

A pioneer "Mustang" (enlisted to officer), he was among the first from the ranks promoted to officer amid a nationwide controversy as hidebound "ring knockers," Academy graduates, tried to prevent the elevation of non-Academy graduates to officer status. He worked with Thomas Edison on Navy inventions and nearly died in an explosion. In the business world, he helped start Pan American Airways and married the daughter of a multimillionaire sugar baron.

Although he came to life with the vivid writing in the book, I wish I could have met Gunner Morgan during his lifetime. The co-authors—Charles Morgan, his grandson, and Jacque Hillman—swept me into Gunner's life from his early days growing up in New Orleans to walking the quiet streets of Somerville, Tennessee; they led me down history's paths through the characters who actually lived it. I highly recommend this book to anyone interested in military history, particularly naval.

—Lt. Gen. John "Glad" Castellaw, USMC (Retired)

This captivating story of the life and remarkable achievements of "Gunner" Morgan grabs hold of the reader from the first to the last word and won't let go. It's easy to become caught up as he enlists in the Navy and, from the start, is determined to become the best sailor he could be—as a gunner; as a diver; as a leader and mentor for other sailors; and as a respected advisor to his Navy leaders. His courage under fire and in dangerous situations is the stuff of heroes. The fact that he was among the first six enlisted sailors to be promoted to officer rank is telling of his reputation throughout the Navy. This is a story well written and worth reading.

—Maj. Gen. Maurice Edmonds, US Army (Retired)

Captain of the Tides Gunner Morgan is written from the first-person point of view. Here we read Gunner Morgan narrate his humble beginnings and rise to fame. The writing style of Morgan and Hillman has resurrected the famous Gunner, as he seems to leap right out of the page. . . . Gunner's story will grab you, and if it does not inspire you, then no story ever will.

—Readers Favorite reviewer Vincent Dublado

Captain of the Tides Gunner Morgan by Charles D. Morgan and Jacque Hillman is the biography of a man living at the right time, in the right place, with the drive, talent, and contacts to achieve his destiny. A historic novel seen through the eyes of Navy Gunner Charles Morgan, *Captain of the Tides* is a story of Morgan's life from the days before the Spanish-American War until his death at ninety-four.

I was fascinated with *Captain of the Tides Gunner Morgan. . . .* The personal letters, original news clips, photos, and other documents left to Charles D. Morgan by his grandfather, Gunner Morgan, ensure a book that is historically informative, readable, and impressive.

—Readers Favorite reviewer Clabe Polk

Library of Congress Cataloging-in-Publication Data

ISBN: 978-1-7333626-7-2

Printed and bound in the United States of America by Ingram Lightning Source

First edition

Cover design and illustrations: Wanda Stanfill

Editing, layout, and design: Jacque Hillman and Katie Gould

The HillHelen Group LLC
127 Fairmont Ave.
Jackson, TN 38301
hillhelengroup@gmail.com

This book is dedicated to the memory of those who lost their lives on the USS *Maine* on February 15, 1898, in Havana Harbor, and to my grandfather, Charles "Gunner" Morgan, who served in the US Navy for more than thirty years, in peacetime and in war. *Captain of the Tides Gunner Morgan* also honors the men and women who serve in our military at home and abroad.

Acknowledgments

For forty years, I've held onto the documents, scrapbooks, and letters in my grandfather's sea chest in hopes of writing a book about Charles "Gunner" Morgan's fascinating life.

Then I asked my lifelong friend, Jacque Hillman, a writer, editor, and publisher, to join me in this project. As we researched Gunner, we found an endless string of new facts and data.

Many thanks to historian Tom Hambright, of the Monroe County Library in Key West, Florida, who shared documents from his own research on Gunner. Hambright also served twenty-one years in the Navy and retired as a lieutenant commander.

Thanks also to Doug Miller, of the Pan Am Historical Foundation, who shared more information about the early history of Pan American Airways. I'm grateful for your continuing support as we wrote that chapter of Gunner's life.

We appreciate Commander Tom O'Bryant, USN (retired), and Commander Debbie O'Bryant, USN (retired) of Cedar Grove, Tennessee, for reading through Gunner Morgan's Navy records and explaining some contents.

Many thanks to our beta readers, Mary Jo Middlebrooks of Jackson, Tennessee; Frances Duquette Davis of Spartanburg, South Carolina; Primrose Bailey of Phoenix, Arizona; and Edward Cohen of Vilcabamba, Ecuador. You kept us straight when we needed it.

I want to thank my brother Jerry L. Morgan and cousin Jerry Teresi for providing important details about Gunner Morgan.

We are grateful to those who wrote testimonials or reviews: Lieutenant General John Castellaw, USMC (retired); Major General Maurice Edmonds, US Army (retired); and our other reviewers.

Finally, thank you to my wife, Paula, who made me laugh when I needed it, has offered wise counsel, and supported me in my lifelong quest to write this book about my grandfather.

You have all helped me make this tribute to Charles "Gunner" Morgan worthy of his life and memory.

Contents

Photo courtesy of the Morgan family

On February 1, 1907, Gunner Morgan was photographed as he looked over the broken propeller of the US torpedo boat destroyer *Hopkins* at the US Naval Station at Key West, Florida.

Prologue

Charles "Gunner" Morgan was my grandfather. I started researching him because I grew up hearing stories of his strange and interesting life. Born in 1865, the year the Civil War ended, he lived in a different time, a different world. His amazing life from age seventeen to ninety-three is centered on the US Navy, Cuba, and Key West.

His world, of which I knew little, has been revealed through the vast resources of the internet and thousands of newspaper articles that he accumulated. I carried those printed reports with me for more than forty-five years, desperately wanting to tell his story. I have his 1881 scrapbook, his passport, his lucky rabbit's foot, his pardon from President Theodore Roosevelt, and a copy of a personal letter from Thomas Edison, among other documents.

Gunner's documents take us through his life growing up in New Orleans in the 1870s, when the family name was Morgani and later changed to Morgan, and four wars: the Spanish-American War, the Russo-Japanese War of 1904-1905, World War I, and World War II. Along the way, he was among the first six enlisted men in the Navy to be promoted to officer, worked with Edison on naval inventions, and experienced romance, true love, heartache, secret naval missions, national fame, extreme wealth, and controversy from the highest levels of the US Navy. From 1898 through the early 1900s, he was America's common-man hero, known as "The Man Behind the Gun."

Later in life, he married the daughter of Jerry Warren, an American millionaire and sugar plantation owner known as "The Sugar King of Havana" with homes in Havana, Key West, and New York City, and interacted with Havana's elite. Gunner worked for Henry Flagler's Florida East Coast Railway to Key West and for Pan American Airways from 1927 to 1937 in Cuba and South America, and he raised his family in Havana and Key West.

I was eight years old in 1956 when my grandfather came to live with us in Somerville, Tennessee. We called him Cap, short for Captain. I often wondered where he had been all my life. Every day, at ninety-two years of age, he donned a white suit, tie, and white straw hat and walked the two miles to town and back. He liked to sit with his friends in the rockers in front of the Reliable Furniture Store. I was amazed when I learned he always pinned a fifty-dollar bill, a significant amount in 1956, to the inside of his undershirt.

He died at the age of ninety-three and was honored with a full military burial. I doubt that many people in Somerville knew how wonderful and intriguing his life was.

This book is written as a historical novel because several pages of his life are unclear due to some family letters missing from his storage box and other documents that are too faded and torn to read completely. I have written this book, *Captain of the Tides Gunner Morgan*, with my childhood friend and an award-winning author, Jacque Armstrong Hillman.

Illustration by Wanda Stanfill

Charles Morgan and his brother Joseph look down the street in New Orleans.

Illustration by Wanda Stanfill

The Morganis sit on their front porch in New Orleans.

"It is a happy talent to know how to play."
Ralph Waldo Emerson

Chapter One

Spaghetti, Baseball, and the Sea

When I reached the steps at Navy quarters, I concentrated on my right foot hitting one step, then my left foot hitting the next step, then my right again, wincing as sweat dripped on my raw skin. The hall stretched longer as I walked, my footsteps echoing in my head.

Pulling off my seaman's dungarees and blouse when I reached my room, I grabbed clean, dry skivvies from my bag and, halfway clothed, I lay back on the cotton sheet, wincing again as my skin touched it. Hours of saltwater, a leaky dive suit, and sweat do a mean job. Washing in rainwater from barrels set out for us divers by the wharf helped.

I shut my eyes, but I saw their faces, the dead men who floated upward from the USS *Maine*'s wreck or surprised me as I dropped a level into the depths. Diving for hours in Havana Harbor, my team and I were surrounded. Most of the crew of the *Maine* had died a day earlier, on February 15, 1898, yet they would live in our minds forever.

The knock on the door delivered me.

"Gunner, it's W. S.," came the soft drawl. "You willing to talk?"

I swung my legs over the side of the bed. My seaman friend, now head of the *New York Herald*'s Havana bureau, leaned on the doorframe, wearing a wrinkled suit that had seen better days. His eyes were kind, and I needed kindness from a friend.

"Certainly, W. S., come on in. You're better company than the dead, anyway."

He straddled the cane chair beside my bed. "You look like hell, Gunner," he said, "and that's a fact. We took a boat toward the wreck, but the Navy launch turned us back. I heard it's really bad, bodies floating everywhere."

"I hope I never see anything like it again," I admitted.

"I heard one of your guys talking about the way the plates were blown," he said. "Sounds like a mine to me, unless you tell me otherwise." His eyes were sharp with interest, yet he would not push too hard.

"W. S., I can't tell you anything about it," I said. "I will testify as the chief diver at the naval board of inquiry."

W. S. sighed, closing his eyes briefly. "To be honest, I heard some of the other divers talking amongst themselves down on the wharf. They don't know me. I know what the consensus is. I had hoped to add your name to my story."

"Leave me out of it," I said, lifting my eyes to his.

W. S. commiserated with me over my raw skin and fatigue. We shared a few lighter thoughts, and then he left.

I became "The Man Who Started the Spanish-American War," due to his fine reporting in the *New York Herald*. That was a long time ago, and W. S. and I remained friends.

We never know what life may hold for us. When I was a boy in New Orleans in 1870, my days were full of playing in the streets, eating good Italian food, and going to church.

Early years in New Orleans

My first memories are of the garden in our courtyard and the sound of water in the fountain. I used to sail paper boats there, pushing them around until they absorbed too much water and disintegrated.

My mother helped me after I tripped on the uneven cobblestones and scraped my knee. She washed and bandaged it, both scolding and soothing me as she did. I was proud to brag about my injury later to the other boys.

My brother Joseph and I raced around our streets with my black dog, named Sailor because he liked to jump into the canal and swim. We found every puddle after heavy rains so we could scuff our feet through the water, even knowing our mother would swat us.

We played in the streets and made plenty of noise. Most of the time there was much laughter, fun, and music. The smell of fresh bread baking, garlic and tomatoes bubbling on the stove . . . spaghetti, sausage—ah, my mother's sausage!

In the middle of those sweet memories, there is another. I was perhaps five years old when I recall my father coming in, a knock on our door. The priest's voice spoke quietly. Then my father's voice answered. The raised voices speared the night, and the boyish dreams I had in my fog of sleepiness rushed away.

People on our street were getting sick from yellow fever. Bonfires were lit, sending clouds of smoke roiling, and flames danced into the sky. Then we would be shut inside the house. It was hot when our mother was afraid to open the shutters and let the wind blow through the house. And the burning pine tar reeked. It was hard to take a breath without coughing if the wind was right. Some of the old ones crossed themselves and muttered about hell and Satan.

My brother Joseph and I, along with my friend Albert Laporte, were the lucky ones—no sickness wrapped its coils around us. I learned early to slide through the back window to meet Albert around the corner at our hideout underneath the back steps of the church. It was cool there when we met to plan whatever activities we could devise to fill our days.

By the time I was ten years old, my father and the other men were talking about Charles Mason, who was the first New Orleans baseball player to sign with the Philadelphia Centennials of the National Association. His name and photograph were often in the New Orleans newspaper.

We knew that was a grand thing to be—in the newspaper, a baseball star. If Charles Mason from New Orleans could become famous, then so could we! Travel the world, play baseball, no school, no work. The world is simple when you're ten.

I don't know who first ran to the park next to the church and found a stick to hit rocks. It may have been Albert, but I grabbed the stick, then Joseph, and we stood there tussling over it and laughing. The other boys saw us and ran to get into the middle of our fun.

We could zing those rocks off the church wall and run bases using the trees and bricks. After the rocks pinged off the wall close to the windows too many times, our priest bought us a baseball and bat and moved us to the vacant lot next to the church cemetery. Father Thomas said the departed souls wouldn't mind our playing. He taught us some rules of the game.

So many boys came that Father Thomas created a church league. He told us, "You'll learn to play, to be honest, to forgive, and to compete, all good qualities in a young man. There'll be no cursing, no cheating." He enjoyed it as much as we did. He ran fast, even in his priest's cassock.

It was joyous to hear the crack of the bat, to run hard around the bases, and to catch the ball—though it hurt your hands. They toughened soon enough. Mother worried over my bruises and cuts, washed my hands, and wanted to put on something to soothe them. No, I needed tough hands, I said.

"You can't catch a ball or raise a sail with soft hands, Mother," I told her.

Those scrapes on my legs from learning to slide into base were rough. You had to hit it right or you landed on your knee and skidded with your skin peeling off. You had to hit on your side. We're lucky no one broke a leg or an ankle. The mothers in the neighborhood created a plan to save our trousers. We dressed to play baseball in uniforms hand-stitched by our mothers.

Father Thomas told me I was good. "You keep on practicing," he said. "No telling where you might go playing baseball."

I'm certain he didn't mean to prophesy, yet he did. Fate came my way with sweat on a baseball field and good hands to catch and throw a baseball.

My brother Joseph punched me hard in my arm after we finished the game and snickered, "You're good, he says. No telling where you might go! Mother will tell you where you might go. So will Father."

Father knew where we were. Everyone on our street knew where we played ball. I'm sure our priest told our parents that we were learning moral principles and a great sport as well. Since it was true, they let us play, and the games were set on days when we weren't expected to be in school or at work. It was a good time, a respite from the pall of yellow fever.

I remember holding my sister Nina's hand when we went to church. She had long, dark hair and wore a blue or red ribbon in it. She stayed at home to help Mother in the kitchen. Later, she got sick, and I just saw her in the bed from the doorway. Both my mother and father were sitting beside her, and Sister Maria was bathing Nina's forehead with wet cloths. We weren't allowed to get too close to Nina. And then she was gone to heaven. I remember the incense at the church, the chanted prayers, and my mother's tears.

My brother Vincent was born and died in the same year. I held him a few times. I could hardly wait to hand him back to Mother so I could play on Toulouse Street. He died from the fever, too. Baptiste, another brother, chased us on his fat little legs when we went to play. We yelled for Mother and shooed him away. The fever carried him off like the others.

Yellow fever was the darkness that crept around corners, the smoke in the wind, the weeping in our household.

Then my beautiful sister Louise came into our lives and lasted.

I wondered if she was a heavenly gift since Mother had a little girl again to dress in lace and ribbons.

I grew old enough to go down to the river and watch the ships come in. Some offloaded on the muddy riverbank. Docks were being built one by one for the bigger ships.

By the time I was twelve, I could sail a boat better than most, fish over the side, and bring a nice catch home to Mother. In contrast with the heat of summer and the heavy, sweet scent of honeysuckle, there was a cleanness in the sea air and the coolness of the water.

I liked diving down deep, gathering oysters or finding shells, and floating on my back in the water, gazing at the blue sky so bright and rich that it filled my mind.

My brother and I liked to race each other, running down the street, and I usually won.

We didn't allow Louise on these excursions, of course, not that I think she wanted to come. By the time she was nine, she could roll and cook pasta almost as well as Mother, and she stayed home to help in the house and the kitchen.

Down on the pier, I met Albert Laporte's grandfather, Mr. Reynaldo Laporte, who was carving wood into detailed ships. I watched him for hours, the way his knife sliced gently into the wood and brought forth this creation of a mast, a bow, that it seemed could sail the waves.

If we had a day off from chores, we could while away the time watching the big ships sail into view and drop anchor.

We liked to follow some of the sailors when they came ashore to hunt for good food and drink. Some chased us off; most were kind, indulging our curiosity and answering questions. Seaman Ellis of the cruiser USS *New Orleans* said that I reminded him of his own son back in New Jersey. After his dinner, he'd sit outside on the low wall surrounding the inn and speak to me of sailing the seas.

I always felt then—and now I know—that he told true stories of how a sailor could stand on the bow and watch the fish jump through rolling waves one day, and the next day he'd have to tie himself to a safety line so he wouldn't go overboard when Mother Nature decided to toss wailing banshee winds, and waves the size of buildings, at the ship.

My father, who had no desire to sail, shook his head over my early love of the sea.

By then, it was expected that if we were not in school learning from the nuns, we were working for the family. I liked school more than Joseph did. I was good with languages and math. Joseph had to help Father in the store. The Morganis were importers. Father's shop was filled with fabrics from Europe on one side, and through the doorway to the other side came the scents of herbs, spices, and oils. He could mix a fragrant perfume for the ladies of New Orleans or create an oil with delicate herbs. The ladies liked to create their own names for their perfumes and oils, and Father would carefully write a tag for each one.

There was too much scent for me. I preferred the smell of salt on the sea air, so I went to the pier to buy fresh fish for Mother. Then I would stay to watch the ships leaving the harbor. I'd drop off the fish, then buy the sausage Mother wanted from the corner butcher. She knew I wasn't going to fit into Morgani's Fine Imports, so she gave me duties that kept me moving.

I owe Mother a debt of gratitude for recognizing early in my life that I would never fit within the confines of a store. Young men often discover their mothers are the best friends they will ever have.

Illustration by Wanda Stanfill

Young Gunner Morgan, his brother Joseph, and friend Albert Laporte go fishing from a pirogue in Louisiana.

"They that go down to the sea in ships, that do business
in great waters, these see the works of the Lord
and his wonders in the deep."
Psalm 107:23-24

Chapter Two

Troubled Waters

When the fragrance of Mother's fresh bread and hot sausage wafted through the house, and I heard my father's deep voice calling for coffee, I would grab my clothes for the new day and all that it promised.

At thirteen, I was skinny. My mother said I ate every meal as though ancient marauders were coming through the hills of Italy, and she had handed me my last plate of food forever.

I said, "*La mia cara madre dolce*, you love me because I love your cooking!"

Then, in a torrent of Italian, she would tell Joseph and me to wash our hands, sit down, eat like young gentlemen instead of heathens, and finish properly before we left the table.

Father began every morning with a prayer asking the saints and angels to watch over us and bless us throughout the day. "And may our business be good today so we can tithe and honor our Lord," he finished daily.

It is always good to have God, angels, and saints standing with you. I believed that then, and I believe it today.

Saturdays were meant for fishing. We would snatch wrapped crackers, cheese, a roll of sausage, and canteens to head for the river. Joseph and I kept cane poles and a net next to the back alley gate, although it was easy enough to cut cane down by the bayou. We had a five-gallon feed bucket that we used for both bait and the fish we caught until we got home to clean our catch for supper.

We liked to go early in the day. It was best. Even then we knew, as Italians, to stay away from the roving white gangs. The federal soldiers had left the previous year around my twelfth birthday. When I was only nine years old, there were bands of white men fighting against the soldiers in the streets of New Orleans. My skin is white. I did not understand then why they hated the government or why we, as Catholic Italians, were targets as well.

Father sat down with us. "Stay away from the streets except those close to home until this is over," he said. "The ignorant feel powerless, and they boil with anger. This will end. I want you safe at home."

Now, from the vantage point of years, I do understand. Life is always about money, power, and who has it. Those who don't, or fear they are losing it, will fight to keep others down. Then there are always some men who are just mean. I tried to stay away from them, too.

We went to the bayou, meeting Albert on the way, and carefully uncovered our pirogue and dipped paddles into water as the gray mists began lifting from the dark water and the rising sun glimmered through the trees.

We put the first hooks into the water before it got hot. We had contests for the biggest fish, the most fish caught, and who would be the first to spot a gator. Blue cat and channel cat were the best. Sometimes we'd catch a mess of white perch or a big redfish. We took off our shirts to try to keep them clean and stuck them in an old saddlebag we'd found.

When the sun was high, we passed around the crackers,

cheese, and sausage, happy to hear seven fish flopping in the bucket. Then we leaned back and talked.

"I'll be rich someday when Father gives me the store," Joseph told us.

I laughed. "You'll be old when Father gives you the store. Don't you want to have adventures?"

"You go have adventures," he grinned, pointing his finger. "I'll be the good son, stay home, and make money. One day you'll come to me wishing you were working in our store that fills a whole block."

Albert Laporte knew he was destined to be a cobbler like his father, but he was glad of it. Antonio Laporte was opening a shoe factory. We knew the Laportes were doing well—a new factory and a new townhouse.

"I'm selling shoes; you're selling clothes, perfumes for the ladies, and spices," Albert smiled. "We need Charles to bring in the lovely ladies, like that *bella carissima* Carolina and her sister Evangeline."

"Not me," I said. "Women don't fit into my adventures."

I had just read Jules Verne's *Dick Sand: A Captain at Fifteen.* What could be better than being captured and taken into a jungle, surviving, and sailing a ship? In the book, Dick is serving on the schooner *Pilgrim*, a whaler, and when the captain and crew go hunt the whale, they are killed, leaving Dick in charge of a ship with no experienced sailors. He has five African survivors from a shipwreck they'd encountered earlier and four passengers.

"I believe I may 'go down to the sea in ships,' " I said, quoting Seaman Ellis's favorite Bible verse. "I may hunt whales or pull in giant squid. I may climb the masts."

Joseph and Albert laughed. But I had a fish on my line, a fat channel catfish, that beat both of their catches that day.

Then the rain came and, with it, yellow fever again. It didn't matter whether it was called Bronze John, Yellow Jack, or the Saffron Scourge. Yellow fever carried away the old, young, and in between. Albert's younger sister, Mariana, died, and so did his grandfather. Yellow fever seemed to be with us every time the heavy rains came. I heard one of the nuns talk about tears falling from heaven.

I tossed and turned in my bed, smelling the smoke of the fires built to kill the evil yellow fever. Someone thought the bonfires helped, so they stayed lit, even if it meant throwing furniture into the flames. The freshness of each dawn turned instead into the wagons going by with the drivers calling, "Bring out your dead!"

Funerals were held in a little chapel beside St. Louis Cemetery No. 1 so that those who died could be blessed before they were buried. No one wanted the infected bodies inside the main cathedral. Some were buried in shallow graves, so when the heavy rains came again, bodies were uncovered. The stench was unbearable.

As I listened to the prayers, I wondered how a just and loving God could let this happen to so many people. Whatever did a small baby, or a little brother or sister, do to deserve such a fate? Why did the elderly Mr. Laporte need to die, a man who sat in his chair whittling and carving beautiful ships and talking to us each day?

My mother said, "We don't question God. He knows why. It is our duty on this earth to pray for understanding."

Yet she cried many tears over the children she lost, and over those of our friends. Her dark hair, always pulled into a neat bun at the back of her neck, had white hair painted by grief threaded into its strands.

When the Saffron Scourge was at its worst, no one came shopping for frivolous ribbons or spices, and Father said our import business was struggling, along with everyone else's.

We watched as people packed wagons and left town. They locked their doors, loaded their trunks and sometimes furniture, and headed inland, away from New Orleans.

My father wanted to send me to live with Uncle Joe in Baton Rouge. Father wanted me off the streets and out of trouble. I had been leaving by the lower back window to go down to the docks and watch people load onto boats to travel the Mississippi River. Often the ship's passengers had to leave behind some of their possessions due to overcrowding. I wasn't stealing because I was raised to understand what was morally right.

One little girl with long, blonde curls tried to fight her mama and run back for her toy chest. Her father lifted her into his arms as she wailed, beat his shoulders with little fists, and drummed her heels.

"Blessed Mary, Mother of God!" he yelled. "Stop it, Jacqueline Louise! Or I will toss you into the river to be eaten by the gators!"

His wife, bawling herself, jerked at his arm. "Don't you tell her that, Alfred! She's already scared. Stop it! You hear!"

I waited in a dark corner by the warehouse. No little girl should have to give up her toys. If she was going to live, she would. Would she remember this day forever? Probably.

If they left something good behind on the dock, I would grab it and run, I thought. If I could sell something to help my family, it would be a good thing.

Thugs with knives slipped from another corner the minute the family boarded the boat. A big one with dirty, greasy, yellow hair dripping into his face squinted around and saw me hiding.

"Here now, who are you?" he whispered. "Come here, boyo. You think you can get this box? Come here and try."

The others with him began opening trunks and tossing clothes onto the wharf. They draped some lace over each other and laughed at the delicate lady things that they shouldn't be touching, items that would have value, if they weren't so stupid. One of them draped a silk ribbon over his head.

A short guy with a big belly found a silver hairbrush and slid it into his leather bag; the yellow-haired leader caught the movement and the glint of something shiny.

"What are you doin' with that?" he yelled, punching the man's arm. "We put everything in together!"

Big Belly thought he'd swing a fist. Big mistake. Yellow Hair slashed blazing fast with a knife and sliced his hand.

"Damn you!" Big Belly yelled.

About that time, the wharf guards came running around the corner of the farthest warehouse. The thieves took off cursing, leather bags slung over their shoulders, lace and ribbons trailing after them. One of the guards, at least, was young enough to run fast after them. The others huffed and puffed and stopped about a block away.

I grabbed a man's silver comb that the thieves had dropped. I felt bad about taking it. I knew it could help my family, and no one else was going to take it except another thief.

If it wasn't one gang stealing, it was another. Once I got a light slice on my arm when the thieves got into a fight over the trunks, and I thought I could slip in to grab a silver flask before it fell between the boards of the dock.

I waited and slipped into the house through my bedroom window. Father was sitting in my chair in the dark. He lit the lantern. I had washed my arm in the church fountain and packed a little moss on the cut. It wasn't much of an injury to brag about. But Father saw it.

"Charles, you've made your mother cry," he said quietly. "Did you think I wouldn't know that you were missing from your bed? The boards creaked under your footsteps. I knew the minute you were gone."

"And your brother Joseph told a lie for you. He knew you slipped from your bed. Did you think you could share a bedroom with your brother, and he sleeps so hard he wouldn't know? So he won't be leaving his work to go enjoy anything else for a while," Father said. It was one thing when he blustered and yelled, and quite another when he was quiet about it. You knew you had really done it.

"I'm sorry I made Mother cry," I said, and I meant it. She had cried so much, and she always was my champion.

That's when I was shipped upriver to Uncle Joe for several months. Uncle Joe was a good-looking man with black hair and a quiet toughness from being outside hunting and fishing at his lodge. He was always watchful. I guess that came from watching the sun rise and set, and the clouds coming over the horizon, as he figured whether Mother Nature would behave herself while he worked.

Louise stood silently next to Mother as I packed my clothes in a battered suitcase. Mother cried when I left. "You behave. Come home to me," she told me.

"*Mia madre,*" I said. "You have cried so much over me that you have surely cleansed my soul. Father Thomas said so."

She smiled and raised her handkerchief to wipe her eyes. "Then the tears are good for something!"

They thought it was safer in Baton Rouge; even so, there were still people dying of yellow fever inland.

"Why are you sending me there?" I asked.

Father was adamant, so I went.

In truth, I was glad to leave the Saffron Scourge in the streets of New Orleans, the rotting corpses above ground, and always the sounds of grief.

I worked hard for my uncle in his hunting and fishing guide business and honored my family. His big, gray cypress lodge sat back in the woods with a wide porch. My room was at the back of the house behind the kitchen. I could slip in and snag hot biscuits and honey early in the morning before the others got out of bed, and Aunt Louisa let me do it, although she'd swat at my hand with a dishcloth as she smiled at me.

On stormy days, I could listen to the rain pouring on the tin roof. Even on rainy days, there was work to be done. Fishing tackle had to be checked. The house had to be cleared for the next group of men coming to fish or hunt. The boat had to be cleaned, knives sharpened, and tackle boxes replenished.

I could work as the second in the boat heading to hunt or fish, and my uncle trusted me. Once I caught one of the hunters drinking steadily from a flask hidden in his pocket. The birds flushed from the reeds, and he grabbed for his gun, nearly shooting his friend in the process.

"You, sir, need to be careful with that gun," I said quietly, before I could think whether I should.

My uncle turned from the lead, saw what had happened, and stared coldly at the drunken hunter.

"You'll not be going out with me again, Mr. Foster," he said, "if that flask touches your lips again while you're in this boat."

Uncle Joe said later, patting my shoulder, "You are good. You keep your eye on the water and on the men in the boat. You've learned how to spot the good ones and the troublemakers. You know exactly what that swirl in the water means, whether it's fish or gator. You hear the sounds of the birds' wings as they lift."

I had learned how to shoot. Uncle Joe christened me the "sharpest shooter I ever saw to be so young." He set shooting targets in the yard and put me against some of the hunters who hired him. I don't know why I had such a clear eye and hand. I just did. Money changed hands, and most often it went into Uncle Joe's pocket.

I went to the Mississippi River docks at night and listened to the crewmen talk and to the easy creaking and rocking of boats in the water.

"I'm not going to chase you down at night," my uncle said.

"I only go to the dock, Uncle," I said. "It's fresh, clean air, and the streets are quiet. I just walk." I was never lost and felt at rest by the water.

"I know where you go and what you do and who you talk to," he said. "You know well that while most of the sailors are good men, there are those who skulk about looking for trouble. It's time for you to go home."

He said no more than that, and he patted my shoulder awkwardly.

I had learned lessons in nature about how to survive. Listening to hunters and fishermen sitting at the lodge dinner table had taught me lessons about women that would make my brother and Albert blush. I became a student of those men with easy banter who made us laugh.

Uncle Joe pressed a leather bag into my hand when I left. "Your winnings," he said.

Shooting a gun was a good way to make money. I left knowing my future was made.

I sauntered to our front door, my leather bag jingling, and I thought about tossing it onto the kitchen table. Next, I'd tell Joseph, "I don't need to work in the store."

When I opened our front door, it was to a quiet house. My mother was sick. The new baby was mewling in a bassinet in the back bedroom.

Sister Marie from the church came rustling down the hall, took my arm, and said, "Your *madre* has awakened every morning hoping you were back."

Mother looked so pale and gaunt. Louise sat in the rocker by the bed, doing cross-stitch. She saw me at the door, and her lip quivered before she looked down again.

Mother looked out her window at the blue, blue sky with a few feathery clouds floating high. She turned her head and lifted her hand to me.

"Come sit with me. Look at you," she tried to smile. "You are a foot taller. What have you been doing with your uncle?"

I sat with her and described everything I could remember. Then she fell asleep as Sister Marie placed a cool, wet cloth over her head. Louise stood slowly and touched my arm lightly as she passed by me.

I whispered, "*Mia madre,* I love you."

Joseph's dog and I sat on the front steps. The black puppy kept nuzzling my hand as if he knew I needed him. We stayed there quietly as the afternoon grew late.

Father turned the corner, walked to me, and sat beside me on the steps.

"I'm glad you're home," he said. "Your mother has gotten sick from some fish, I think. We can't seem to get her well."

He went inside the house to sit with Mother.

Sister Marie heated some stew and bread for me, and Louise

served us in the kitchen. We ate in silence for the most part, except when I asked Louise about a friend of ours. Sister Anna came in after supper to stay the night, while Sister Marie went back to the church.

Joseph came home later, when I was sitting at the kitchen table alone. I had been reading my Jules Verne book again.

He slid into the chair across from me, his dark brown eyes as serious as I'd ever seen them. "I don't think Mother is going to get better."

Each day for a week, I sat with Mother and read stories of adventure aloud, leaving only when Sister Marie changed Mother's bedsheets and washed and re-dressed her. Sister Marie fed Mother small spoonfuls of chicken broth and a little warm tea and honey. Then she took care of the baby, carefully feeding little Mathilda goat's milk.

Louise sat with the baby and changed her. I looked in once or twice at the tiny red face.

Mother's voice became a whisper as the fever squeezed her in its grip. "I love you, my son."

Joseph and Louise pressed close, and she turned her head ever so slowly from the window to look at each of us. "I love you."

Then our priest came to read Scriptures to comfort Mother as she weakened. I heard his quiet voice several mornings murmuring to her. He prayed with her almost daily. I hope it eased her soul.

Mother died two weeks after my fourteenth birthday. During her funeral, the stained glass window, lit by the sun, cast brilliant colors across the church altar. I thought it must have been angels watching over her.

After the funeral, Louise, Father, and Sister Marie greeted friends and relatives at the house. Joseph and I escaped to the bayou and rowed the pirogue to our fishing hole. We watched the gray moss drift toward the water, listened to the fish plop, and told stories about Mother. We brushed our tears away and looked fiercely at any little thing.

In September, we buried little Mathilda. Louise wept as she placed her favorite pink satin ribbon tied to a few roses on the tiny casket. Father, Joseph, and I stood with dry eyes.

Quiet blanketed the house and smothered my breath until I would race outside at daybreak for fresh air and the comforting noise of the streets.

Illustration by Wanda Stanfill

Gaetano Morgani, Gunner's father, said the Louisiana legislature—the crooks, he called them—tried several schemes to deal with the river levees, assigning the duty first to the Board of Public Works, then to a private corporation called the Louisiana Levee Company, and finally to the Board of State Engineers. Millions of tax dollars were funneled into the projects, but not much was achieved. The rains came, and the floods swamped New Orleans.

"The sea is everything. It covers seven-tenths of the terrestrial globe. Its breath is pure and healthy. It is an immense desert, where man is never lonely, for he feels life stirring on all sides."
Jules Verne

Chapter Three

Rivers Rising!

At fifteen, I caught fish for the local market, made twenty cents a day, and had the chance to take home some of my fresh catch.

By sixteen, I had a crew of three friends working for me.

The day *My Dolly* came back into harbor with a full load of fish and one of its seamen, Mick Maguire, was carried onto the dock with one leg half gone, I remember thinking, "Poor guy. That will never happen to me."

It didn't.

Man may rule or ruin the earth. Once we leave the seashore, the deep blue ocean, with its fearsome denizens, and Mother Nature's tempests will reign.

I remember Father, Mr. Laporte, the Messinas, and others talking about the river, the proposed levees, and what the government would or wouldn't do to change the river flow. They would drink their coffee and debate. Mostly, it seemed the government and politicians talked, the newspaper wrote about it, and nothing ever happened, which I thought was good for our bayous, canals, and beloved Mississippi River.

Father said the Louisiana legislature—the crooks, he called them—tried several schemes, assigning the duty first to the Board of Public Works, then to a private corporation called the Louisiana Levee Company, and finally to the Board of State Engineers. Millions of tax dollars were funneled into the projects, yet not much was achieved. Someone made money on it.

Father said the Irish had their hand in the till. Mr. Messina muttered about one or two of our Italians making their profits. I don't know. Nonetheless, levees that had been damaged during the Civil War still weren't fixed.

The New Orleans gangs were causing trouble. Once the Irish gang—well, some of the younger boys anyway—got into a warehouse, grabbed tomatoes, and lobbed them at the houses in our Italian neighborhood. They yelled that it was blood from the Italian criminals they'd kill someday.

Joseph, Albert, and I had to wipe down the walls by our front door with vinegar to clean the mess. Our eyes watered, and we smelled of it. We made big plans for what we'd do to get back at the midget redheads.

At seventeen, I wasn't an engineer, although I could have been. I understood math, angles, and trajectories for my hook to land and pull in that catfish. I was already, as my Uncle Joe said, "a fine sailor." I could quickly calculate my point of sail and tack my boat relative to the wind, and I felt I could handle almost anything.

Even those simple lessons would be good for later. Later came much more quickly than I thought it would.

"Father, I'm going to join the United States Navy. The USS *Kearsarge* is coming into harbor. They will pay me a wage," I said. "I'm going to sea."

Joseph patted my shoulder. Father shook his head sadly. Louise, at thirteen, was already a dark-haired beauty who kept the house. Father had asked our cousin Elizabeth to stay with us after her parents died. She was in her twenties, and if circumstances had been different, Father said she might have already been married and had her own household.

"She's grateful to have a home and good company for Louise," he said. "Show her respect."

And I did. Yet we were in close quarters in our house, with Elizabeth and Louise sharing a bed in their room and Joseph sleeping in the other bed in our room.

Father knew there was enough work in the store for Joseph and that mixing perfumes, or unrolling and measuring fabrics, wasn't work I would want to do.

Before I left the house, I opened my bottom drawer and grabbed the leather pouch with the silver dollars I had won for my shooting skills. I handed it to my father.

"I won these fair and square from my shooting contests at Uncle Joe's," I smiled. "They're yours now. I don't think the Navy will think much of my bringing a bag of coins on board. Use them as you see fit or give them to Joseph."

We hugged awkwardly, and I walked toward my new life.

Charley Morgan

When I signed my name on the line at the USS *Kearsarge* on January 24, 1882, I decided in that instant to drop the "i," changing my name to Morgan. I was handed two uniforms and an empty seaman's bag, and stepped to the side with another group of third-class apprentice seamen.

A big Scotsman named Skip Beveridge stood next to me in line. "Call me Skip," he said, looking over his shoulder. "You'll never get the real Scots sound of my name, 'Eyetalian' guy."

I recognized an Irishman from Irish Town who signed on when I did. He knew I was a Morgani. Why would that matter? Why should it? Because Italians can cook—like my mother. Or so he thought, nudging me as he went past.

"You're the cook," he whispered with a smirk.

When I rolled from my hammock at dawn the next day, I reported for my new duty assignment: I was a "jack of the dust."

That meant I usually had flour on my hands or face. When I was not in training on the ship, I made biscuits. And I was good. You couldn't stand in a kitchen with my *madre* and not learn something about cooking, which was easy when we were in port.

Fresh fruit, vegetables, fish—the officers ate well. The men ate satisfactory meals of baked bread and fish. They needed some basil, oregano, rosemary, more salt and pepper, and some sweet and spicy Italian sausage.

And so, I went to save the world and learned to save a skillet of fish. I thought of Dick Sand, saving a ship and her people at age fifteen, in Jules Verne's book. My copy was dog-eared on the small table next to my bed at home. And I laughed. Captain of all I surveyed! Rolling pin, flour bags, a stove, and metal trays.

While the ship took on supplies and the ship's commander, Captain Johnson, visited with New Orleans government representatives about building more docks, my new mates and I began training on board.

The days when we arose with the dawn were full of new lessons, words to learn, commands to follow, and finding out that being quick to respond was not only a lesson but a way to survive and live longer.

Every day we stayed in port, we watched twilight fall and the lights of New Orleans flicker and remind us of home so nearby. Once or twice, I heard a sniffle that quickly stopped in the night. I thought of the families hanging on to feed their children, the yellow fever, and the smoke. I was glad to be on my ship.

Late one night, Skip and I were above decks leaning on the rail. "Do you miss it?" I asked. The big Scot was always laughing heartily; still, I could see sadness behind it.

"No," he said. "My family is dead. My father brought us here for a better life. I'm ready for anything better than death." It was the only time we mentioned it.

The *Kearsarge* was nearly ready to sail. Repairs had been made to one sail and a metal plate had been rewelded.

The officers were getting anxious to go to sea. First Mate

Andrew Blackstock said we were headed to the Caribbean and Panama to show the world the might of the US Navy.

"When we sail into port, the world pays attention," he said. "We'll fire the guns in practice while we're a few miles out. You seamen might get to go ashore."

Skip and I began talking about what we would see in the Caribbean. We didn't know how much time we'd get off the ship. We thought at least a day and a night maybe.

The heavy rains began. The water began rising from up north and coming down the Mississippi. The captain brought a newspaper back onto the ship.

"The newspaper boys called the headlines on the corner," he told the first mate. "This looks to be a bad one."

I looked over his shoulder as I served the bread.

"Rivers rising!" The headline blared in giant black letters.

In Cincinnati, heavy rains began on Sunday night, February 19, 1882, and lasted for two days, causing the Ohio River to rise at a rate of two inches per hour. The newspaper boys left the streets for higher ground.

Downstream, we waited, and our time came. People were loading sandbags, which was like putting a thumb in the dike.

I thought of Uncle Joe upstream. He would be better off than most with his boats.

The captain and his officers met to discuss what our ship might do to help.

First Mate Blackstock called Skip, some Irish Town boys, and me to his cabin. "You know the canals and rivers and docks. We'll send a boat to see if we can ferry any people to safety."

The water easily broke through most of the levees, buried towns, and killed livestock. People climbed onto the roofs of their houses. In some places, the overflowing Mississippi River transformed communities into fifteen-mile-wide lakes. Yes, there were private steamboat companies, the Army Corps of Engineers, and the Quartermaster Corps rescuing some stranded by the flood.

In the streets of New Orleans, I watched a boat offload its

goods onto the second floor of a warehouse. We kept our boat going from daylight until dark for several days, saving anyone we found stranded and taking them to higher ground. We listened for the sounds of people trying to break through roofs to be rescued. We even tried to lasso horses and pull them to higher ground. Sometimes we managed to get the horses into a warehouse as well. Some panicked and went underwater.

We took some families to the upper floors of empty warehouses, where they found shelter. The images of their fearful, shocked eyes were seared into my brain, along with the cries of women and children. The Quartermaster Corps brought rations when they could. Finding fresh water was not easy. Some provided bottles of wine or ale because there was nothing else. No one wanted to drink water with dead cows floating in it. The gators were getting fat.

There is something about watching a mother's body float by with a baby in her arms that forever changes your understanding of the fickle attributes of Mother Nature, who can give life and take it away so quickly.

The Morgani's Imports business was flooded. I saw my father once on the dock. Our streets in Little Italy were passable by boat.

"We moved the goods from the bottom floor to the third floor, so we have goods to sell. But I don't know who will be buying," Father said. His eyes were worried, and he looked tired.

The plantations were flooded. Small restaurants and businesses were gone. Those who survived were working from their second and third floors. Thousands of people moved north because they had nothing left.

Joseph looked as haggard as Father did while we talked. I had only a little time. The captain had said it was time to sail. We'd done what we could.

Father said, "It will take months for us to come back from this, maybe years. Sons, I'm not certain how we will make it. If they bring in construction crews, we can still sell spices and some foods. Some families will need to replace lost clothing. We may have to barter these items for things we need if there is no money. We will figure it out."

That was the last I saw of them for two years. We wrote letters. They told me that true to Father's prediction, people coming into town to rebuild were buying in the store. Slowly, people were coming back.

As for me, I was sailing the seas and working like a sea dog. There's nothing easy about being the low man in rank, I can tell you that.

My Navy number was 817. As a third-class apprentice seaman, I was paid nine dollars and thirty cents per month. They deducted three dollars for food and thirty cents for hospital insurance.

Photo courtesy of the Morgan family

Gunner Morgan is photographed in 1890, eight years after he joined the US Navy.

"The secret of getting ahead is getting started."
Mark Twain

Chapter Four

Going to Sea

At eighteen, I was always hungry. Serving on the sea stirs dreams of hot meals, maybe a hard biscuit with warm gravy. A sailor's dreams could sometimes center on a cold biscuit or two, when we didn't heat the stove because of the ship's heavy roll in the storm.

Yet it was a good way that I started. Eventually, I delivered meals to the officers. You hear things, and if you listen carefully, you learn. They were wary of making open comments about the men on the ship when I knocked and came in with the trays. Once I heard one say, "If only they were all as good on the big gun as . . ." Or a complaint, followed by the captain's terse order, "Make him train harder."

Skip, the Scotsman, started training with me on the deck. He could toss a giant mop across the deck just so some of the cold spray would slap my back. I could work a rope so it caught his ankle and sent him thudding onto his backside.

"Morgan! Beveridge! Do you think we are sailing this ship for your entertainment?" the first mate yelled. "Do you think your playtime will save a man in rough water or when the enemy is firing upon us? You'll climb the rigging a hundred times today!"

We did it only once. I did not have to hear that particular dressing-down again. Nor did Skip. And we said nothing about our hands bleeding from the ropes later.

We learned our lessons and succumbed to the Caribbean, which calls to the sailor like a woman draped in blue silk. She's tempting. That blue, blue sea! Ah, the wind and the ship moving through the waves! Every free moment I could leave that hot kitchen below decks and go to breathe the salt air, I did.

The intense training began. When Mother Nature decided to toss storms upon our ship, and the ship was rolling deeply from one giant trough of a wave into another, everyone had an assigned duty post to keep us sailing. Being a jack of the dust meant I cooked below decks. On deck, I had work to do like every sailor on board.

I had listened to Seaman Ellis and others back in New Orleans often enough that I thought I knew the sailors' lingo. It's not the same when the commands are shouted, and the wind is high. You catch a syllable and figure out what the shout was. You'd better be quick.

We had to make certain a rope was wound perfectly. That fact could make the difference if the mast swung free in a blast of wind; a sailor might be able to duck or could be killed. A swinging mast could crack a skull. A poorly coiled rope could whip a foot and break a leg or dislocate a shoulder. Those same ropes were lifesavers when the deck was awash in a high sea.

"Did you hear what the second mate yelled?" Skip asked me one day. "I didn't. Nearly got beaned."

The first day the big guns fired, I thought we were at war. The ship vibrated.

Skip looked at me, his eyes wide and red hair askew. "Is this it, mate?" he asked. Then he grinned. "Adventures ahoy!"

"Whoever it is, we'll win the war!" I said. "We are the United States Navy!"

I believe we have a destiny—and mine was set when those guns roared over the sea. It was practice, not war. Listening to the commands fired to the men and the running feet, and feeling the ship taking the impact of the big guns' roll, inspired a voice in my soul that said, "You are meant to be here." I understood better than many new seamen that the wind, angles, and trajectory affect the range of the guns. Whenever I could, I listened and watched and found I still had much to learn.

I wanted to learn to shoot the big guns. For now, I had to learn to cook in a ship's galley.

Little Rob O'Connor, whose pride in being an Irishman was so big you had to walk two feet around him, pestered me constantly in the galley.

"Is that the most you can roll at one time? We have hungry men on board this ship! You paltry Italian, you only know how to eat noodles. What you need to eat is an Irish potato to put meat on your bones!" O'Connor said, tossing a potato at my head.

I caught the potato with the quick skill I used on the baseball field and in one motion sent it back toward his head. He wasn't as fast and took a clip to his ear.

"Look out, mate! That's some fast hands you've got," he grinned, rubbing his ear.

"Get your hands back into those slippery fish guts, Irish," I said. "That's where your hands belong, not trying to pitch a potato like a baseball."

"What do you know about playing baseball?" he laughed. "You're an 'Eyetalian.' "

"More than you do, mate, since that's you rubbing your ear," I said, smirking at him.

"Enough! Get the food ready," bellowed Second Mate John William. "The officers are hungry."

"Aye, aye, sir," I said.

Irish muttered into my ear, "The officers, begging your pardon, are always hungry."

"So are we," I reminded him.

My father and mother taught me that no man is better than another, although some will surely puff up their pomp and circumstance. A man's character shows in his actions.

And so, as we fed our officers, I saw which ones led by good example and which ones skewered the sailors under them with wisecracks about their performance. It was a weaker officer who made fun of others. My mother's wisdom about the boys in the streets of New Orleans held just as true for grown men.

I saw Seaman Harry Stonewall, who was sick with the fever, try to hide his illness. Lieutenant Alfred Dunagan accosted Harry. "You there, leaning against the gun! Get on that mast and climb it now!"

Captain Johnson happened to be coming on deck. He watched Harry struggle to begin his climb.

"A word if you please, Lieutenant Dunagan," Captain Johnson said quietly, looking Harry over and seeing the pale skin and sweat draining down his face. "Seaman, stand down."

He spoke to Lieutenant Dunagan quietly, and we didn't hear what he said.

The young officer walked over to Harry, looked him over carefully, and said, "First Mate, this man is sick. Get him below. Find someone to take his watch."

Captain Johnson expected the best and demanded it. He saw to it that the good men stayed, and though it might take some time, the poor ones were transferred. Lieutenant Dunagan was a good man, though inexperienced. He learned, and he stayed.

I watched the captain's expressions whenever he issued commands, and when he met with his officers and I served them. I watched their table manners. The way you hold your fork and knife makes a difference—no scraping your plate and no pouring hot tea into a saucer to cool it.

He noticed me watching him once, assessed me in a moment, and didn't break stride in his conversation. I wondered if I had overstepped.

Skip laughed when he realized that I was worried. "They

have much more to think about than you watching them. Are you that important now?"

I decided that he was right, and I was sinking into my own puffed-up importance, which I vowed never to do.

When we docked, Skip and I were among the lucky ones who got shore leave. The chief mate gathered us on board and gave us a talk about the women in the port that had my ears turning red. I'd heard plenty among the men—it was quiet talk in the night, not this booming voice declaring that women with certain attributes were every sailor's downfall!

"Yeah, you know what they say," he bellowed. "Women are a good man's downfall. You boys, who think you are men, keep your hands to yourself. Stay away from their huts. You could find a knife in your gizzard and your balls falling off. If you catch the sickness from playing in the swamp, you'll lose your bunk on this ship!"

"Quit grinning, Irish!" Chief yelled. "You don't know your head from your arse. God pity the woman you latch onto!"

The lush women were off limits to us. I could admire them all the same.

Skip elbowed me the first time we saw a barefoot woman with fruit in a basket on her head as she sashayed down the path. Her long, black hair hung down her back. When she turned into a shanty home, her attributes showed well in the sunshine.

"Now, we haven't seen a woman like her!" he whispered.

"It's true," I said. "And Father Thomas would tell us we're going to hell for looking! Sister Cecelia Marie would hit us both on our heads!"

The women on a street corner in New Orleans had a harder, leaner look. It was tough times at home. I heard it wasn't so at certain houses—at least, my brother claimed he knew because he'd made a backdoor delivery and gotten a peek inside.

The women's clothing in the Caribbean was simple washed cotton. Simplicity can shape a form into an ode to elegance. It was good, I guess, that the missionaries had taught the women to cover themselves. I heard the first mate bemoan the "lovely flowers that no longer bloom in our view."

As for me, I felt guilty for looking. I didn't do as well at that as I should have.

There wasn't much to do in the shantytown port. The mud streets turned into ditches in heavy rains. Pigs wallowed in the mud. The natives sat on tree stumps in their yards in the sunlight and shucked pineapples and coconuts as a few chickens clucked in the dirt.

Many houses had open sides with woven reed wall hangings. They seemed fragile, but when the storms blew in, the wind and rain blew through. The people would roll the reed hangings and sweep away the water with a handmade broom and palm fronds. The men were mostly fishermen sailing in small boats every day to bring in a fresh catch. The old men sat and mended ship sails. Boats were always waiting for caulking and repairs near the dock.

There was a beach, and we had a baseball and a bat. We'd walk down the beach to move any hidden rocks or sharp, broken shells. Our men soon gathered and broke into teams. The slant to the sea made playing baseball an interesting challenge, running from the incoming waves as the tide changed.

Skip and I joined one team, and Irish another. There was more than one Italian on the ship, and we were good. Running on sand was easy for me after running on cobblestones in New Orleans. Other city boys huffed and puffed their way around the bases.

The young native boys, barefoot and wearing cotton pants, always came to watch and cheer. I figure bringing baseball to the islands was a great gift from America. The captain had decided to buy supplies of extra baseballs and bats for each port.

A few boys knew words in English, Spanish, Portuguese, and French, and wanted to learn more English. I learned a little of each language from talking with them.

Skip and I taught them most baseball terms, pointed to items around us, and gave their English names.

"Run the bases fast," Skip said slowly, then added, grinning, "like my friend here does."

They would repeat the words slowly. If one of the boys got the phrases right, I handed him a tiny ship I had carved from pieces of driftwood I'd found. The small leather bag I tied at my waist always held a treasure to share.

Abuejo, one of the older boys, learned quickly and was the first to win a small ship. "Thank you," he said shyly, in perfect English.

When the game was over, we'd show the boys how to pitch and hit. We baseball ambassadors for America always left the boys smiling.

Our next port of call was Panama. It was not anything like I expected: the grand colonial buildings, the cobblestone roads, so many large homes behind tall walls, and elegant carriages. Between Spanish and French colonization, there was much wealth. Many native people had fled to the jungle in the early days and were replaced by African slaves.

Standing in line to buy pineapple at the market and hearing all the languages spoken around me was a heady moment. I grew to love the taste of that fresh fruit and the coconut.

After we bought supplies for the crew and officers, we sent them back by horse-drawn wagons to the ship. We strolled along, looking at the market vendors' textiles and jewelry.

"I would like to buy this cotton fabric and the silver jewelry to send to Morgani's Imports," I told Skip.

"And your pockets are full of gold and silver to buy it with?" he grinned. "If so, I hope you'll let your friends know where your treasure chest is."

"These prices are low, at least not as high as in New Orleans," I said. "No, my pockets aren't filled with gold and silver. More like they have lint and sand in them."

Still, I made lists in my leather-covered journal of what I saw because I knew one day I'd be back, and I'd have the pay to buy some fabric and silver jewelry.

A wealthy Spanish merchant arrived in his carriage with his wife, an elegant woman wearing a day gown that any woman in America would have wanted. Even from where I was standing, I could see the lace of her mantilla was delicate. Their burly driver stepped down to haggle with the vendors, who rushed from behind their tables to bring the woman whatever caught her attention.

"Quiero las botas de cuero," she demanded. They brought her soft, supple leather boots in a tiny size. *"Y quiero el cinturón de cuero."* Then the matching belt.

We leaned against a stucco wall to watch the bartering. When the merchant handed down his coins for the pieces, the native vendor moved a bit too slowly. The driver pulled out a leather sap or cudgel and whacked the man on his shoulder. The vendor hustled and quickly handed over his handcrafted leather with his head bowed.

The last of the coins were tossed at his head. The Spaniards drove on into the crowded street.

I watched the native man gather his coins and look up with hate in his eyes.

"No wonder we've been warned to hustle back to the ship if any fighting breaks out," I murmured to Skip.

He nodded. "The rich and powerful may find themselves in trouble here," he said quietly.

The great talk was about the canal the French were building that would give ships an easier route to the Pacific Ocean. In the middle of those plans were groups trying to take over the government.

Every day we remained in port, the commander went ashore and met with the diplomats at the French and Spanish embassies, and with the Panamanian government leaders. The progress on the canal was the reason. Construction under the French was slow. The United States wanted that route completed as quickly as possible, but building the canal was a treacherous undertaking.

One night, from the ship, we heard gunfire and saw fire glowing from a house in town. We were ordered on alert. Our men were on board, so we watched from a distance.

"Double the watch," Captain Johnson said. "Be alert for anything."

When daylight came, he sent two men ashore to get a report. They returned swiftly.

"Coming aboard, sir!"

"In my quarters, Lieutenant," the captain ordered.

We had the news quickly enough. Shut the captain's door and scuttlebutt will soon tell the story or a tale will be concocted. A native rebel group had attacked a Spanish compound. The well-armed Spaniards had demolished the small group of native fighters in short order.

Still, the captain said it was time to be on our way. We were well provisioned and expected in Florida, South Carolina, and New York.

"This is not our fight in Panama," the captain said to his officers assembled at breakfast. "At least, not yet."

Our destination was to be the new Navy training school in Newport, Rhode Island.

Some seamen groaned and worried about the new Navy training. Until that year, training had been on the ships. By the time we sailed along the East Coast to New York Harbor, some of my younger mates thought we'd know everything we needed to know.

"We're the best in the Navy," bragged the youngest, "Windy Little Man" Manetti, another Italian from New Orleans. He was so skinny we'd seen a gale force wind blow him over, but his safety line saved him from going overboard. Windy was only fourteen. I had been one of the oldest recruits at seventeen.

Seaman Allen Edwards from Boston had been at sea for two years. "We don't need to go to school," he vowed. "We've been through terrible storms, lost men overboard, and kept this ship going."

The first mate guffawed at both of them. Hearing the captain's command, the chief mate relayed the command to hoist sail.

Knowing that some ship's captains are better than others, I thought if they pulled some of the best ones to teach, that could be good. I planned on learning everything I could. The galley was not where I intended to stay. Every minute I could, I watched the gunners. I heard their commands and watched to see who hit their targets.

Gunner Reagan from New York was the best. I tried to be his faithful shadow.

"What are you doing here, Morgan?" he'd growl.

"Sir, I want to be prepared to fire the guns," I said.

"Don't you have biscuits to make so I can eat?" he demanded, his gray, bushy brows merging as he frowned. He was an old, weather-beaten gunner with broad hands roped in tough, leathery skin and scars everywhere, but he knew more than the other gunners did.

"The biscuits are done, sir," I said. "I added some cheese to yours, sir."

He paused and considered the waves rolling past the bow.

"You'll need to know the wind direction, the ship's speed, the depth of the waves, and have a sense of timing that others don't have, Morgan," he said. "Eventually you'll know if any of your guns have anything peculiar that affects the shot.

"You believe you are learning quickly. See that vast ocean? What you know is a tiny bit of froth on that one wave at starboard," he said. "You'll have to learn about explosives, keeping the magazine clean, checking your inventory. Do you know why we have so many promoted to gunner? Because the last one got blown up. Pay attention."

He growled again, "If you don't know anything about adding numbers or angles, you're wasting my time. And every gun is different. You don't start on the Big Mother."

"I'm good in math, sir," I said. "And I've noticed you've not been blown up yet. I figure you're the one to teach me."

He cut me a quick look. "Smart and smart-assed. Well, maybe you'll live," he said, and the corners of his mouth twitched once.

I was right that this school was about to change my life. Yet I never could have predicted what would occur within the next few years.

Life has a way of throwing curve balls.

Photo courtesy of Library of Congress

Gunner Morgan trained on the USS *New Hampshire*.

"There is a witchery in the sea, its songs and stories, and in the mere sight of a ship, and the sailor's dress, especially to a young mind, which has done more to man navies, and fill merchantmen, than all the pressgangs of Europe."
Richard Henry Dana Jr.

Chapter Five

Sink or Swim

Sailing into New York Harbor for the first time is something a young seaman never forgets. We'd crossed the bar into many harbors, yet New York was far beyond anything I could have imagined.

Skip and I jostled each other's shoulders as we watched the city come into view. We'd been watching the shoreline change from green-leaved forests and coves and beaches to lines of buildings marching along, pointing our way north.

"Look at that, Skip!" I grinned. "I think the world comes to New York."

"Yes, and here you are, Jack o' Dust, coming into town like you own the place." He slapped my shoulder, laughing like the big Scotsman he was.

Seaman Edwards was so glad to be back home, or near to it, that I thought I saw him swipe his palm over his eye.

He caught me watching. "Something in my eye," he muttered. I nodded and looked away.

Edwards, one of the quiet ones, told us that he hoped he

would get to see his family again for the first time in two years.

It was a fair, brisk April day with a following wind snapping our American flag. We were headed to Newport, Rhode Island, to the US Naval Recruit Training Station on Coasters Harbor Island. First, we were to drop anchor in New York. The sight of so many ships at dock had us nudging each other at the railing. The city noise shifted on the wind, sharp voices yelling orders, ships' whistles, and trains rumbling.

The masts were tall, pointing to a crystal blue sky against which the ship boilers belched clouds of smoke. Against the big ship outlines, small sloops tacked busily on the water, while seagulls called and swooped into the middle of the melee.

Windy Manetti was almost stuttering in excitement when he shoved beside me at the rail. "Look!" he exclaimed in awe.

"Oh, to be sixteen again," I said to Skip.

Gunner Reagan, who was from New York, had walked along with us to watch.

"And there you have it, men," he said. "Not just any city, but my city. I can tell you that it offers the best roast beef stew at Sally's Place for a good price. And the bread! You'll smell that baking before you get close. You will have shore leave for the day. I'll give you the directions, and you can walk to it. Just follow your nose." He grinned. "Sally will take good care of you. Stay away from the ale. It will kick your young selves to the wall."

The young men groaned, and the older ones guffawed. "Tell 'em, Gunner," Seaman Shadowes said.

"Tell us about Sally," Skip said, shoving one red curl away from his green eyes, which glinted with mischief. "Is she a lovely New York lassie for the likes of me?"

"That you can find out yourself, Seaman Beveridge," Gunner said, shaking his head slowly. "I wouldn't presume to know what kind of lassie you like, nor do I want to know!"

"Keep your money close in your pocket," Gunner added, his dark eyes intent on each of our faces in turn. "New York also has more than its share of grubby street children. They'll ask you for a few pennies more like. A few may try to steal it from you. Watch yourselves. Report back here at dusk. Tomorrow you'll transfer for your ride to Newport."

He startled us with a mild laugh. "Ah, you young men make me feel old," he said.

Skip and I glanced at each other. On any given day, Gunner would be scowling at a hapless seaman who got in his way. Seeing New York had stirred even Gunner Reagan to smile. I didn't mind his stern scowl when he was training me. I hoped I would move up in the ranks when I finished training school. So far, I'd had good marks in my record.

We were dressed in our best Navy uniforms, the only ones we had, looking clean in our whites. We were impressive lined up on deck. The ship had been cleaned and polished for days before we arrived. New Yorkers, men and women, stopped to watch as we came into port with our American flag unfurled in the wind. Some were there for our officers who were going ashore, others for the enlisted men.

I would miss some of the better ones who were being transferred, like Lieutenant Dunagan. Skip and I were going on to training together, so I'd have a friendly face beside me for a while longer.

When the whistle blew and we were dismissed, we headed toward the dock and Sally's.

"Your cooking's good, Jack o' Dust," Skip said, tossing the remark over his shoulder as he pushed through the crowd, his wide shoulders plowing the way. "But not that good!"

I considered swatting his head, except I'd have to reach to hit him. With so many people watching—and some lovely ladies among them—I didn't.

We walked past Edwards, whose wife and mother had come to see him. If a man could smile any bigger, I don't know who it might be.

Windy shoved himself ahead, and being smaller than everyone else, he made it to the front of our crowd before turning back to laugh. Then he tripped on a rough board and landed flat on his posterior. There is nothing worse than your shipmates laughing in your face. I extended my hand and jerked him to his feet.

"Windy, you're Italian!" I said. "You're a good-looking boy who doesn't have a grain of sense in your head. But try to pretend like you do!"

Three blocks down the street, as we walked on the wooden sidewalks past importers, exporters, and shipping companies, we found a line of shops—a leather maker whose tanning dyes made our eyes and noses water, a furniture maker, a bookseller, and a spice shop that swamped me with memories of Morgani's Imports.

Turning another corner, we smelled the bread. The sign over the door read "Sally's Place."

Skip led the way in, with Windy shoving past me. We stepped inside to see a room filled with rough tables and chairs. Dockworkers and gentlemen alike were seated at the tables with wooden bowls filled with stew. Big platters laden with bread sat in the center of each table, and small plates held rolls of cheese and butter.

There was a bellow from the bar. "Look here! It's the Navy!"

A short, mostly bald man with a fringe of white hair stepped around the bar's end, grinning and wiping his hands on a once-white apron. He was as broad as he was tall.

"Hey, boys, welcome to my place! I'm Sally, and there's a long table over here always saved for the Navy!"

Seeing our expressions, he laughed. "You young sports thought you was going to meet a fair woman? Well, Gunner Reagan got you again! Never fails!"

"Tom, get some bread on the table," Sally ordered a young man in an apron, swinging through the kitchen doors.

Skip led the way over to the long table, and the eight of us slid onto the benches.

"Hey, Betsy, get these boys something to drink. Water for the younguns," Sally said, ignoring the groans from our table.

Mindful of our white pants, I looked at the bench. A tribute to Sally, the bench was spotless, and so were the walls, floor, and tables. He was retired Navy. Some things you don't forget after years on a ship.

Betsy, it turned out, was Sally's daughter, older than we were and still young-looking. Her black hair was pulled back with a silver comb, and she wore a neatly pressed blue skirt with a pleated white blouse.

She brought a heavy tray, managing it like a master on a ship, swinging past customers and yelling at a waiter, "Tom, bread platter over here!"

"Gunner is here?" she asked with a distracted smile.

At our chorus of yeses, she nodded. "He'll be by later to get his own bowl of beef stew, and he'll ask how each of you behaved, so be good."

"Does that mean you're not interested in a good-looking Scotsman like me?" Skip grinned.

"Yes! I'm not! No young seamen for me who are always at sea and never home! I spent a lifetime waiting for Father to come home!" she said, smiling, and a dimple suddenly appeared. "Now I spend a lifetime getting orders in the kitchen."

When the bowls were passed around, we tore into the bread to dunk into our stew. Talking slowed down to a few words here and there.

Then I heard music to my ears. The men at the table next to us were betting on their baseball teams.

The New York Gothams had just been renamed the New York Giants. Tim Keefe, "Sir Timothy," one of the best pitchers ever seen, and Dude Esterbrook, who usually played third base, had joined the Giants. The owner, John Day, had moved them over from his other team, the New York Metropolitans.

Of course, the Giants were going to win the World Series! The men at the table were talking about some huge bets—at least to a Navy jack of the dust like me with a few coins in my pocket, they were bigger-than-life bets.

Keefe was an Irishman, so anyone who said anything against his pitching record in front of our Irishmen on the ship was likely to get a knuckle in his face. Not that anyone wanted to say anything bad about Keefe. Two years earlier, he'd pitched in a doubleheader against Columbus, and he won the first game with a one-hitter. The next game he won with two hits. A year later, he'd won thirty-seven games and lost seventeen. He was a dynamo on the pitcher's mound!

At another table close to us, businessmen wearing brown tweed sack suits with wingtip collars and four-in-hand ties conversed about a new yachting race and the speed of the ships.

Skip nudged my elbow as we looked over their style. Serious money there. At least we, who had little to none, thought so.

The younger gentleman brought up a new sport coming over from England called polo. There was talk of an international polo match the next year in Newport. "Best horses in the world will be there," he said.

"A Navy man doesn't need a horse," Skip whispered. I nodded.

We were like clay to be molded, watching the men and eavesdropping on their conversations about England, India, and the world.

After looking over the tables and seeing that everyone was served, Sally sat down, leaning over the table. "The days I was on board ship, we raised the rigging as fast as we could, and my team usually won! We raced our ships to see who could get the sails up first. We were tough. I'm not so sure about you young men. You look pretty pallid and weak to me!"

Oh, that got us going. We hooted and pointed, flexed muscles, and dared him to test us.

"Old man, sir," said Mickey Coffey, grinning back. "We can race you anytime and anywhere!"

"And do you know how to play baseball?" Skip chortled. "Because my friend here can put a spin on a ball that you can't even see it's so fast, my man."

"Baseball? Oh, that sport," Sally laughed. "I've got my money on the New York Giants, boy. And you ought to. That doesn't mean Navy men ought to be thinking baseball is their new training. Running bases and throwing balls, sure now. That's the way to build muscle to climb a ship's ladder in a heavy storm."

"Better eat some more of my beef stew to put some meat on your bones, you tiny lad," he roared. He yelled for Betsy to bring us more stew and bread "on the house, though these young Navy whelps don't deserve it, to be sure!"

Sally took good care of us and told us which stores would be best to visit in our Navy uniforms, like the candy store with cheap sweets for sale. When you're in the Navy, you have no money. But adventures! Oh, you couldn't place a price on our adventures.

Heading back to the ship just before dusk, we had a ragtag group of boys following us. One caught up with me, pestering me with questions about being on a ship. Jeremy was his name, and he had holes in his shoes and dirt on his face.

Remembering my old friend Seaman Ellis in New Orleans, I waved the others on and found a wooden bench outside a solicitor's office. I sat there with Jeremy for about an hour until I knew I couldn't delay any longer.

"Can I join the Navy now?" Jeremy asked, his eyes wide as I talked of the islands.

"No, Jeremy, you can't," I said solemnly. "You're not old enough and you need to grow more. Here, take this bread roll I have in my pocket. Good luck to you, boy."

I watched him run down the street, turn at the corner and look back for a moment, lift his hand and wave at me, and tear off again. I hoped he would stay unharmed and have a good life.

At dawn the next morning, I eagerly climbed on board the ship that would take us to training. Some of us weren't so eager. Mickey, for one, was puking his ale over the side the night before. Typical Irish.

Next day, it was yelling all day and bells ringing in the yard.

"On your feet, sailors! Roll out, seamen! Today you become better than you have ever been!"

Double time to the mess hall. At least they fed us well.

We ran miles. We swam miles. I had to grab Windy once because he was about to sink. Skip wasn't much of a swimmer. He pounded the water with each stroke like he was beating it into submission.

"Are you winning this battle with the water?" I asked cheerfully as I sat on the dock, having beaten everyone on our laps.

"I get where I need to go, don't I?" Skip wheezed as he pulled himself from the water.

We learned to row boats—as though we needed that lesson. We learned it was to be a competition between our squads, and we pulled together.

The boat drills were never-ending. Going to the piers and learning to climb down ladders to waiting boats as quickly as possible, and climbing as fast as we could, only to start over again. Sweat dripping down everywhere. Calluses on our hands. Even our feet were sore. Fair weather or rough weather, it didn't matter; we kept training.

We already knew that you could lose a man trying to get him on board a ship that was in a heavy swell. We'd seen one poor seaman lose his grip and get caught between the boat and the ship. He was lucky it didn't kill him. It was weeks before he recovered. He resigned at the next transfer station.

Skip and I learned how to set sails on the USS *Constitution*. It's true. What a grand old ship! There will never be another like her. She retired from active duty in 1881, a year before I joined the Navy. When she was at Portsmouth Naval Shipyard in Kittery, Maine, I spent some weeks on her.

Eventually, we were living on the USS *New Hampshire* for training, rotating from shore to the ship. There were 750 seamen, and Commodore Luce was in charge. When we lined up for inspection, it was spit and polish.

I liked the training weeks we had at the Naval Torpedo Station in Newport. We all had to learn how to load and fire a torpedo. We went out to sea on the USS *New Hampshire* for gunnery exercises in the bay. I worked hard at the gunnery exercises and had letters of commendation in my file. Gunner Reagan had taught me well.

We went ashore when we had leave. I don't like being around drunks, particularly drunks named Miller who yell about "stupid Italians" just because I caught him out on third base on the baseball field earlier in the day. I didn't throw the first punch; I threw the second and probably cracked his jaw. I didn't box much because I saved my hands for baseball. When you catch baseballs in your bare hands, you have calluses, big knuckles, and tough hands. Miller landed on the floor, and Skip stepped in. It was over when the officer of the day walked into the bar. My misfortune was that Second Lieutenant Johnson knew where we were headed and arrived just in time.

Miller had a reputation for fighting; I didn't. Second Lieutenant Johnson wrote Miller up as the instigator and said that I had a right to self-defense, but we had created a disturbance. The next day, we were standing tall in front of our squad commander. I lost ten days' pay. It was Miller's second hearing, and I never saw him again after that incident. That was a true testament to why you should never drink alcohol in a bar. I had never touched hard liquor, and I still don't today.

After that incident, I didn't move to the higher ranking I had hoped for as quickly as I could have.

Skip and one other sailor from Connecticut caught the eye due to their size. We were a short bunch of men. Most of our recruits were sixteen years old, maybe five feet four inches and 115 pounds; I was an old man at eighteen.

When I graduated from training, I would be nineteen, and my pay would be fifteen dollars a month as I became an apprentice second class. That's what I thought anyway. For another year, I was a jack of the dust on the USS *Swatara*.

We sailed to Colón during the Panama rebellion in 1885 along with the USS *Tennessee*, the USS *Galena*, and the USS *Alliance*. The rebels had taken several Americans hostage and wanted to trade them for a steamship loaded with guns. Two of those hostages were US Navy officers from the *Galena*. Our orders were to keep the peace, remaining neutral, and to protect the railroad, while rescuing the hostages and saving Americans from the rebels who set the city on fire. Two hundred Marines were added into the mix and sent from New York. I was assigned to a shore patrol to gather American citizens for safe transport to the United States. Whatever else happened as we protected ourselves and our citizens is not part of the Navy record. I was twenty when I saw several rebels hung.

When we sailed back to America, I knew I had found my calling in the US Navy. Someone had to protect America's interests abroad. I wanted to serve. I re-enlisted as a seaman on September 11, 1886, in Portsmouth, New Hampshire.

Photo courtesy of Library of Congress

In March 1897, the USS *New York* arrived in New York in preparation for routine maintenance at the Brooklyn Navy Yard. The day before the scheduled docking, a fire broke out in the coal next to the magazine. Gunner Morgan and his team put out the fire at great risk.

Photo courtesy of Library of Congress

Gunner Morgan served on the USS *New York* in 1898.

"That's all a man can hope for during his lifetime—to set an example—and when he is dead, to be an inspiration for history."
President William McKinley

Chapter Six

Fire! Fire!

The wind snapped the pennant in the March breeze as I walked on the deck of the USS *New York*. A sailor grows accustomed to the quiet of a tropical island's bay, and lights reflected on water that mirrors the life asleep on shore, then taps lifting on the wind at nine o'clock.

Never in New York. It could be midnight, and amid the sound of ships creaking at their moorings would be dock workers yelling orders as they worked. The men were restless, knowing that we would head back to sea before long and sail to Fort Monroe in Hampton, Virginia, and to Charleston, South Carolina, our base of operations in 1897. We missed those southern nights under the stars. First, we had to get to our berth at the Brooklyn Navy Yard for a week of repairs. At least, we hoped it would be a week.

A merchant ship lay at anchor farther away in the harbor. They would move in to offload early in the morning and were probably headed through the bay to the Hudson River and Jersey City. There's a rhythm that becomes obvious once you've come into as many harbors as I had in the past fifteen years. I could hear the harmonica being played on their deck, notes floating over the light slap of small waves heading to shore. The night watch was alert, even in safe harbor.

I wasn't the night duty officer; clearly, I was restless, too.

"Good evening, sir," Seaman Robert Elroy said as I approached him on the bow.

"Good evening, Elroy," I smiled. "All's quiet, except for that harmonica player nearby."

"Yes, sir," he smiled, his unruly blond hair drooping over one eye. We had accused him of practicing that look for the women in town.

"I have been enjoying the music myself," he said quietly.

The USS *New York* was a beautiful ship, part of the North Atlantic Squadron, under the command of Captain W. S. Schley. We sailed up and down the coastline, protecting the United States at the orders of our commander in chief, President McKinley.

I had passed my examinations for gunner in 1892 with a high score. When American guns were trained on an enemy, the enemy would fear us; they'd fear my crew's deadly accuracy.

I had learned about the US Navy instilling fear and respect in January 1894, when I served on Admiral Benham's flagship, the USS *San Francisco*, under the command of Captain J. C. Watson. We sailed to Rio de Janeiro along with the cruisers USS *Detroit* and USS *Newark* to protect American interests because a Brazilian Navy revolt was underway. Several American ships had been fired upon.

The Brazilian Navy had been warned; yet they continued with three attacks on American merchant ships in the harbor. The USS *Detroit* under Commander Willard Brownson fired a first shot that inflicted minor damage. The second shot at the *Trajano* hit near her sternpost. That brought the conflict to a quick end.

What protection could our country need when we weren't at war? The simplest answer is that I've learned we're always facing conflict somewhere. Americans aren't always welcome when we dock in a country's harbor. At age twenty-nine, I had come to believe nearly every island and country in South America would—sooner or later—have a power struggle simmering, exploding, and catching the unwary in its blast. That meant Americans would come under fire and their businesses would be threatened.

Yes, the tropical islands are beautiful.

Even so, I was glad to be breathing fresh air on the USS *New York*'s deck as we anchored near Tompkinsville, Staten Island, waiting for our berth to open at the yard.

"Sir," Elroy said quietly, "I hope someday to become a gunner myself. I've read about a ship that was boarded recently and the men jailed in Cuba because they were hauling guns to the rebels. Are we going to war?"

"Elroy, that question goes to Washington, DC, to the president and vice president," I said. "They'll decide. We serve our country at their orders. I have read also that it's bad in Cuba."

I added, "We have our own issues here in our country, though we don't want to talk about it. We can't do anything about the unions trying to organize. Everyone's mad at the Polish immigrants working in the mines and wanting more money. These are uneasy times. We can be glad we don't work below ground, for certain."

"Yes, sir, I am glad to be on a ship and not coal mining!" Elroy said. "I just want to be a gunner like you, sir."

"Seaman, we'll do our job and make certain that at sea, our merchant ships are safe from marauders," I replied. "I've read that same story about some ships being boarded."

"I'm turning in," I said. "Keep good watch. Do your job, and maybe I can get you some training on the guns."

"Aye, aye, sir," he saluted.

He was so young. Wanting to go to war and save the world. What would the Navy do without the ones who want to be heroes?

I went below and crawled into my hammock, listening to the snores and Seaman Andrews talking in his sleep. The men were merciless in the daytime, making up stories to tell Andrews about what he had said. He was a good sort who laughed about it. He said, "I wish my life was that full of ale and wild women!"

At daybreak, the crew was already stoking the boilers, making our move to the Navy Yard. Captain Schley was on the bridge with the first mate beside him.

Suddenly, voices yelled, "Smoke in the shell room!" Running feet everywhere. What happened to the new automatic fire alarm? Someone sounded the klaxon.

Lieutenant Berry, his voice stone cool, ordered the crew to fire quarters instantly.

I muttered as I ran, "God watch over us all!"

Ensign Sticht ran three hoses down to the powder magazine. I raced to the platform deck above the smoking magazine and flung open the hatch. The roiling smoke from the charred chamber choked us as I ordered my crew—Whipkey, Casteen, McDermott, and Mackinn—down the ladder. The inch-thick Norway pine was already blackened as we poured water.

"That's it! Keep working," I ordered, not feeling any greater rush of heat or rumbling that would mean we were in the jaws of death.

Our faces blackened, hair singed, my men and I searched the chamber to make certain the fire was out and the shells were safe. Topside, we drank water, poured more water over our heads, and thanked God and His angels that we stood on a solid deck.

Captain Schley strode among us. "You will be recognized for your bravery today," he said. "You will be expected to report to the board of inquiry that I will call immediately."

We snapped to attention and saluted, a more bedraggled, soot-covered motley crew than I had ever seen. Who cared? We lived.

"Lieutenant Capeheart, walk with me," Schley ordered. "It's a great day when we've saved the flagship of the North Atlantic Squadron. And it's a poor day when we have to save it from exploding!"

And what would this board of inquiry discover? That bituminous coal had ignited next to the shells due to spontaneous combustion, which happens when the coal reaches a certain temperature and has enough oxygen and moisture. The hot spots are created when the coal absorbs the oxygen and heats. That's why seamen are assigned shifts turning the coal. Spontaneous combustion had happened on the *Cincinnati* and on the *Indiana*. We were the "new Navy," they said. Yet we were still storing coal next to the magazines. Nor had the woodwork of the USS *New York* been treated so it wouldn't ignite. Our biggest fear as gunners was to have the magazine explode.

Casteen pulled off his filthy cap and nudged McDermott, who inspected a singed hole in his uniform sleeve.

"A special Navy board has already investigated, forward and backward, and here we are today. Nothing's changed," Casteen said. "The coal is still next to the magazine."

McDermott, glad he was still in one piece, said, "I'm here. So are you."

He whipped off his kerchief and blew black from his nose.

"McDermott, you're a nasty soul, aren't you?" Casteen smiled, white teeth gleaming around black smudges.

"You'd best keep those thoughts about Navy boards to yourself," I said. "We know it. They know it. What I think is that because this is Captain Schley's ship, and the third ship recently to have fires, something will be done."

"Let's go below and wash. The captain will want us spit and shine before we dock," I added.

We were a little late sailing into the Brooklyn Navy Yard. The point is that we made it.

The seamen lined up on deck cheered mightily when we docked. A Navy repair crew walked on board to assess our damage. Some plates of the bunker wall were warped; the shells hoisted from the wetness were safe. Some of the powder was damaged but not much.

They'd be asking how often we moved the coal, but our records were accurate. I made certain of that. If you don't move the coal, the heat will build. We had a regular schedule, and we stuck to it. Why it didn't work that morning, I don't know. The fire didn't spread, which would indicate that the coal, except in one corner, was in good shape.

If they asked my opinion, I would tell the ship's engineers to relocate the coal. They wouldn't. Stacks of experts had already written and reported, "Move the coal!"

We'd done what we were supposed to do. We stayed on the ship for the board of inquiry the next day. Then my crew was given a day in the city. We had been absolved of neglecting our jobs. The admiral concluded that the last collier supply ship had offloaded to us some older coal, mixed with fresh. The Navy was going to offload all our coal and bring in a fresh supply before we set sail again.

I caught the streetcar along with Lieutenant Capeheart and my gunners Casteen and McDermott, and we headed over to Peter Luger Steak House off Broadway. My cash weighed heavily in my pocket, and I wanted one of those two-inch-thick steaks.

"You need it," Capeheart said. "You're skinny and overworked, Morgan."

"Still, the ladies love him, Lieutenant," chortled Casteen. "They look at his—what was it that girl said in Charleston?—melting brown eyes."

I rolled said melting brown eyes, still slightly bloodshot from the smoke, at them.

"The only thing you need to worry about is whether you want your steak rare or done. And not charred."

The steak and stacks of bread were so good that I left a small leather pouch on the table with one of my tiny ship carvings inside. Smothering a small belch with a glass of water, I laid the pouch near my tip.

Lieutenant Capeheart watched me and said, "Isn't that a bit much for a waiter, Gunner?"

"I started as a jack of the dust and served officers. Cooking and serving is hard work, even if the ship's deck isn't rolling in a heavy swell."

I told our waiter that it was for him. He followed me from the restaurant, saying, "Sir, I can't take this. It's a grand carving."

"Do you have children at home?" I asked.

"Yes, sir, my boy is three years old," he said.

"Put it away until he is old enough to have it in his room," I said. "He can look at it and imagine the breeze filling the sails and dream of going of sea."

Photo courtesy of Library of Congress

The USS *Maine* after the explosion shows ships and divers nearby.

Photo courtesy of the Morgan family

The USS *Maine* dive crew includes Gunner Morgan, second from left.

Photo courtesy of the Morgan family

All but one member of the USS *Maine* championship baseball team perished in the explosion in 1898.

Photo courtesy of Library of Congress

The USS *Maine* anchored in Havana Harbor in 1898.

Photo courtesy of Library of Congress

Gunner Morgan was lead diver on the USS *Maine*. In this photo, he enters the water.

"Remember upon the conduct of each depends the fate of all."
Alexander the Great

Chapter Seven

Starting a War With Spain

In February 1898, I was serving on the USS *New York*, flagship of the North Atlantic fleet, lying off the Dry Tortugas, sixty miles from Havana. Thanks to my reputation as a good baseball player and, on most occasions, a skilled shortstop, I had been ordered to participate in a game on February 14 during Mardi Gras in New Orleans. The Navy also thought it would be good to have a hometown boy playing against a local nine.

The USS *Maine* baseball team was the US Navy's champion. The *Maine* players had won the Navy championship in December 1897 in Key West, Florida. They beat the USS *Marblehead*'s team by a score of 18–2. William Lambert, a black man and left-hander from Virginia, was the *Maine*'s best pitcher.

They were in Havana to play an all-star Cuban team. The Spanish government, despite the Cuban insurrection, had allowed a baseball season. All things in their time—shoot and torture the Cubans, and play ball whenever possible.

I was to "stand by" and wait for the torpedo boat *Cushing* to take me off the *New York* to go on board the P&O steamer *Olivette* and proceed to Key West with the mail. From there, I would go to the USS *Maine*.

It was one of those moments, knowing I had joined the Navy to make a living and save the world, and I got to play baseball. I was smiling into the wind, thinking of the Mardi Gras game coming up.

The past year, I'd played in New Orleans during the Navy's Mardi Gras demonstration game. It was one of the good times when I could see my father and brother, who came to the game to cheer for the Navy.

"Aren't you special now," Joseph grinned, "getting sent over here to play baseball."

"Did you doubt Father Thomas back when we were young?" I ragged him. "A man of the Lord? Who said that I was a good Catholic boy destined for greater things?"

"He had to hold to something good," Joseph smiled. "It was his job to find something good in every boy."

He handed me a small leather pouch. "For you to place your dainty, little carved ships inside," he smiled, "in case you lose another one."

On that trip a year earlier, I had been given permission to take the next morning off to meet my father and Joseph at the Italian restaurant on the corner, where we devoured sausage and pasta and talked baseball. I was eager to hear about the latest news about the top players and teams. Willie Keeler was leading in batting for the Baltimore Orioles. Kid Nichols was the leading pitcher for the Boston Beaneaters, who were set to win the National League, but the Orioles were not far behind.

Afterward, I headed back to Key West to return to the USS *New York*. It was a great memory, and I relished it while we rode on the waves of the *Cushing*.

The wind was up, and above me, a thundercloud mumbled to its brothers. As we left Morro Castle in Havana, we rode one wave and then another headed toward the ship. Suddenly we smacked into a bigger roll, and Ensign Breckenridge, the son of General

Breckenridge, bounced back, hit his head, and fell overboard. The propellers caught his legs.

We pulled him from the water and wrapped his legs in cotton sheeting. He was in bad shape, unconscious and bleeding. We headed back to port in Havana as fast as we could. We got him on shore, and he had immediate medical attention. No one could have survived those grievous wounds, and he died.

My schedule was canceled, and I headed for the sailors' boardinghouse to await my next orders. Basically, the game would go on. The ship would sail to New Orleans. The Navy doesn't stop because one man died. I was to embark on the *Olivette* and go then to the USS *Maine*.

As twilight fell over the bay, I stood on the quay looking at the sunset, hearing the quiet creak of boats at anchor and voices floating over the water. I turned in and sat on my bed, watching the light fail. I reflected that no man knows what is his last day on this earth. There is a tide that controls our destiny.

I heard a faint sound of taps from the USS *Maine* at 9:10 p.m.

At 9:40 p.m., the USS *Maine* was blown up in Havana Harbor and destroyed. Two hundred sixty-six officers and enlisted men died. Most were killed outright; some drowned after the ship sank. I should have been on it. Only Ensign Breckenridge's grievous injury had kept me from being on the *Maine*. I knew many of those men.

I had trained as a diver in Newport and was highly ranked in my performance record. The more skills you learn, the quicker the promotion.

At daybreak, I was sent on another boat, assigned to lead the dive team to go on board the *Maine*. Captain Philip Cosgrove Sr. of the lighthouse tender *Mangrove* had sailed from Key West within an hour after hearing of the disaster. His son, P. L. Cosgrove Jr., served as first mate.

They anchored near the wreckage of the *Maine* at daybreak, and surviving officers and men of the *Maine* came on board. Captain Cosgrove shared his clothes with Lieutenant

Commander Holden, whose uniform had been torn and burned in the explosion.

The superstructure of the *Maine* was still above water. In the twisted steel, they found a leg, an arm, a head, and an eye.

Captain Cosgrove summoned me to speak with him before we began the dive. The naval board of inquiry led by Captain William Sampson was already preparing to meet, and I would report to them.

"You look carefully at the ship's destruction," Captain Cosgrove said. "Write your notes each day when you come back topside. There are major decisions in Washington that will be based on your report.

"The Roosevelt Board was meeting on the *Maine* regarding the Cuban request to be freed from Spanish control. The documents were on a table in the captain's cabin and need to be found and retrieved. Find the papers. Bring them to me," he said.

"You may be called to give your report in person to Captain Sampson, especially if there are any questions, so be quite certain of what you see!" he concluded, slapping his desk. "The Navy has lost fine men. There must be someone to answer for it."

I saluted and turned to leave but overheard the captain say, "First Mate, go ashore to find Clara Barton, the president of the American Red Cross. She is in Havana, and I'm told she's at the San Ambrosia, the Spanish military hospital, seeing to the wounded.

"Find out what they are telling her, the poor ones who can speak. We'll want her report as well," he said, adding in a lower voice, "even if we have to bury it."

"Yes, sir." The first mate saluted and left at the same time I did, as I thought, "Bury it? Why?"

Unspoken was this: Someone would be blamed. No one in the Navy wanted it to be Captain Sigsbee of the USS *Maine*, his officers, and his crew. There would be questions flying and answers demanded. Sigsbee could lose his command.

With a prayer from my heart to God, and wearing my

200-pound suit and metal helmet, I dropped down into the murky Havana Harbor. I had only a foot or so of visibility in the silt stirred up.

Then the *Maine* was in front of me. It was horrible! As I descended into the death ship, the dead rose to meet me. They floated toward me with outstretched arms, as if to welcome their shipmate. For the most part, their faces were bloated with decay or burned beyond recognition. Here and there, the light of my lamp flashed upon a stony face I knew, which when I last saw it had smiled a merry greeting and now returned my gaze with staring eyes and fallen jaw.

The dead choked the hatchways and blocked my passage from stateroom to cabin. I had to elbow my way through them as one does in a crowd. While I examined the twisted iron and broken timbers, they brushed against my helmet and touched my shoulders with rigid hands, as if they sought to tell me the tale of the disaster. I often had to push them aside to examine the interior of the wreck.

I felt like a live man in command of the dead. From every part of the ship came sighs and groans. I knew it was the gurgling of the water through the shattered beams and battered sides of the vessel. The sounds made me shudder, echoes of that awful February night of death. The water swayed the bodies to and fro and kept them constantly moving with a hideous semblance of life. Turn which way I would, I was confronted by corpses.

On the third night, Captain Cosgrove had his own fright. He was sitting on the *Mangrove*'s deck when he heard tapping over the ship's side.

"Was it someone setting a bomb to the *Mangrove*? Was it a mine floating against the ship? That was my first question," he said. He went to the pilothouse quickly and told the quartermaster to train the dark searchlight down over the side of the boat. "I told him to put the light on when I struck a match. I went into my cabin for my pistol and ran back to the side where I had heard the tapping.

"When it came again, tap, tap, against the ship's side, I struck a match. The searchlight beamed down over the side. I looked down and saw a human body. The head was striking against the side with the rise and fall of the waves."

By sunrise, the water within 300 feet of the *Maine* was practically filled with bodies. Nearly every body was nude. The explosions had blown off their uniforms.

Awash in pity and anger for these men, I worked many hours a day in shifts diving on the *Maine*. A four-hour day was usually fatiguing enough for a Navy diver. Four hours weren't enough to bring any trapped bodies to the surface and hand over the remains to be buried with honor.

I found the documents on the captain's table in a leather pouch and brought them as directed to Captain Cosgrove. I never saw that pouch again.

Before long, my skin was raw and burned from the heat, the rubbing, and the salt. Still, we kept diving. My team included Powelson, Smith, Olsen, and Lundquist. Later, we added Reddlin of the *Maine* and Schulter of the *New York* as relief divers. They were strong divers, and I was glad to have them.

One of my team, Eddie Lewis, was a good man who kept an eye on me. He knew I was driven. We all were. If he didn't tap my shoulder for us to ascend, I'd tap his. Having a watchful partner in the depths can keep a diver alive.

When we were pulled onto the boat deck and a crew member took off our helmets, we'd wipe sweat from our red-rimmed eyes and sit quietly. Sailors brought us water.

"You okay, Gunner?" Eddie asked.

"I'm okay, Eddie. You?"

"We're limp as seaweed, slimy and everlasting," he said with a grimace.

"We're on the deck," I said, lifting my eyes to the late afternoon tropical sun. "That counts."

Two of my men got sick and were relieved. They ended up in San Ambrosia Hospital with the survivors, who were dealing with burns, missing limbs, and severe cuts. Many who made it ashore were dying from infection.

Two fresh divers were brought on board. "Reporting for duty, sir," they said.

"Suit up," I replied.

They might have been a little alarmed at our haggard faces and the raw splotches on our arms and legs. They kept their thoughts to themselves. No need for conversation.

Fresh water was poured over our heads. We asked for it because the salt water burned every raw, rubbed piece of skin.

At the end of two weeks, a Navy doctor came aboard to examine us. He gave us a supply of medicated ointment to use at night.

"Doc, I don't want this sweating down my body and turning me into a slippery mess," I said.

"It will sink in overnight," he promised. "I got this remedy from native divers who wear no suits and dive daily for fish and shells. It works."

I had my doubts and used the ointment sparingly, telling my divers to do the same. The salve did what the doctor said and sank into our poor skin.

I couldn't sleep well because the images of the bodies were burned into my brain. If I managed to sleep, I ached as though I was sick. Some thought I would turn to drink, but I didn't drink or smoke. Never did. That is why I was a better diver than most and became the chief diver. To endure the weight and the heat, you had to be in excellent physical condition, and I was, or I had been before this!

For forty-nine days, we went down into the warm waters of the harbor, into the filth, and climbed through the hull of the *Maine* to bring the bodies to the surface. Around us floated body parts that we claimed with nets.

No matter how long I spent below, if I abruptly encountered a man I knew, his eyes staring, my soul was hit by a fist. By day's end, I'd feel my heart was bruised.

And yet, we kept on. No choice. I wrote my report and turned it in to Captain Cosgrove first. He was leafing through handwritten notes from Clara Barton.

"She writes that the officers and the men said they escaped from the ends of the ship, where the boilers were. They say the blast came from the center. They were burned by fire, not steam. We'll pass this on," the captain said, stacking Clara Barton's notes with mine.

Yes, the plates were blown inward by something outside. It had to be a mine in the harbor. As I stood before Captain Sampson, I thought of those men. I knew nothing they did or didn't do had created this disaster. It was Spain.

The board of inquiry on the *New York* off Key West issued its finding on March 21, after twenty-three days, and the finding was approved on March 22 by the commander in chief of the US Naval Force on the North Atlantic Station. The conclusion was that regulations had been followed in the magazines and shell rooms. The torpedo warheads were stowed and did not cause the destruction of the *Maine*. Nothing combustible was near the scene of the explosion. The coal bunkers were inspected daily, and it was noted that there had never been a case of spontaneous combustion of coal on board the *Maine*. The two after-boilers of the ship were in use with a low pressure of steam and had a reliable watch.

The *Maine* was destroyed at 9:40 p.m. on February 15, 1898, in Havana Harbor. At the time, she was moored to the same buoy to which she had been taken upon her arrival.

Lieutenant Holman, the navigator and ordnance officer, gave his report. He said there were two explosions of a different character, with a short, distinct interval between them, and the forward part of the ship was lifted to a marked degree at the time of the first explosion. The first blast was more like a gun's report, while the second explosion was more open, prolonged, and of greater volume. The partial explosion of two or more of the *Maine*'s forward magazines caused the second blast.

Lieutenant Commander Wainwright, executive officer of the USS *Maine*, confirmed the reports of Holman and our team. Wainwright had been placed in charge of the *Maine* since the wreck. What he'd seen and heard that night haunted him. His gaunt face and shadowed eyes testified silently.

We were not allowed in the board of inquiry at the same time. We testified separately, which made sense because they didn't want us to repeat what we might have heard from each other. Having begun my career as a jack of the dust, I could talk to the seamen serving the officers and hear some of what went on after I testified.

The court determined that the bottom plating break described by my dive team could only have been produced by a submarine mine exploding under the bottom of the ship, causing the partial explosion of two or more of her forward magazines.

The loss of the *Maine* was not due to fault or negligence by any officers or crew members. The court added that it had not been able to obtain evidence that fixed responsibility for the destruction of the *Maine* upon any person or persons.

M. Sicard, rear admiral, commander in chief of the US Naval Force of the North Atlantic Station, approved the findings of the board of inquiry.

It was at those hearings that I first saw Assistant Secretary of the Navy Theodore Roosevelt in the hallway following a break. He looked me straight in the eye and said, "You honor the US Navy, Gunner Morgan, with your exemplary service."

"Thank you, sir," I said, saluting sharply.

Later that evening, I was called to his cabin for a quiet discussion about what I had seen, and what I had heard in Cuba about the cruelty of the Spanish.

"You will not share this conversation, Morgan," Mr. Roosevelt said, his gaze sharp and assessing. "I expect your discretion."

"You need not ask, sir. You certainly have it," I said. I was glad to be of service to a man I respected for his knowledge and progressive reforms.

Even far away from Washington, we had heard that Theodore Roosevelt wanted a new and better Navy, more ships, advanced weapons, and more highly trained men. William Randolph Hearst's newspapers said Roosevelt believed the time had come for America to rule the seas.

Later, I heard that my friend J. H. Bloomer was the only survivor of the USS *Maine*'s baseball team. It was many years before I saw him again and clasped his hand. The years vanished in a moment as though that brilliant blue sky over us in Key West reflected upon the grim wreckage of the *Maine*, and I stared into eyes as haunted as I'm sure mine were in that instant.

The newspaper headlines read, "Remember the *Maine*!" On April 25, 1898, the United States declared war against Spain.

In those newspapers, I became "The Man Who Started the Spanish-American War."

US Naval Historical Center photo

The dive crew works on the wreck of the USS *Maine* as seen from aft looking forward.

Photo courtesy of Library of Congress

The mast and part of the USS *Maine*'s deck were exposed in the bay.

Photos courtesy
of the Morgan family

This letter and the photo of Admiral Sampson on the USS *New York* are from Gunner Morgan's old sea chest full of documents.

Navy Yard, Boston,
September 20, 1900.

Dear Mr. Morgan:

I have just received the two photographs of a very interesting incident, which you kindly sent me. Allow me to thank you sincerely for your courtesy.

Very truly yours,

W. T. Sampson

Chief Gunner
Charles H. Morgan, U.S.N.,
Torpedo Station,
Newport, R. I.

"A good Navy is not a provocation to war.
It is the surest guaranty of peace."
Theodore Roosevelt, December 2, 1902,
second annual message to Congress

Chapter Eight

Ready, Aim, Fire!

At night, when my hammock swung in the ship's easy movement, and Glendale was always snoring, I fell asleep and saw the bodies of the *Maine* seamen and officers floating in the deep, murky bay toward the light of the water above. I saw them lift into the blue sky. They fell back into the bay and floated toward the ship.

I awakened shivering in the night and listened to the breathing around me. When could I aim my ship guns toward the villains who killed these men and blasted them away?

The next day, the opportunity for war was edging its way onto the horizon.

America declared war against Spain on April 25. Then we received a message that on May 1, Admiral Dewey's fleet had been victorious over the Spanish in Manila Bay, with only one man lost. They decimated the Spanish fleet of Rear Admiral Patricio Montojo in only two hours. American merchant ships would be safe in the Pacific, and there would be no threat to the West Coast.

We were headed to blockade Cuba in our search for the Spanish fleet of Rear Admiral Cervera. Admiral Sampson believed the Spanish would go from the Cape Verde Islands to San Juan, Puerto Rico, to get coal. Neutral nations would offer only limited amounts of supplies at their ports, but San Juan belonged to Spain, and it had a fortified harbor.

The monitors *Terror* and *Amphitrite* and the cruiser USS *Detroit* would join us off the Cruz del Padre lighthouse. Admiral Sampson ordered the battleships *Iowa* and *Indiana*, the cruiser *Montgomery*, the torpedo boat *Porter*, the armed tug *Wompatuck*, and the supply ship *Niagara* to join us.

All hands were called on deck at three in the morning on May 12. We breakfasted at three thirty, fueling for the day's events.

At four forty-five, First Officer Erickson muttered under his breath as he left the captain's quarters.

"Chief Gunner, gather your crews, double time! Roust them! Even those on night duty."

"Yes, sir." I snapped a salute and sent out the call.

"We are headed to shoot the coast fortifications at San Juan into ruins," the first officer said. "No one has seen the Spanish fleet yet. The admiral is certain they'll refuel in San Juan."

When the *New York* sailed past the harbor, we knew the Spanish fleet wasn't there. Admiral Sampson honored me by asking me to fire the first gun at the fortifications. When I gave the command, my heart was swelling with joy, and also pain, that this would not be enough to bring 266 good men back from their graves.

We began our rounds of the fortification batteries, following behind the *Iowa* and the *Indiana*.

For three hours, we bombarded San Juan's fortifications. My newly implemented improvements to the breech on our rapid-fire guns worked beautifully.

We took heavy fire from the Spanish, but we escaped being hit for a time. The enemy's marksmanship was off in estimating the range. Most shells passed over the ship.

Seaman Bartholemy shouted, "Ah, you bastards! Can't shoot, can you?"

The catcalls rained over the ship. "Can't see the target either?"

"Blind gunners with no guts!" yelled Seaman Reginald.

Whistles began. "Here, boy! Here, boy! Hey, we're over here!"

"Steady now," I said.

The damned Spaniards got lucky when we were on our third pass of the batteries. The battle continued as we opened fire at 7:29 a.m. on Castillo San Felipe del Morro—or El Morro, a citadel built between the sixteenth and eighteenth centuries—about 2,900 yards distant. At 7:40 a.m., a six-inch shell came aboard about six feet above the after end of the superstructure deck, taking off the top of the after stanchion on that deck, and exploded near our crew at the port waist eight-inch gun. This destroyed the fourth cutter and the port searchlight, and pierced the ventilators and smoke pipes in many places. Shell fragments also struck the whaleboat and second steam cutter. The shell was fired from the eastern battery, about 5,000 yards distant.

Almost everything worked well on board the *New York*, but some primers jammed in the vents of the eight-inch guns, causing the lock extractors to break. In the after turret, the locking catch on the faceplate of the right-hand gun jammed and had to be repaired, leading to considerable delay in firing.

When Lieutenant Commander Potter wrote his report to the secretary, he observed that a spare lock should be provided for each eight-inch gun, there being only one on the ship for six guns.

The shell fragments flew forward and spread. A fragment of exploded shell struck and killed Seaman Frank Widemark, and seven others were hit. I was standing nearby commanding my gunnery crew when I had my cap shot off. That day was not my time. Head wounds bleed freely, so I looked worse than I was.

"You have a thick skull," Dr. Randolph said. "And you bleed like a rascal."

"I've been told that before, sir," I said, wincing as he cleaned the cut. "About my skull, that is. I try not to be a rascal."

I'll tell you this. We had crew members who joined us as we sailed around the seas. I served with Japanese, Chinese, and

Filipino men who enlisted while we were in their homeports. Although they were not native-born Americans, each one fought bravely and well, and they loved the flag as much as any American from Boston, Chicago, or anywhere else.

A man run over by a streetcar in a city would groan and moan and exhibit his suffering. The eight men of my gunnery crew, maimed and distressed, shot down in the midst of their comrades, never murmured. They joked about the Spaniards getting lucky with their shots.

Later, when I visited Bartholemy in the ship's medical bay, he said, "Why, Gunner, we had to show every seaman we were willing to die. Why would we caterwaul and shake them up? They had a duty to do." His leg was broken, and he'd had shrapnel removed from his chest.

Reginald added from his bed, an arm wrapped heavily in gauze bandages, "Our crew had to keep firing, sir. They had to take over the gun. If they had hesitated, it would be disaster."

I laid my hand first on one man's shoulder and then the other, and nodded to the others who were conscious. "Thank you all."

Back on the deck, I received and compiled reports from my gunnery crew. Captain Chadwick commented that having so few injuries was "extraordinary, considering the incessant fire the ship was subjected to for so prolonged a period."

The concussion from our eight-inch guns blew away part of the flooring on the starboard side, the starboard waist searchlight, and the starboard life buoy, and it shattered the wings of the afterbridge that were stowed on edge alongside the superstructure.

We got underway again. Later we heard that there had been some civilian casualties in San Juan, and an errant shell—not from my gunnery crew, I may add—hit an old Catholic church.

That did not go over well anywhere. There is an unwritten international rule that we advise civilians of upcoming bombardments so they can leave for safety. That Sampson ignored this rule of ethics angered Puerto Ricans and Americans, who felt that the admiral wanted a victory regardless of the women and children who might be in harm's way. The newspapers claimed he wanted to have a victory like Admiral Dewey's at the Battle of Manila Bay a few weeks before.

To the critics, Sampson said, "I am satisfied with the morning's work. I could have taken San Juan, but I have no force to hold it. I only wanted to administer punishment. This has been done. I came for the Spanish fleet and not for San Juan."

We left our patrol along the Bahamas and ran quickly for Key West. The seas were calm as the USS *New York* lay at Key West on May 29, 1898, taking on coal as quickly as possible from two lighters on either side. Rear Admiral Sampson had developed his strategic plan of attack.

The USS *Oregon* had just arrived, setting a record for her 14,000-mile voyage in sixty-six days from San Francisco after leaving there on March 19 with Captain Charles Clark in command. She had traveled along the West Coast, through the Straits of Magellan, and then north to reach our squadron.

Captain Clark came aboard the USS *New York* to report to the rear admiral. Sampson had a table set on the deck to catch the sea breezes, so he sat with the captain and his officers. The chief gunner also came aboard, as Sampson had requested. I stood with the chief gunner, a few feet away from the table.

"Are you ready for a fight, Captain?" Sampson asked. The USS *Oregon* had thirteen-inch guns, the largest in the fleet, along with the USS *Massachusetts* and the USS *Indiana*.

Clark said, "Sir, I have the finest crew a captain could want. To save fresh water for the ship's boilers, the men drank feeder warm water from the boilers. Before we put into Callao, we had to deal with a coal bunker fire. My men worked in ten-minute shifts digging through the coal for four hours to get to the fire until they uncovered and extinguished it. We never slowed our engines during this time. My men have done everything I've asked of them and more."

They had faced gales in the Straits of Magellan and the news that the Spanish torpedo boat *Temerario* was possibly stalking them. As the *Oregon* coaled in Rio de Janeiro Harbor on April 30, the Brazilian Navy patrolled outside the harbor entrance to watch for any Spanish vessels. The Brazilians had placed guards on the coal barges because Spanish spies with explosives had been captured on board recently.

When the *Oregon* left Rio on May 4, Captain Clark received a dispatch from the secretary of the Navy that four Spanish armored cruisers and three torpedo-boat destroyers had left the Cape Verde Islands heading west, possibly searching for the *Oregon*.

"I ordered the woodwork and mahogany paneling thrown overboard to lighten the ship, and the ship painted wartime gray," Clark said. "We saw that sailor, Joshua Slocum, on his sailboat, *Spray*, trying to set a record. He's sailing alone. Brave but foolish. And in a war zone."

Slocum had set forth from Boston in April 1895 to become the first person to solo circumnavigate the globe. "Sitting down with him to talk would have been a rare treat," Clark said. "We were racing to get here, and that was just not possible. We wished him fair seas for sailing and urged him not to get blown away!"

Shortly after May 14, they arrived in Bridgetown, Barbados, recoaled, and left as quickly as possible.

After chasing across the seas and keeping their location as secret as possible, Clark told Sampson, "We were nearly undone by the American consul in Bridgetown who cabled that we had arrived and were coaling. Somehow he got it past the censor. Our presence had been a secret until that man thought he'd be so helpful to Washington, DC! We left the harbor with our lights, and then I ordered full dark, and we changed our course."

Telegraph operators were notorious for sharing information that they saw with newspaper reporters who paid well for it. Chief Gunner Allison and I shook our heads at this foolish and dangerous collapse in wartime security.

"I'll be certain I bend the ear of the secretary," Sampson said. "Obviously the consul is no military man."

"To your question, sir, I respond, we are ready for battle. We need no major repairs," Clark said.

Dispatches arrived alerting the admiral that the Spanish fleet had put into Santiago Harbor. Admiral Sampson was concerned that if we concentrated our naval forces outside one harbor, the Spanish could land arms and supplies for their army on another beach and prolong the war. He wanted the Spanish fleet bottled up without all our ships outside the Santiago Harbor entrance.

We trained our gunners daily to keep them sharp. I knew from mess-room scuttlebutt that Admiral Sampson had sent a message asking Commodore Schley to sink a collier in the narrow channel at the harbor entrance that would trap Admiral Cervera's squadron inside. Schley had apparently ignored the suggestion.

When Admiral Sampson paced with his pipe in hand, we knew something was afoot.

Then he discussed with Lieutenant Richmond Hobson, our assistant naval constructor, a plan to rig ten torpedoes outside the collier *Merrimac*'s bulkheads, steam into the narrow passage in the early hours of the morning, turn the ship ninety degrees, set off the torpedoes, and sink the ship, blocking the channel.

I was chosen to lead my gunner's gang to create torpedoes that would explode from batteries and wiring. Hobson went to work. The torpedoes would extend around the vessel, resting lengthwise, about twelve feet below the water surface. Each torpedo had a hogging line plus two lashings to keep it close to the side and at depth. All were on the port side so the inrush of water would be more rapid as the ship turned. The crew would abandon the ship on the starboard side.

The crew was to open doors, hatches, manholes, and cargo ports to guarantee sinking.

The admiral approved the ten torpedoes, but Hobson wanted two more inside the *Merrimac*, next to the two most important bulkheads. Their connections would be inside so they would be less susceptible to enemy fire.

"No," Admiral Sampson said. "Two hundred pounds of

guncotton on the inside would blow everything to the devil."

We needed the ship to block the harbor, not disappear in pieces.

The harbor entrance was narrow with a long channel. The *Merrimac* was approximately 333 feet, and the width of the channel ranged from 350 to 450 feet where it was narrowest. The crew on board would have to swing the vessel across the channel to catch and hold her there.

A minimal crew of six volunteers would be on board, with one man at each anchor held by lashings so they could be cut quickly with an ax to drop and swing the ship, one man at the wheel, and one to assist with the torpedoes. They would signal by cord pulls, one for "stand by" and three for action.

The plan included a lifeboat in tow at the stern. The first man would pull in the long painter line and jump aboard, and then the other men would jump overboard and get into the lifeboat, which would have rifles and ammunition. The torpedoes were to be fired when the ship had reached her position.

Hobson and another crew spent half a day scouting the enemy's battery locations on the slopes.

We had signaled our vessels that we needed an electric machine for firing the torpedoes, which were ready. The captain brought the *New York* close by, and Hobson went to explain the plan to the *Merrimac* crew. We sent over half our deck force to prepare the anchors, chains, belt, and hogging lines.

My crew told me that *Merrimac* Captain J. M. Miller had no idea until then that his ship was about to be sunk. He was not pleased. He directed his officers and crew to prepare to leave the ship while he left to see Admiral Sampson.

After Miller arrived on the USS *New York*, he saluted the admiral. "Sir, I would like to remain with my ship, with Lieutenant Hobson and the men chosen for this valiant attempt. It is my right as commanding officer."

"I respect that claim, Captain," Sampson told him shortly. "You don't have enough time to be instructed on the plan. We have kept the crew to a minimum. If they end up in the water and under fire, they'll have to swim to safety. I understand your commitment to duty. A man of your training and experience is needed elsewhere."

Hobson set aside new Manila rope for the elastic hawser winch, and more for beltlines and hogging lines. He said he stored it in a safe place because another crew would be coming aboard to strip the *Merrimac* so nothing useful would go down with the ship. A seaman always looks for gear to pillage if he needs it to do his job.

When Hobson came back aboard the *New York*, I reported that we did not have an electric machine available. Our vessels with electric machines were north of Cuba, so batteries of cells would have to suffice. We had only a few spare firing cells aboard, and we set a test firing to be certain this method would work.

Hobson left for the *Merrimac*. Hours later, darkness began to set in. I watched the sun glowing hot on the low horizon, followed by that flashing green fire before the sun pulled down the shades and lavender lengthened to gray and black.

The heat was horrendous. The first team of men felt exhausted from transporting the torpedoes.

In our final test on the *New York*, the battery could only fire six primers, so Lieutenant Hobson knew he had to pick the six most important positions for those torpedoes.

I wish I could tell you this military exercise went well. When we went onto the ship to start with the fresh second team, the men sent to strip it had done a first-rate job.

Seaman Brooks scratched his head and looked at me. "Gunner, there are only two poor lanterns left. The tackles have been stripped. The lines they've already put over are tangled. They'll have to start over. The damn strippers pillaged the gear that the lieutenant ordered put aside. The hogging lines are missing."

"Well, Seaman, you're here as a dynamo man to run the wires. That's your job. The pillagers are gone, so let's get it done and get back to the *New York*," I ordered. "They're already letting in water below decks."

The work went on rapidly. The men were smoothly hooking the longer wires to the shorter wires from the torpedo.

Robertson cursed a long string of profanity that would have done Gunner Reagan, my first trainer, proud.

"What now?" I demanded, leaning over the side.

"We're running out of wire, sir," Robertson said.

"Walters, stop handing down the wire and start searching for more," I ordered. I hoped, even searching in the dark with only a little moonlight and a lantern held close, that we might find it.

The extra roll of wire was not on board. Either the pillagers got it or not enough wire had been transported.

The plan to have the ship ready by midnight June 1–2 was not going to happen.

The *New York*'s steam launch remained near, so Hobson went hunting for wire. He didn't find it there. He did find an insulated wire on a Norwegian steamer nearby that we hoped would do.

We finished wiring and boarded the steam launch. Soon, we left the *Merrimac* behind in darkness. Heavy black clouds were moving in from the southeast, and the moon was dressed in a mist fitting for this night's dance on the seas.

About three in the morning, Admiral Sampson took the launch back to inspect the work on the *Merrimac*. At that point, the *Merrimac* was about five or six miles from the harbor.

Our deck watch reported some unknown craft in the area, and the first mate sent a torpedo boat to find out who they were. We discovered they were vessels belonging to the press, with reporters waiting for guns to fire and blood to flow.

We kept an eye on the steam launch and waited for Admiral Sampson's return. The launch's propeller caught one of the lines linking the lifeboat with the *Merrimac*, and it took an hour to clear it. By that time, it was four o'clock, and dawn stroked the sky.

Hobson pushed the speed on the *Merrimac* because they had to reach the channel quickly. The lifeboat broke loose and capsized, and the crew couldn't take time to save it. The admiral lowered his eyeglass briefly.

"They're brave men, and they will be able to swim to the shore," he said. "But it is too light. They cannot attempt this with dawn breaking. Order them to return to their previous location."

A torpedo boat, the *Porter*, carried the message. They would wait another day.

The watch saw an unknown ship heading toward the harbor. We laid on full power on the *New York* and, with smoke pouring from our funnels, the chase was on. The other vessel had a ten- to twelve-mile start, but we pressed forward at full speed with the *Porter* joining us.

Whatever country she was from, she was fleet, and she vanished over the horizon, not wanting to encounter our guns.

We sailed back to the *Merrimac* under a cloudless sky with heat beating down. The *Porter* came alongside with a message: Hobson wanted to try for the harbor channel at sunset.

Admiral Sampson sent Hobson a message to board the *Porter* and come to the *New York*. We had found more firing cells, so we sent four more torpedoes over when Hobson went back. We also sent another lifeboat to be slung from a cargo boom.

Our executive officer ordered provisions and a bucket of coffee for the *Merrimac*'s small volunteer crew. Our fleet surgeon sent two canteens of water mixed with quinine.

For the final time, my crew and I went on board the *Merrimac* with the coffee and provisions so we could check the explosives. Three of the torpedo connections were not responding, so we had seven that could be used. At my direction, we moved the cells in hopes of having a better effect on the wiring. Would the insulated wire do the job?

We transferred to the steam launch, and I looked back once at the condemned *Merrimac*. So much had gone wrong with this plan thus far.

I'm not particularly superstitious, even though I'm from New Orleans; however, I didn't have a good feeling about this.

Here's what happened. At dawn, the Spaniards began shooting from the bluffs above the harbor at the sailors working on the

Merrimac. A lucky shot from the Spaniards sheared the anchor that would have swung the ship into place, blocking the harbor. The ship sank—not where it should have been. We didn't know that until later.

The lifeboat capsized and floated away, but Lieutenant Hobson and his crew were able to hold onto a catamaran from the ship. As the sun rose bright overhead, Admiral Cervera and two junior officers and crew appeared in a launch boat, holding rifles on the men hanging onto the catamaran in the water. Lieutenant Hobson surrendered to the admiral as a prisoner of war, and our other men were also pulled on board, including two with injuries. On the admiral's ship, the *Reina Mercedes*, they were given clean clothes, food, and medical care, and were treated well. Hobson said he became friends with Captain Acosta. Unfortunately, they were then imprisoned in Morro Castle.

"I was placed in a barren cell full of flies and insects where it was clear the last prisoner had died," Hobson later told Admiral Sampson on board the *New York*. "We were accused of killing fourteen men and wounding thirty-seven. As you know, we had no guns! Every indication to me is that the Spaniards firing at the *Merrimac* hit their own men across the channel. The Spaniards did not want to believe me when I told them we had no guns."

British Consul Ramsden stepped in to provide cots and blankets in the cells, pitchers for water, a table, and chairs. Our men were fed frijoles, rice, a piece of sausage, and bread every day, and it became clear that the Spanish officers received the same food.

In the report he made later to the admiral, which I was standing tall to hear myself, Lieutenant Hobson said only two torpedoes worked due to the batteries and that we had needed an electric machine, which we didn't have. He said the substitute wiring wasn't what it should have been—thanks to our own men who carried off the extra coils of wiring. He sounded bitter and said he knew those adverse actions could never happen again.

Hobson and our other men were fortunate not to be killed in the bombardment of Morro Castle. Spanish General Linares had informed Admiral Sampson that our men had been moved. Nonetheless, they were still prisoners there.

"They intended to leave us there and make you our executioners!" Hobson said grimly.

Hobson complained to General Linares about their treatment in the castle prison, and they were moved to Santiago. The one good point was that as Hobson stood on his cot and looked out the small window of his cell, he could tell what effect our guns had on the batteries—very little, it seemed, unless there was a direct hit on the gun. But the *Reina Mercedes* was on fire. We thought one of our shells might have triggered a magazine fire.

By June 7, they were headed to Santiago, marching under a guard of thirty soldiers, to be imprisoned at the barracks on the eastern edge of the city beside the military hospital. The British consul checked on the men again; the crew was allowed to have more food, clothes, and other provisions brought to them.

The consul had just been to a funeral for Captain Acosta, who died on the *Mercedes* after his leg was shot off.

Hobson mused to me, as Sampson took a report from his executive officer, "It is a fact of war that men die. It was hard to hear that the first Spanish officer killed on the *Mercedes* was Captain Emilio J. de Acosta, who had been so courteous. He showed me photographs of his wife and children. We talked about what our lives might be once this war is over."

"Yes, Lieutenant," I said. "We have met and sailed with good men on our ships and their ships who are gone."

Our fleet won against the Spanish on July 3. My team and I, along with Lieutenant Capeheart, took the launch to sail quietly into Santiago Harbor just before daybreak to locate and destroy Spanish mines in the harbor. On July 4, under Lieutenant Roy Smith, I gathered a team of four to prepare countermines on the collier USS *Lebanon* off Santiago. Both of these exercises succeeded—first, clearing the harbor so our ships could enter, and second, leaving mines that would attach to Spanish ships.

Lieutenant Hobson and his crew were exchanged on July 6,

marching to cheers from soldiers lining the road while the Army band played "When Johnny Comes Marching Home Again!" They reached General Joseph Wheeler's camp and were sent on to General Shafter.

From there, they arrived back at the *New York* on the *Harvard*, and Hobson made a first, brief report to Admiral Sampson below decks in his cabin. A second, longer report followed the next day when I was present.

My crew and I were honored for our efforts, despite equipment losses affecting the outcome.

Lieutenant Hobson and his brave crew were highly honored for their attempt, and what was a failed mission became a Navy success due to the newspapers and the public.

So much time and effort went into a plan that didn't work. That thought remained in my head, a silent communication reminding me that simpler is better. The more complex a plan is, the less likely the elements will come together at the same point for the desired conclusion.

Or, as Seaman Brooks concluded: "It was mucked up from the beginning, sir."

Photo courtesy of the Morgan family

Gunner Charles Morgan, USN, standing alongside an eight-inch gun on the USS *New York* in August 1898, was named by Walter Scott Meriwether as the original 'Man Behind the Gun.'

Theodore Roosevelt

President of the United States of America.

TO ALL WHO SHALL SEE THESE PRESENTS,

Greeting:

Know Ye, that reposing special Trust and Confidence in the Patriotism, Valor, Fidelity and Abilities of Charles Morgan, I have nominated, and by and with the advice and consent of the Senate do appoint him a Chief Gunner in the Navy to rank with but after Ensign from the 1st day of October 1901 in the service of the UNITED STATES. He is therefore carefully and diligently to discharge the Duties of a Chief Gunner by doing and performing all Manner of Things thereto belonging.

And I do strictly charge and require all Officers, Seamen and Marines under his Command to be obedient to his Orders as a Chief Gunner. And he is to observe and follow such Orders and Directions from time to time as he shall receive from me, or the future PRESIDENT of the United States of America, or his Superior Officer set over him according to the Rules and Discipline of THE NAVY.

This COMMISSION to continue in force during the pleasure of the President of the United States for the time being.

Given under my Hand at Washington, this thirteenth day of May in the year of our Lord One Thousand Nine Hundred and Two and in the 126th year of the Independence of the United States.

Theodore Roosevelt

By the President

William H. Moody

Secretary of the Navy

Photo courtesy of the Morgan family

President Theodore Roosevelt promoted Charles Morgan to chief gunner in the US Navy on May 10, 1902.

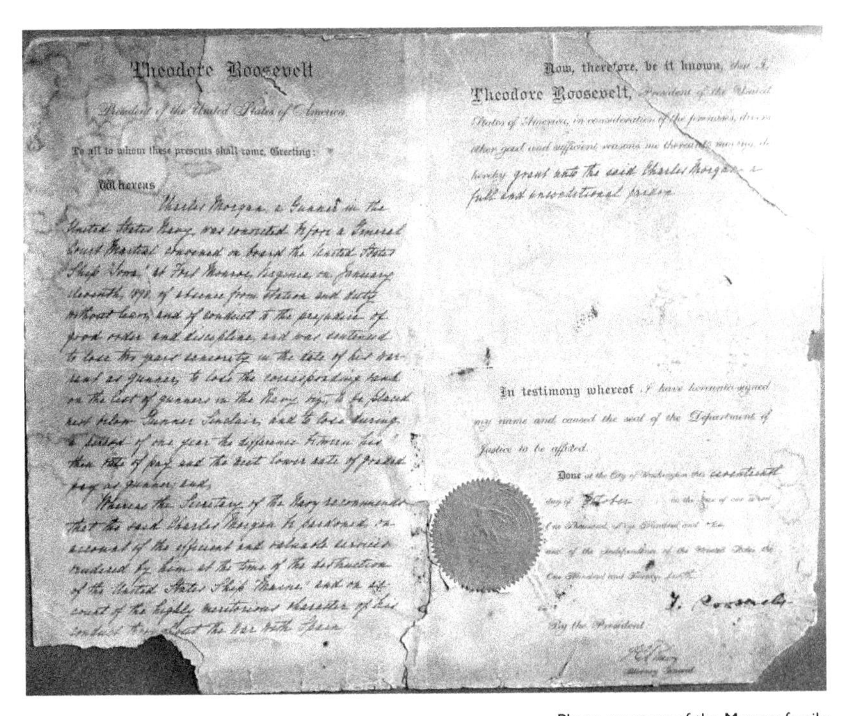

Theodore Roosevelt

President of the United States of America

To all to whom these presents shall come, Greeting:

Whereas

Charles Morgan, a Gunner in the United States Navy, was convicted before a General Court Martial convened on board the United States Ship "Iowa" at Fort Monroe, Virginia, on January eleventh, 1898, of absence from station and duty without leave, and of conduct to the prejudice of good order and discipline, and was sentenced to lose two years seniority in the date of his warrant as gunner, to lose the corresponding rank on the list of gunners in the Navy, [illegible], to be placed next below Gunner Sinclair, and to lose during a period of one year the difference between his then rate of pay and the next lower rate of graded pay as gunner; and,

Whereas the Secretary of the Navy recommends that the said Charles Morgan be pardoned on account of the efficient and valuable services rendered by him at the time of the destruction of the United States Ship "Maine" and on account of the highly meritorious character of his conduct throughout the war with Spain

Now, therefore, be it known, that I, Theodore Roosevelt, President of the United States of America, in consideration of the premises, divers other good and sufficient reasons me thereunto moving, do hereby grant unto the said Charles Morgan a full and unconditional pardon.

In testimony whereof I have hereunto signed my name and caused the seal of the Department of Justice to be affixed.

Done at the City of Washington this seventeenth day of October in the year of our Lord One Thousand Nine Hundred and [illegible] and of the Independence of the United States the One Hundred and Twenty [illegible].

T. Roosevelt

By the President

[illegible]
Attorney General

Photo courtesy of the Morgan family

Gunner Morgan received a presidential pardon from Theodore Roosevelt.

Photo courtesy of the Morgan family

Newspaper cartoons across the country depicted Gunner Morgan as the everyday hero of the US Navy, a top gunner, and Admiral Sampson as a snobby aristocrat who said any Navy man who hadn't attended Annapolis couldn't represent America well as a US Navy officer. Most editorials proclaimed that Americans wanted heroes who could fight in wars, not a man who could balance a teacup on his lap at high society events.

"If Admiral Sampson is the author of these endorsements,
he is a conceited ass, and he ought to be marked down as such."
Senator William V. Allen, Populist from Nebraska

Chapter Nine

Man Behind the Gun

My mother raised me to believe that I am as good as any other man when I perform my duty well and behave as a gentleman would. I have always believed my mother.

On March 2, 1889, I had married the beautiful, burnished red-haired Mary Noonan of Erie, Pennsylvania. I was twenty-four then. Mary came from a good family; she was a good Catholic woman, lace curtain Irish.

A man gets lonely at sea. I met Mary at church, where I was praying for young Seaman Windy Manetti, who, I'd just learned, had gone overboard in a gale, like we'd predicted with laughter those few years ago. I wasn't laughing anymore.

Mary spoke to me on the steps of St. Patrick's, and I invited her to lunch. Next I worked on a picnic by the lake while we listened to the stirring music of John Philip Sousa.

"You are so brave to go to sea," she said, smiling gently at me. The kindness in her blue eyes brought some welling of deep emotion, a desire to be warmed by that kindness forever.

And I was done.

I talked her into a wedding at the courthouse before I left to go to sea again. With my *madre*'s wise words about being a gentleman, I loved my beautiful Mary gently. I believed we could build a marriage on love.

Her mother never forgave me for that courthouse wedding, nor did her sister Elizabeth or her brother James.

"Charles, you need a bit more money, my man, to keep my sister in style," said James Noonan, who owned a printing business. "You could leave the Navy and work for me. I'd get you out of that Navy uniform and into a high-quality sack coat and trousers."

James thought dangling a man's business suit would be like chum in the water. He leaned back in his favorite Queen Anne damask-covered chair near the fire as he sipped his hot tea.

"We can talk about that," I said, hoping I looked seriously interested. I enjoyed the warmth of the fire in the grate—not the chill in his eyes.

Now, I liked the idea of more money, but I had left New Orleans because I knew I would never fit into a store. That had not changed in those hard years of training in the Navy. If my own father and brother couldn't pull me in, James Noonan certainly could not. I had no intention of leaving the sea.

Except the Navy wasn't dispensing promotions and raises.

Meanwhile, Mary and I were living in her old bedroom in her family's home, "just until we can find our own home," she smiled at me across her mother's dining room table with its porcelain china. The silver comb that held back her glorious red hair glinted in the chandelier's soft light.

The next week, I got my orders for more training at Portsmouth Navy Yard in Kittery, Maine. I would be housed on the USS *Constitution*, now a receiving ship at dock. They had built a house over the grand old ship, and the Navy kept her repaired so she didn't leak.

I told Mary upstairs in our room, since it was a conversation for us, not the household.

Mary paused and then tied her hair with a blue ribbon, straightened her pleated blouse sleeve, and turned to face me.

"I'm staying home with my mother," she said, blinking those deep sea-blue eyes. "I'm not going to Maine."

Her skirts swished past the doorway as she walked downstairs for dinner.

The maid was pouring hot tea, the family gathered at the dinner table, and James ladled pot roast, potatoes, and carrots onto each plate. He looked at her face and mine and kept on ladling.

After the maid left, he looked up again.

"Mary and Charles, is there something you wish to share?"

I looked at him and said quite clearly, "I'm to be stationed at Portsmouth Navy Yard for some time. I leave next week."

"Then I take it you're not seriously considering working for me," he said quietly.

"No, I'm not. The Navy is my life."

"I can't live alone near a Navy base while you sail the seas," Mary said in a quiet, gentle voice.

"And you shouldn't," James added with finality. "You'll be safer and better off here at home."

Mary clenched her lace handkerchief tightly and dabbed at her eyes. "If you'd only take a job with James, Charles, we would be fine."

Her mother sipped her tea and watched me over the rim of the cup. That woman, well, she was *una donna difficile*, like my *madre* used to say of some church women. Lord save me from the self-righteous woman.

Lace curtain Irish wasn't for an Italian from New Orleans. Was I a good husband? Not really, if I was supposed to leave the sea and go to work for her brother.

Ten years later, I faced my mistake and filed for a civil divorce. Mary never forgave me. She called herself Mrs. Morgan when she wrote to the Navy after she read my name in the papers. The US Navy didn't care. I only saw the letter some months later in a packet of mail forwarded to me.

I never forgot James Noonan telling me I couldn't keep his sister in style.

The US Navy was my life, not Third Avenue in Erie, Pennsylvania.

And so, when Congressman Melville Bull, a member of the House Naval Affairs Committee, suggested that I write a letter to Admiral Sampson requesting my promotion to ensign from warrant officer, I did it. Congressman Bull said because of my heroic actions diving on the USS *Maine* in 1898 and during the war, I should be commissioned an ensign.

In his letter, he wrote: "If that valiant action doesn't prove that you are officer material, I don't know what would. We need brave men leading our Navy. Vice President Roosevelt feels the same. It is time for our Navy to embrace reforms, and Roosevelt is determined officer promotions will be part of that change."

Secretary of the Navy John Long liked the idea of recognizing exceptional ability in the ranks and had a bill introduced in Congress authorizing the promotion of six warrant officers to the commissioned rank of ensign. Roosevelt, as former secretary of the Navy, was likely in the background on the bill.

My former commanding officer, Admiral Sampson, was Captain Sampson when he placed me in charge of the crew of divers assigned to dive on the USS *Maine* for forty-nine days, exploring the hull and bringing forth the bodies.

War was declared April 25, 1898, against Spain, and we were firing in San Juan, Puerto Rico, on May 12, when a Spanish shell hit the *New York*, not fifteen feet from where I was standing. Seven good men died. My cap was blown off.

Then there was my work under Lieutenant Richmond Pearson Hobson, creating the torpedoes and ordnance designed to sink the collier *Merrimac* at the mouth of Santiago Harbor in order to bottle up the Spanish fleet. We had some success, even though the Spanish guns had sheared the anchor.

I had done my duty and, according to my records, performed it well.

Dear Sir:

The new bill whereby six gunners are to be commissioned ensigns tempts me to write you, trusting you will pardon the liberty I take in so doing. As I served on the flagship "New York" during your command of the fleet, you will know whether my abilities, whatever they may be, are of such merit as to warrant me in filling the position of ensign. I would say here that I never use tobacco or liquor in any form. If, in your estimation, I am worthy of this position, I would be most grateful to you if you would recommend me to the department. I am, very respectfully yours,

CHARLES MORGAN, Gunner, U.S.N.

Skip Beveridge read about the resulting furor in the newspapers and wrote to me from his post on the USS *New York*. "My friend, you have stepped in it now. Listening to those politicians will muck up your brain! You need the fresh ocean air to scrub off the barnacles. Yes, you deserve the promotion. But, Gunner, you need to get back to sea, man!"

Instead of treating my letter sent through mail delivery as the private matter it was intended to be, Admiral Sampson sent it through Navy channels with his comments: "In time of peace, the Navy function consists, to a certain extent, of representing the country abroad. The Navy's representatives should be representatives of at least refinement. While there are perhaps a certain few among the warrant officers who could fulfill this requirement, I am of the opinion that the vast majority of them could not. Once commissioned, they will have the same social standing as other officers. The consequences that would rise might not redound to the credit of the Navy.

"I hope no warrant officers would be commissioned."

In February 1901, Congress held hearings on the military appropriations bill. Senator William V. Allen of Nebraska read my letter in the US Senate, so I'm now part of the official congressional record.

The congressional record states: "Mr. Allen in the US Senate read a letter purporting to have been sent by Chief Gunner Charles Morgan of the Navy to Rear Admiral William T. Sampson requesting him to forward to the Navy Department his application for promotion to the rank of ensign under a provision of the pending Navy appropriations bill. Five other enlisted men were also recommended for promotion."

Mr. Allen also read to the other senators Admiral Sampson's endorsement, which said that while he recognized my technical and professional ability, Sampson was opposed to promoting warrant officers to the grade of ensign because they had not enjoyed the social advantages that Sampson believed a commissioned officer of the Navy should have enjoyed so that he might properly represent his country, particularly in foreign countries.

> *"I do not mean to detract from the sterling worth of the warrant officers of the navy: I merely mean to suggest to the department that unfortunately for them, they have been deprived of certain natural advantages, and in consequence, their proper place is that of leading men among the crew, and not as representatives of the country in the wardroom and steerage. I request that this may be brought to the personal attention of the Secretary of the Navy."*
>
> *W. T. Sampson, Rear Admiral, USN Commandant*

The newspapers reported Senator Allen's response. "If Admiral Sampson is the author of these endorsements," declared Mr. Allen with vehemence, "he is a conceited ass, and he ought to be marked down as such. We are not bringing up in this country a race of snobs. If I am correctly informed, there was a time when Sampson was no better than Charles Morgan, the gunner. He came from no better stock. I am glad to repeat that we are not raising in the United States a class of jeweled aristocrats. If this rank and arrant coward is to be believed, the time may never come in this country when a poor boy may attain such a position as his abilities warrant his holding."

The *New York Journal*'s headline said: "Congress to Investigate Journal's Exposure of Sampson's Snobbery to Our Brave Sailors."

I was depicted in cartoons as a fighting man, "The Man Behind the Gun," and Sampson was depicted sitting in a parlor with a teacup on his lap, "The Man Behind the Teacup."

During this difficult time, my good friend Walter Scott Meriwether, nicknamed Skipper, cabled that his photo of me on the USS *New York*, taken in August 1898 with the eight-inch gun, was going to have a big impact in this "ludicrous" debate with Admiral Sampson.

> *YES. YOU, MAN BEHIND THE GUN, DESERVE THE PROMOTION. I WILL HELP. W. S.*

W. S. and I served together as seamen on the USS *Kearsarge*. He left to become a reporter for the *New York Herald*, and he was in Havana at the newspaper's bureau when the USS *Maine* exploded. He got the nickname Skipper because he loved to write about the Navy.

One evening after I had spent a day diving into the sunken *Maine*, he asked me: "Shorts, you're leading the Blue Jacket Divers on the *Maine*?"

He was a good man. He called me Shorts half the time because I played shortstop and talked baseball to anyone who would listen or share a current newspaper.

"W. S., I'm so tired I can barely lift my fork to this red snapper and pineapple," I said.

W. S. sat on the empty bed next to mine and asked what had happened. I gave him an outline of what I'd seen on my dives, although I didn't tell him everything.

He took off on his boat, the *Vamos*, for Key West, to send dispatches to New York.

Later, during the publicity about Sampson's pronouncement

that warrant officers were too unsophisticated to be promoted to ensign, W. S. came to see me on the USS *New York*, which is when he took that picture.

I didn't ask for his help. He jumped in.

"Gunner, you've sold so many newspapers we should be paying you some of the profits! I admit that Sampson's poor choice of words has hung him out on a mast waving in a gale, but that's not your fault," W. S. said.

When I wrote that letter asking for consideration to be promoted, I had no idea I'd be starting another war! I meant it as a simple letter to my former commander.

The *New York Journal* wrote: "Gunner Morgan, a man as Sampson admits of admirable character, good education, temperate habits, and professional ability, applied for promotion. Admiral Sampson, the unparalleled idiot of American life, vetoes the man's application on the ground, if you please, that he is 'NOT A GENTLEMAN.' "

I visited Admiral Sampson at the Charleston Navy Yard in Boston the first week of February. I talked to him privately and made certain he knew I bore no ill will and did not consider his statement a personal affront. We had a good conversation. Afterward, he refused to talk to reporters.

I was pursued relentlessly, and finally I thought giving a statement might make the reporters go away.

I told them, "I came to Boston to see my old commander and to express to him my friendship, which is as strong as ever. He is an exceptional officer. Admiral Sampson gave me a very high personal recommendation in his endorsement of my letter. I wanted to thank him for this and to express to him my entire friendship for him as of old; that is why I came up from the station at Newport today. I did not know but perhaps he might think I took the endorsement as a personal affront. I entertain no such feelings."

I felt better after spending the hour talking with Admiral Sampson about the entire affair.

Then Admiral Dewey openly supported making it possible for men like me to become commissioned officers. Admiral Dewey was the hero of the Battle of Manila Bay. Admiral Sampson had not particularly cared for Admiral Dewey, although they were polite in public.

The bill passed in Congress.

Meanwhile, life goes on. Newspaper battles in print soon vanish. Ships will set sail. In port, ships are repaired. Seamen go ashore for training or train on board. The Navy wouldn't come to a halt because of my application to be promoted. Life still happens, whatever our duty station may be.

I was sent to League Island Navy Yard on the Delaware River in Philadelphia and assigned to the cruiser USS *Minneapolis* as deck officer in June. I felt proud to do that duty.

There was so much going on in America.

The northern guys on board ship talked quite often about the steel mills and the unions that formed to guarantee higher wages and benefits.

J. P. Morgan, my cousin—that's what I told the youngest seaman, Henry—had formed his corporation, United States Steel. Someday his billions would be lining my pockets.

"Oh, sir," Henry breathed, his eyes wide. "Will you share it with us then?"

I looked at him seriously and said, "Do you doubt me, Henry? I take care of my seamen friends first! It's the US Navy! Now get on with you and get that deck cleaned."

Behind him, Gunner Caslow muffled his laughter and turned it into a snort or sneeze.

What was more important was that the American League had declared itself a Major League. The baseball wars were in full swing. There were rumors that the National League and the American League were going to create eight teams each, make peace, and set rules about player contracts. They talked about creating two teams in New York City and competing for the championship.

That was the grand news!

Fall was coming, and the crisp air on the sea would make a man sniff the wind like an old dog with his eyes halfway shut.

And suddenly, the news was terrible.

Our flags were lowered to half-mast. A great man, our commander in chief, died from his gunshot wounds.

A crazy Polish anarchist, Leon Czolgosz, shot President William McKinley on September 6, 1901. The president was shaking hands with the crowd at the Pan-American Exposition with three Secret Service members close by. Czolgosz approached and acted normally. The president reached out his hand and was shot in his chest and abdomen.

One bullet hit his suit button and glanced off. The other one lodged in his body, and the doctors couldn't find it. Gangrene killed him. That's a nasty death. I've seen it kill sailors.

We protect our country at sea and around the world from military incursion. When our ships' guns are trained on a target, the fear is real.

How can you protect against one crazy man with a gun? You can't. And he was crazy. He said it just came to him that day to go kill the president.

McKinley died at 2:15 a.m. on September 14. That afternoon, Theodore Roosevelt became president. Some politicians called him "that damned cowboy." Maybe he was a cowboy, but he believed in men being treated fairly if they worked hard.

Both President McKinley and President Roosevelt supported enlisted men being promoted to officer in the United States Navy if their records showed meritorious service.

I had missed my train once and was late reporting to duty from leave, for which I lost a pay grade. That caused an issue. There was a reason for my tardiness. Oh, I know. Everyone says they've heard that one before. I have told many a seaman that same thing.

President Roosevelt pardoned me on October 17, 1901, for missing my ship.

THEODORE ROOSEVELT
PRESIDENT OF THE UNITED STATES OF AMERICA
To all to whom these presents shall come, Greeting:
WHEREAS

The Secretary of the Navy recommends that the said Charles Morgan be pardoned on account of the efficient and valuable services rendered by him at the time of the destruction of the United States Ship "Maine," and on account of the highly meritorious character of his conduct throughout the war with Spain.

IN TESTIMONY WHEREOF I have hereunto signed my name and caused the seal of the Department of Justice to be affixed.

DONE at the city of Washington this seventeenth day of October in the year of our Lord One Thousand, Nine Hundred and One, and of the Independence of the United States the One Hundred and Twenty Sixth.

T. ROOSEVELT
President
T. E. Knox
Attorney General

Our nation mourned President McKinley, and we honored and celebrated our new president.

As the air turned cold, and snowflakes drifted here and there, it was time to celebrate Christmas. I was stationed at Newport, Rhode Island, and Admiral Sampson notwithstanding, we Navy men knew how to create a grand event. The enlisted men on duty at Torpedo Station Rhode Island decided to hold a grand ball and banquet in Newport at the State Armory.

The *Army and Navy Journal* edition on December 3, 1901, described it as a "perfect palace of lights, bunting flags, and ordnance." We draped the sides of the hall with stars, signal flags, and international code signals. Chief Electricians Hamilton and Ferguson and Class Electricians Cordes and Henry planned all the Christmas lights. We hung streamers of red, white, and blue lights across the ceilings. At the west end of the hall were four light designs, and under the gallery was a star in lights. At the end of the hall, we put together a platform for the torpedo station men and their wives. On the port side, we placed the musicians' stand and set evergreen plants.

Chief Gunner's Mate Durgin managed it. Commander Gleaves led the grand march with Miss Annie Brennen. Lieutenant Capeheart and his wife walked behind the commander, and after the other lieutenants and their wives, I escorted in Mrs. Camp and Mrs. Blackwood, both lovely ladies celebrating the holidays as best they could with their husbands at sea. Commander Gleaves made certain Mayor P. J. Boyle and our Navy friend, former Congressman Bull, were invited.

About 180 couples attended the ball, and as we finished the grand march, small American flags fell from the ceiling into our hands. I danced with both ladies. Yes, I could dance. I learned by watching the officers.

Lieutenant Capeheart was dancing the two-step to Sousa's "Washington Post March" with his wife. Then the band swung into a Boston waltz.

How hard is it to walk down a dance floor anyway? Not hard. I didn't step on Mrs. Blackwood's feet once.

When the band swung into "I Love You Truly," I enjoyed the song and watching the happily married couples slow-dance.

Christmas can be a melancholy time for sailors everywhere, separated from their loved ones, yet I enjoyed the night. Once you've been to war, you learn to savor such respite and take each moment as it comes.

At midnight, they served the buffet and I brought plates to my companions. I carefully placed dollops of escalloped oysters, turkey, ham, French rolls, butter pickles, croquettes, chicken salad, and potato salad on the plates. No gobs of anything for the ladies.

I brought them ice cream, cake, sherbet, and coffee.

Next to each lady's plate, I placed a small leather pouch holding a carved sailing ship. "For your children," I said, smiling.

"Oh, Gunner Morgan, you shouldn't do this!" the two of them chorused.

"It's a small token of my esteem for allowing me to escort you both this evening," I said. I was glad the commander had asked that I fulfill this duty because it was a grand event.

Somewhere there is a photograph of me in my dress whites, dancing with Mrs. Blackwood. I like to think I wasn't a ruffian, and I performed well to whatever Admiral Sampson expected.

The holidays over, it was back to work and a new assignment for me.

In 1902, after twenty years, the Navy diving school at Newport was growing. Gunners' mates were instructed in simple diving because this was our additional duty. We had to help test and recover the torpedoes once the Navy began using them. Our maximum depth for descent was sixty feet. The USS *Maine* had been at twenty-five feet. Our dive times had been short. There were many bodies trapped in the wreck that we couldn't remove. My dive team and I had brought up 171 bodies; sixty-three were still in the wreck.

Nothing happens quickly in the military, but at last, work began on better diving equipment. I was ordered to shore duty at the school, describing our dive team's difficult work on the USS *Maine*, hampered by our equipment. Talking with the engineers daily was a great exercise.

"What we need, Gunner Morgan, is a lightweight helmet so you can do a better job," said Chief Gunner Heathcott, looking at some designs with the engineers' team.

I had never met him before, but that meant nothing. We changed ships every two years like ants crawling from one anthill to the next, and sometimes we shifted sooner than that.

I was—too rapidly—approaching the age when the Navy wouldn't ask me to dive. I wanted our future gunners to be safer than we were.

"It would be excellent if we didn't drown, Chief Gunner," I said drily.

"You led the dive team on the USS *Maine,* didn't you?" His eyes sparked with interest.

"Yes. It wasn't deep, but the suits leaked and our skin got raw. We need better suits," I said, looking at the engineers from Morse Diving. They nodded wisely. I determined that most of them had done some diving themselves. They weren't idiots with titles and no toughness.

That duty completed, I was assigned to another Navy yard, and I longed for the sea.

So it was that on May 4, 1903, I found myself helping present a captured Spanish cannon in Towson, Maryland. Mr. William Tyler Page, clerk to the minority in the US House of Representatives, had become my friend during the promotion controversy, and the *Baltimore American* wanted our photo together. Mr. Page, who had unsuccessfully campaigned to be elected to the House the year before, was a principled man of renown. I stood at his right in the photograph.

The commentary in the newspapers about whether enlisted men knew how to behave in polite society and whether this was important had repercussions for the Navy, although certainly not bad ones. The first banquet and ball of the enlisted forces of the US Naval Torpedo Station took place on February 5, 1904.

I never meant for the controversy over my potential promotion and that of any others who were under consideration to create the distraction it did.

Other articles and headlines only told part of the stories of the times. There are things even today that I'm not supposed to share about my service to President Roosevelt. I will tell you that I signed up for the new Naval Intelligence Service. What better cover than to be a gunner traveling the world on Navy ships?

I went to sea again, leaving from San Francisco. As we left the port, dolphins raced us through the white-capped waves. They seemed as excited as I was in that moment.

My family went through a period of fear and grieving when they thought I was dead in 1905. Along with thirty-four other gunners, I was sent to teach the Japanese how to fire the big guns. I served on the *Mikasa*, commanded by Captain Hikojirō Ijichi, under Admiral Tōgō Heihachirō, who was commanding the 1st Fleet.

Then the Treaty of Portsmouth was signed, and I disembarked from the *Mikasa* at Sasebo. Six days later, on September 12, 1905, the *Mikasa* sank at her moorings after a fire and magazine explosion, killing 251 crewmen.

I've heard some call the Russo-Japanese War the first modern war because the weapons, from mortars to artillery to hand grenades, became more lethal.

In other words, we learned to kill more men more quickly.

I can summarize this for you succinctly: The Russian czar wanted to control the Far East. Japan wanted a foothold on the Asian mainland. Russia wanted Port Arthur, a warm water port.

After about 150,000 soldiers, sailors, and civilians died, the two countries came to the treaty table—actually, they met first on the president's yacht, the *Mayflower*, in Portsmouth, New Hampshire, in June 1905.

Our president didn't want Russia to take over Port Arthur during the Russo-Japanese War. President Roosevelt convinced Japan to withdraw her indemnity demand and to split the island of Sakhalin with Russia. The treaty was signed, but thousands protested in Japan that Russia wasn't going to pay war damages.

Meanwhile, President Roosevelt won the Nobel Peace Prize for helping to end the war.

My job was to be a gunner—and whatever else I did was no one's business except mine and the president's. There may be some documents hidden in a corner somewhere. The president sought men who would do their duty and keep their mouths shut. I did that.

Trust my brother Joseph to go to Captain Merrill, who commanded the New Orleans Navy Yard before Captain Singer, and ask him outright where I was. Captain Merrill told Joseph, so the family knew I was in Japan. And my brother, who was well known for working with my uncle at Morgan's Camp at the Rigolets during busy times, told the press.

"Thirty-five gunners were sent over to Japan, including my brother," Joseph said. "Understand that? They had orders to go. Who sent them, I don't know. Captain Merrill said each gunner was paid $500 and is to receive a handsome bonus at the end of the war. I last heard from my brother eighteen months ago when he was in Newport, Rhode Island. A few weeks later, I heard he was in San Francisco. From there, I'm sure he boarded a ship for Japan. I never had any doubts he was in their navy when I heard what good shooting they were doing.

"If the secret history of that war is ever written, I think it will be written that the men behind the guns were Americans. There were thirty-five of them—enough to direct the gunnery of the entire Japanese Navy.

"I'm glad to know my brother isn't dead. And he's not a traitor to his country by being there. He's always followed orders. That's why he was a hero on the USS *New York* and in Havana, Cuba, and in the Battle of Santiago. In San Juan, he nearly lost his life when a Spanish shell hit the *New York*, killing several men and blowing his cap off his head. He loves the United States Navy. That's all I need to know."

I'm glad my brother was so proud of my shooting. I'm sorry that my father suffered for months thinking I was dead. Joseph was still angry that I had disappeared with no word.

The *Washington Times* reported about me on Sunday, September 17, 1905: "After twenty-two years in the Navy, he retired in disgust. Admiral Sampson's refusal to recommend Morgan for a commission on the ground that his social standing disqualified him for such a position was the real cause of his retirement."

Yes, I sent a letter home to my family about my resignation. It was necessary. I couldn't be in the US Navy and join the Japanese Navy to help them shoot the big guns.

The next time I went home, our first dinner together was strained until my father said, "Humph. You're home. You're safe. God has blessed us. Say the dinner prayer."

We didn't talk about my "promotion." I never intended to hurt Admiral Sampson in any way, I'll say that right now. He was denied promotion from his rank of rear admiral. I'm sorry for that. He had died a few months after I spoke with him.

Did I get my commission as an ensign? They delayed so long that by the time the furor was over, I had passed my thirty-fifth birthday and was over the maximum age for ensigns. The Navy created a new commissioned rank for me, chief gunner, and I did get that on October 17, 1907.

Why it took six years to make this happen, I can't tell you except that Congress and the military move slower than tortoises in the islands as they creep onto land to give birth.

There is that. And there was my service in Japan. I'm grateful that I could serve my commander in chief.

Photo courtesy of the Morgan family

Jerry Warren, center; Rudolph, left; Sybil; and Vivian pose for a family photo without Mrs. Warren.

"A foolish consistency is the hobgoblin of little minds, adored by little statesmen and philosophers and divines."
Ralph Waldo Emerson

Chapter Ten

Riding Fortune's Seas

The US Navy placed me on the retired list on June 8, 1903, in Key West. The ostensible reason was they weren't happy that I wore glasses. Some papers declared that I reported to duty in charge of the Naval Magazine at Rose Island off Newport, Rhode Island. In the Navy, you resign before you re-up. So yes, I had resigned in the official records. Any documentation after that is as murky as the silt stirred in a Louisiana bayou when a gator slides to the depths.

Meanwhile, I traveled to Japan and did what I was "hired" to do. Since the Japanese didn't allow any Americans to join their navy, we were there secretly. We stayed in barracks at the port, and quiet, courteous women served us hot tea or *sake* and baked fish in rice most often.

Once I was invited to visit a Japanese gunner's house, located down a tiny dirt lane. The ornate wooden gates opened into an equally tiny garden with flowers, herbs, and a fountain. We sat on the wooden bench and drank tea in a quiet, serene moment. He knew little English. I knew little Japanese. But we could lift a teacup in a toast to life. I met his wife and two little black-haired boys, who bent low and giggled as they ran back into the house.

I learned quickly to say, "*Kashikomarimashita,*" which means, "Yes, sir," when speaking to Japanese officers. You learn the key words if you want to survive on board. A few officers spoke English, and they had little patience with any seaman who didn't run to perform his assigned duty.

Once I got involved in this thing with Japan, I spent many a night in my hammock wondering what the end goal was.

Many people have a false impression that because military men take orders, they follow blindly. That was true of some who wanted to get their pay, go ashore, drink or gamble it away, and find a woman for the night. But most of us read and studied newspaper accounts if we had access to US or British newspapers. We wanted to know the reason we were leaving port like a five-alarm fire was blazing, and only the US Navy could put it out.

It was far better to be educated about the country and the port into which we were sailing than to arrive uneducated and drop anchor blind to another tinpot revolution.

President Roosevelt wanted to expand America's power worldwide. He wanted an improved US Navy, and he convinced Congress that we needed new ships, more men, and bigger guns. I placed a copy of his speech to Congress on December 6, 1904, into my documents.

He said: "Chronic wrongdoings, or an impotence which results in a general loosening of the ties of civilized society, may in America, as elsewhere, ultimately require intervention by some civilized nation, and in the Western Hemisphere the adherence of the United States to the Monroe Doctrine may force the United States, however reluctantly, in flagrant cases of such wrongdoing or impotence, to the exercise of an international police power. . . ."

Spend much time in the US Navy, and you realize there is a balance of power that must be maintained. Our job was—and is—to maintain order. Japan was angry that Russia had allied with China in 1896 to extend the Trans-Siberian Railroad across

Manchuria to Vladivostok. Japan had increased its ground troops; then Russia reneged on an agreement to withdraw from Manchuria.

Under the Treaty of Portsmouth, Japan would control the Liaodong Peninsula, Port Arthur, the South Manchurian Railway that led to Port Arthur, and Sakhalin Island. Russia agreed to leave southern Manchuria, which was restored to China. Japan would control Korea.

The Japanese protested for weeks after the Russians were not required to pay war reparations. Thirty thousand people protested in Hibiya Park in Tokyo on September 5, 1905. According to the headlines, seventeen people were killed, more than 500 were injured, and 350 buildings were damaged. The protesters believed America had sold them out.

Whoever has power over the highways, the railroads, and the seas can control the world.

We had our own share of protests in America. The Chicago Teamsters strike that started in the spring left twenty-one people dead and more than 400 injured. Sad days when the only solution to progress in the United States is violence.

Plenty of our seamen turned to the US Navy as an escape from the steel mills and the mines.

I recall Seaman Paul Wisniowski—Wiz, we called him, eighteen and wild as a March hare—letting epithets fly when his mother's letter arrived, telling him that his brother had broken a leg in the last protest and asking Wiz to come home.

I was out at the Key West Naval Yard handling records in the administrative office, retired and working as an aide to Commodore Beehler. Wiz walked in from the mess hall reading his letter, shaking his head, and slapping the paper on his leg. He had sailed on my last ship, the USS *San Francisco.*

"They beat my brother bad, Gunner, sir," Wiz said, looking at me with angry eyes as we stopped to talk. "Mother says I'm needed. I don't want to go home. There's nothing for me there. I'm supposed to ship out in two days."

"Look, Wiz," I said. "You've already re-enlisted. The US Navy isn't going to let you go home. You try going home and you'll be placed in the brig."

You have to spell it out for the young seamen. Wiz rocked back and forth and slapped the letter on his leg again.

"Two days from now I'd be at sea and not able to answer her," he muttered. We looked out at the tropical blue sky, so bright that we both blinked, and then toward the palms waving slightly in the sea breeze.

"What you have to do is tell her the truth," I said patiently. I'd been that young once. "Your ship is sailing, and the Navy won't let you leave. Tell her that you know she wouldn't want one son in the hospital and the other in jail. Mothers don't understand the military life much, Seaman. You need to lift this burden on your heart for the simple reason that you can't go."

He nodded and set his shoulders. "Thank you, Gunner, sir. I love the Navy. I belong here."

"Yes, you do," I nodded back, remembering that the Navy had saved me when I was seventeen.

A few days later, with Wiz safe at sea, I hoped, the newspapers mentioned the Wright brothers' third aeroplane, *Flyer III*, stayed in the air for thirty-nine minutes with Wilbur as the pilot in Dayton, Ohio. He landed safely when his fuel ran out. Now that, I wish I'd been there to see.

The newspapers paid less attention after the earlier less successful flights. I picked up a copy of the *Washington Evening Star* at my favorite newsstand. They had a story on page fourteen titled "FOR AERIAL FLIGHT," and buried deep in the story was a mention of the Wright brothers under a small headline that read, "Flying Has Been Done."

The great news was that Henry Flagler began extending the Florida East Coast Railway to Key West in 1905. *National Geographic* magazine had predicted in 1898, in a story with the headline "Across the Gulf by Rail to Key West," that this would become "one of man's greatest achievements."

I planned on being part of that action, building track and placing railroad cars on ships to take them to the next offloading dock, where the railroad cars exited onto other tracks and continued on their way. We were talking about engineering feats that no one had ever considered. Train traffic to Key West and Cuba was Flagler's plan. His Florida East Coast Railway was called the eighth wonder of the world.

Some Key West businessmen, friends of mine, recommended me to Flagler's project chief, Joseph Parrott, as someone with good Cuban contacts.

"You're that Gunner Morgan," Parrott said when I met him in a private dining room at Mr. Flagler's Royal Palm Hotel in Miami. "You've received many awards from the Cubans for your valor at the sinking of the USS *Maine*."

"Yes, sir, I am," I answered.

"Can you get the necessary clearances in Havana and get Cuban officials and businessmen to support this project?" he inquired crisply. He crossed one leg over the other and leaned forward with his hands clasped as though I had the secrets of the universe at my disposal.

"Yes, sir, I certainly can," I responded. "Most assuredly. Having the best means for shipping freight or transporting people is clearly a moneymaking opportunity. Reasonable businessmen will want to invest or create their business related to the railway."

We spent about two hours discussing what I would have permission to reveal about the Florida East Coast Railway, a monumental engineering project that would take years to complete. We talked about Parrott's view of what needed to be accomplished over the next two years in promoting the venture and gathering customers. I gave him a brief outline of how I would approach the project.

"You're hired," he said. "For the foreseeable future, we're in Rooms 128–130. Our bookkeeper, Mr. Robert Belcher, is there now. Your best job title will be representative for FECR."

Parrott pulled out a small leather notebook and wrote a note with my name on it and "representative's salary" beside it. "If you accept our offer, please stop by as you leave," he added.

"I certainly accept, Mr. Parrott," I said. I needed a job.

We stood, I shook his hand, and thus began my adventures with Flagler's eighth wonder of the world. Some called it Flagler's folly. Sometimes I still consider how my life would have changed from age forty onward if I had not become Flagler's representative and gone to Havana.

My friend Skip Beveridge had his own company in Jacksonville, Florida, working as a freight middleman and booking shipments for companies on the best routes available. Skip would want his customers to learn about a route to ship by railway to Cuba and South America.

I had heard that Mr. Flagler placed a ship order that involved joining the Plant Line to offer a regular shipping schedule. The Plant Line had steamships based in Tampa, Florida, that served Cuba by way of Key West; Mobile, Alabama; and two local routes.

After I met with Belcher, I spent a few minutes touring the Royal Palm Hotel, which had been open for about ten years and offered electricity, elevators, and a swimming pool—only the best for Henry Flagler's enterprises.

I knew I could like Parrott and enjoy working with him. As a military man, I appreciated straightforwardness.

Back in the lobby, I ran into Mr. Whitaker, a haberdasher, and Mr. Stevenson, the funeral director, nice men from Key West who talked too much.

And here it came: "Why, hello, Captain Morgan, what are you doing here at the Royal Palm on this beautiful day?" Whitaker's eyes gleamed with curiosity. I'd swear his mustache twitched. Stevenson stuck his hands into his coat pockets and rocked a bit as he waited.

Due to my good friend and ace newsman W. S. Meriwether, I had to be tactful in public. After he plastered my name across America as "The Man Behind the Gun," people felt I was public property. Folks thought they had a right to know what I was doing. I found that along with fame came those who wanted to ask questions and get close to the famous or infamous, and were offended if I walked away without giving careful reasons.

As I stood there contemplating my future with Flagler, I realized these two old gossips could spread the word faster than a newspaper or a club social.

"I'm representing the Florida East Coast Railway and will be speaking soon about this extraordinary opportunity and the money to be made," I said.

"Really?" Whitaker smiled, eyes gleaming. "Very interesting news, Captain."

Parrott and I agreed that I would have a letter introducing me when it was needed.

One week later, I spoke at Mr. Whitaker's businessmen's lunch in Key West. There was no need for me to stir interest in Miami. Henry Flagler was already famous there for bringing the first train to the then-fledgling city in 1896, working with Julia Tuttle to develop the city, and building the first luxury hotel.

I was called back to active duty to fill in at the Naval Yard in April 1906. When you retire from the military, they can call you back, and I was okay with that. At forty-two, it was good to feel needed. It was usually for a six-month stint.

Parrott liked that I'd been called back to duty. Even though I couldn't speak about FECR while wearing my Navy whites, when I talked to various business groups, I would be introduced as retired Chief Gunner Morgan.

In fall 1906, I traveled to Cuba, where I talked with Havana officials and pulled together my contacts, who proved highly useful. I spent a week forming a consortium of interested parties who wanted to benefit from shipping freight and people.

At the Havana Yacht Club, I met Jerry J. Warren, the Sugar King of Havana. Puffing on an aromatic Cuban cigar, he held a snifter of an after-dinner brandy and stood among several businessmen whom I'd made it my goal to meet. He wore his power well, as he was tall and sharply dressed in a casual suit.

"You're working for Henry Flagler? That's an interesting project he has going on," Mr. Warren grinned. "If anyone can get this railway built, it will be Flagler. I'll get our sugar company owners aligned to use your trains for freight. But I would be surprised if this will happen anytime soon. Why don't you stop by my office tomorrow afternoon?"

When I arrived at the Havana Vedado neighborhood address, Warren's assistant showed me into a large office with ceiling fans turning idly, dark green and white marble floors, and windows open to the terrace with its brilliant, vividly colored frangipani and orchids. A large fountain soothed the senses with the splash of water.

Inside the office, a small group of men, most wearing white linen suits, sat on the sofa and clustered chairs. A maid carefully poured Cuban rum into crystal glasses and added a sprig of mint to each glass.

"Ah, there he is! Gentlemen, meet Mr. Charles 'Gunner' Morgan, of US Navy fame, and now working for Henry Flagler. Are you interested in a drink, Mr. Morgan?" Warren asked.

"I'm interested in water, Mr. Warren," I said. "It's such a warm day today." I decided to leave for another time the fact that I don't drink. Never have.

He waved a hand toward the maid, who reached for a pitcher of water and a little bit of mint.

I was sitting in a room with five men who owned or ran sugar plantations and import and export businesses.

Behind his massive mahogany desk, Warren leaned back and unbuttoned his coat.

"Let's talk about this Florida East Coast Railway," he said.

By the end of the hour's meeting, I had six customers for Mr. Flagler, including Warren and his sugar shipments to America, and an invitation to come to the Vedado Tennis Club to discuss the next baseball championship. The other men left for their dinner engagements, but Warren asked me to stay behind.

"You played on the Navy's touring baseball team." Warren

pointed his finger at me, with that wide smile that brought people around him like dragonflies on the frangipani. "You know how the game is played, whether you're on a Navy ship or a baseball field. You've dealt with Navy officers. And yes, I've read many articles about your promotion in the newspapers. You worked the press like a charm."

"Mr. Warren, I didn't work the press," I began, tamping down irritation.

"Sure you did. Maybe you didn't intend for your letter to become public. But it did. You handled it well, being humble and letting the uproar seethe around you. You just pitched the ball to the press and let the hitter hit, the runners run, and the umpire call it."

Baseball speaks a universal language. I determined the scoreboard would be in my favor.

I smiled. "Sir, that's one way of looking at it."

I bought a white linen suit and Panama hat. I thought briefly of James Noonan of Erie, Pennsylvania, and how he might laugh that I had finally realized the value of a business suit.

Meanwhile, Henry Flagler's team was proving they could do what they promised. Key West's harbor offered vessels with a draft of thirty-three feet the deepest harbor south of Norfolk, Virginia. Construction called upon Flagler's engineers to prove their worth and more.

The September 1906 hurricane hit us hard. A quarter boat used at Long Key Viaduct escaped from its mooring and broke apart in the waves. Of 150 men aboard, 100 died. The rest were rescued by other ships.

We organized teams to search for the men. I helped pull five men from the water, sunburned, exhausted, and sick; at least they were alive.

Some were rescued at sea and ended up on a freighter headed for Liverpool, England. We found them only when the rescue ship cabled a passing US freighter.

I was called back into the Navy Yard to help put things right after the storm damage. My months were divided between the Navy Yard and being off for my other career.

In June 1907, I was on duty at the Navy Yard when a request came in at 0700 hours: Meet the ship from Havana with Mr. Jerry J. Warren's daughter Vivian aboard, and see that she receives all courtesy and care.

The order was simple enough. Because it was Jerry Warren's daughter, I would take the launch out myself. It was a morning blessed with a brilliant sun and a few white-capped waves out in Key West Harbor.

I took her hand and escorted her on board for the brief trip to land. Vivian C. Warren Weld was a lovely woman with a high forehead that showed her intelligence. She was also married and pregnant. As the wind lifted her white lace collar to blow against her cheek, I followed the collar's delicate point to hazel eyes that held a clear assessment of me as they danced with warmth, a hint of laughter, and fatigue.

"You're the famous Gunner Morgan," she smiled. "My father has told me so much about you. I feel like I know you already!"

"I'm not so famous," I smiled in return. "But thank you for that. We'll see you safely to the hospital, or are you headed to your home?"

"My home," she said.

I held her arm as we walked to her car, making her laugh as I described my first purchase of a white linen suit.

She patted my hand and said, "You're still Gunner Morgan, dressed in Navy whites or white linen."

We walked upon the dock; suddenly, there must have been a swell under my feet, because I felt my heart lift, roll, and settle again. A brisk wind lifted a curl of her sun-lightened hair against the sky. And I knew. The knowledge settled into me, a message I'd been wanting for years.

Yes, she was married and pregnant.

Both situations were temporary.

She looked at me and smiled again. "You've been visiting with my father, and somehow we haven't met. Perhaps in the future, I'll be in Havana when you come to talk business."

I escorted her to her chauffeur, waiting in front of the snazziest Pierce Great Arrow I'd seen so far. Cream leather upholstery. Brass polished to a shine you could see your face in. I have great respect for a man who knows how to polish his brass. You can't spend twenty-four years in the military and not admire the brass.

"I'm Gunner Morgan," I said, extending my hand.

"I'm Harry Brown," the chauffeur said. "I was Navy at one time myself. Everyone knows who you are, sir."

"No sirs here, Harry. I'm just Gunner," I said.

I helped Mrs. Weld onto the seat and relinquished her hand perhaps a few seconds later than I should have.

"Please let me know if you need anything while you're here, Mrs. Weld," I said politely.

"Thank you, Gunner, I certainly will."

With that, she went back to her life, and I went back to mine.

Photo courtesy of Library of Congress

The first Florida East Coast Railway train arrives at Key West, Florida, over the sea on January 22, 1912.

Photo courtesy of the Morgan family

Gunner Morgan was well known for his hand-carved ships, which he gave away as gifts, once to a seriously ill young boy and another time as a prize to the newspaper delivery boys for the *Key West Citizen*.

Carpe diem, quam minimum, crudelo postero.
"Seize the day, put very little trust in tomorrow."
Horace, *Odes*, 23 BC

Chapter Eleven

Who Cares About Key West?

Critics of Flagler's plan for the railway didn't ask whether he could build it, but why he would bother.

"Who cares what's in Key West?" I heard more than one time.

Those of us who loved the island decided to change that.

I talked with Key West businessmen George Allen, Dr. J. N. Fogarty, and V. Johnson, and our goal in October 1908 was to bring national baseball to Key West. They loved the all-American pastime as much as I did.

Because I had been the shortstop on the Navy team, I'd met and played exhibition games against national teams. More than one professional player became my friend. When we played in New Orleans, I always took them to the best Italian restaurants. If we were in New York, I'd suggest Peter Luger's for the steaks..

I wrote to Christy Mathewson of the New York Giants. Mathewson and the Giants had won the 1905 World Series over the Philadelphia Athletics. My friend Matty had pitched three shutouts in six days while giving up only 14 hits. You could say he was a national baseball sensation, and he was. He was also a kind man of great principles. Due to his Christian beliefs, he never pitched on Sundays.

He sent me this letter that I offered to the local newspaper to reprint and stir plenty of interest in the game.

New York, Oct. 3, 1908
Charles Morgan, U.S.N., Box 55, Key West, Fla.
Dear Sir:

I wrote you a few days ago but possibly you have not had time to reply. Since then I have had an offer to play a few games of ball in Norfolk, VA., and may consider going to Havana for railroad to Port Tampa.

I would have to leave Key West for Cuba on the 29th or 30th, as we have to play there on November 1.

Now that would give us any date from the 26–28 of October to play one or two games in Key West.

We will carry only about twelve men so if you get a team to play us, I will, if absolutely necessary, lend you a pitcher and catcher. My team will be composed entirely of New York National League players.

I would like to have you cable as soon as you get this unless you can reach me by letter before the 12th.

Very sincerely,
Christy Mathewson

In reply, I cabled:

Christy Mathewson, 87 St. Nicholas Place, New York City.

You arrive here on the 26th. Play the 27th and 28th. Your conditions accepted. Have sent letter.

Morgan

My friends Johnson, Fogarty, and Allen helped select good players for our team.

Bad news arrived at the last minute; the Giants did not come.

Their trip to Havana was canceled, so that meant their trip to Key West was off as well.

When we began our baseball enterprise, Fogarty was president; I was vice president; Edmund T. Crittenden was secretary; and Dr. William Warren was treasurer. We named our group the Key West Amusement Association. We looked for a site for a ballpark, including the Gato property at the corner of White Street and the County Road. We also planned to build a racetrack. Our efforts would promote the city's business and attract tourists.

Once we got baseball started in Key West, we had the Cincinnati Reds come to play November 3–4.

Jerry Warren went to the Royal Palm Hotel in Miami and stayed a week, then sailed his yacht over to Key West for the game.

The Reds' manager, Frank Bancroft, became a good friend starting with that first round of exhibition games. We also invited the Cubans to bring their teams over to Key West.

The Reds' lineup for the first game was Dick Hoblitzell, first base; Miller Huggins, second base; Hans Lobert, third base; Rudy Hulswitt, shortstop; Jean Dubuc, left field; Mike Mitchell, center field; Bob Spade, pitcher; and Admiral Schlei, catcher. Backup catcher Bunny Pearce shared the other outfield position with the non-starting pitcher for the game.

Lobert had a record of having run bases in 14 seconds. If you've ever seen him run, well, he's known as the fastest man in baseball. We had read the headlines. On September 27, Lobert was the first Reds player to steal second base, third base, and home plate in the same inning. Spade was a crackerjack pitcher, the new man on board for the Reds, and he was doing well.

The crowd had a grand time. We counted about $1,600 in ticket sales—a dollar per ticket. The best seats cost two dollars per ticket.

I made certain the players and their wives had a good trip. I took them to dinner and then on a moonlit cruise in the harbor. The 9th Artillery band played during the cruise.

The next day off, I took the team to fish, and we went to Boca Chica to have the fish cooked.

"I ate at least a hundred fish," Lobert said when we got back.

I grinned. "The better to slow you down, sir."

His teammates laughed at me. "Nothing slows down Hans!"

They were right.

Bancroft had a great time describing the game to a reporter afterward. "I have read of many peculiar plays in baseball, but I think the best of them all was pulled off at Key West," he said.

"Three sides of the field were fenced in, and the sea served for the fence on the fourth side. Dozens of boats were anchored off center field territory, loaded with spectators to watch the game. We were at bat and Bunny Pearce made the longest hit ever seen in that country, knocking the ball clear into the gulf. The Key West left fielder was sort of a daredevil. When he saw the ball strike the water, he dove in after it and a few seconds later appeared with the ball in his hand. Pearce got around the bags and was presented with a pair of shoes for pounding out that long one."

I put up the first investment in the ballgame, and I made it back three times over on ticket sales.

When he saw me in the lobby at the Royal Palm, Jerry Warren laughed over the profit report in the newspaper and waved his hand with a cheroot between his fingers. I was on my way to meet with Parrott at the time.

"Play that game, Morgan. Keep playing it," he grinned.

An invitation to Havana

Another afternoon when I met Warren in the hotel lobby, he had a lovely blonde with him who I knew wasn't his wife.

"Gunner, this is Mrs. Valerie Blackwell, who is new to Miami, and a widow as well," Warren said. "We're discussing the social life in Miami and Havana."

"Good evening, Mrs. Blackwell," I said. "You will have an excellent guide in Mr. Warren."

She nodded, her wide-brimmed, finely woven hat with its parrot feathers dipping slightly as she turned her light blue eyes my way. A beige linen jacket with ivory buttons topped her cream silk blouse, a russet tie was lightly folded at her long neck, and her blouse was tucked into a pleated linen skirt. She looked a picture, and she knew it.

"Mr. Morgan, the Navy hero," she smiled. "Why don't I see a beautiful woman on your arm?"

I turned the comment quickly, pointing out, "There aren't any who could possibly compare with you!"

She laughed and the moment passed.

I rarely escorted a woman due to the gossips who always wanted to pair me with someone. I'd gladly escort two wives to a social event when their husbands were gone, and they needed to attend. If anyone pressed too much, I'd explain that I was divorced, and it had been an unhappy time.

Yet the ladies seemed to find that even more interesting. Miss M. L. Cappick invited me to participate in an exhibit at her art studio on December 10. I took a few pieces of my hand-painted china and silk scarves and oil paintings.

Dr. Fogarty and Edmund came because they heard I was part of the art show.

"What else is it that you do?" Edmund demanded to know. "Or better, is there anything you can't do, Gunner?"

"It is somewhat hard to see your knotted baseball hands with a delicate paintbrush," Dr. Fogarty admitted in his slow drawl.

"I learned well during my time in Japan," I said. "In between firing guns and playing baseball, I found I'd rather take painting lessons and drink tea. Painting is quite calming to the spirit."

I had given away my hand-carved sailing yachts to little boys I knew through the years. My hands bore plenty of tiny white scars as well from the carving.

"Mr. Morgan, we are so glad you're here!" Miss Cappick said, her red curls bobbing around a heart-shaped face that blossomed when she smiled.

As sweet as she was, something about Miss Cappick reminded me of my long-ago ex-wife. I was unfailingly polite in return but kept my distance.

Curve balls in 1909

At the beginning of 1909, the Florida East Coast Railway construction headquarters moved to Marathon, Florida. The first office was a quarter boat; the main office was built and opened for the staff that summer.

When you consider what Flagler wanted to do, it's no wonder he had a plenitude of doubters. The route for his railway would be built over twenty-nine islands before reaching Key West, and it would cross forty-three stretches of water.

Flagler needed men experienced in these waters, the channels, and the tide, and if he didn't have them on staff, he sent me to find some of the old men well versed in the sea and the channels to give advice to the engineers. It helped that I could talk with them about my years in the Navy. Some old-timers guffawed over the entire project, and I'll give them that—it did sound weak on feasibility. A favorite saying became "a man and his money . . ."

Meanwhile, I offered advice to my friends in real estate in Key West because I knew that Flagler was a man of vision. This railway would happen. Property values would rise. Now was the time to buy.

"You're a man on a mission every single day," Fogarty said at lunch one day in the Seabreeze Café with Crittenden and Warren.

"J. N., we all have to make a living, and I like what I'm doing," I said lightly.

"What have you got going today?" Crittenden asked.

"The usual, Edmund. I reported to the engineers early, talked to Captain Sam, that old sea dog, for a while, and here I am with you, working on another baseball season for us," I said.

"Glad you are working with us, Gunner!" Fogarty grinned. "Never seen a man with as much energy as you have."

Just when you're tooling down the road of life, you hit a pothole. I always try not to wake anticipating trouble. I'm grateful for every day, and I wake anticipating the best.

We were getting a lot of good work done in June; even so,

I'd had a restless night. I was at home drinking coffee right after daybreak when my phone rang, never a good sign.

"Charles," my sister said. "I hate to give you bad news."

She paused.

I braced for news of my father's death. "Tell me, Louise."

"Brother Joseph was on his boat yesterday with Albert Snowden, one of his usual crew, and apparently, they hit a sunken log after the storm. Joseph slipped, hit his head, and never opened his eyes," Louise said. "I got the call late yesterday afternoon, and Father and I went to the hospital in Baton Rouge. We sat with him last night. He passed early this morning. Father is bearing up, but he's terribly sad."

On the beautiful day that was June 18, 1909, my dear brother Joseph, age forty-seven, passed from this life.

I took the next train to New Orleans to Louise and Father. We buried Joseph in the family mausoleum. The priest of our young days was long gone, but Father Brennan knew our family well enough and was a kind soul.

In the blink of an eye, a moment on a boat under a sunny sky, my brother was gone.

"At least," I told Louise and Father, "his last view was of the water and the sky, and no doubt he was walking forward to check that darkness in the next wave when it happened. I believe he's in heaven, looking down and wondering why, after all these years, one sunken log did him in."

I went to the bayou, intending to sit on the old dock and talk to the water, sky, and gray moss for a little while. The dock was gone, and the storm had churned the mud.

You can't go back, even if you think you can. I returned to Louise's townhouse and sat in the living room with her and Father, reminiscing over the scrapes we boys had gotten into running and playing in the streets.

"I wish you would stay for a bit," Louise said the next day.

Father had stayed with her overnight in her pleasant townhouse, too. He wouldn't leave our old cottage on Marais

Street, so Louise had a housekeeper for him, which he needed at seventy-eight. He looked shrunken, with deep circles under his eyes. He and Joseph had sold the import business, knowing I had no interest. Joseph had invested in his own freight business.

"Father walks down to the business most days," Louise said. "The young owners even have a rocker in place for him so he can enjoy watching for a while."

"They're doing well," Father said. "They have plenty of energy to run the business."

He looked at me a bit fiercely under his bushy white eyebrows.

"I never expected to bury Joseph before my time," he said. "I've lost years worrying over you. Yet here you are in the peak of health! I'm glad for it, son, but we've lost Joseph. I just never thought that would happen anytime soon."

His voice wavered.

"Father," I said gently. "I wish I could promise you that I'll be here for a very long time. You know, and I know, that life can change in an instant as it did for Joseph. I'll do my best to last for some time."

"Are you going to marry and have children?" he asked. "We have a family line to carry on."

"Someday," I heard myself say. "No hurry."

"Louise, it's best if I get back to work," I said. "Staying busy helps. Thank you for taking such good care of Father."

I patted his shoulder as I left, hugged Louise, and left her pleasant, three-story brick townhouse to return to Key West. Louise had a husband to take care of and seemed happy in her life, and I needed to go back and be happy in mine.

Visiting with the Sugar King

Jerry Warren invited me to the Vedado Tennis Club for a holiday baseball game in 1909 and to his home for a weekend. I arrived as the sun silhouetted the palm trees. We drove past the Havana Yacht Club, where boats bobbed in the marina.

I handed my hat to his butler, walked down the marble-floored hallway to the parlor, and halted abruptly as I saw Vivian Warren Weld sitting on the rattan sofa, a teacup before her on the delicately carved teak table. She wore an emerald green silk and white lace evening dress for dinner. That mesmerizing picture will remain in my mind forever.

"I believe you've met my daughter," Warren smiled as he rose from a damask-covered Queen Anne chair.

"Yes, I have," I said, walking over to extend my hand to him.

"And how are you and the baby?" I inquired, turning slightly to Mrs. Weld.

"Warren is a holy terror who's been terribly spoiled by his grandfather," she smiled over the rim of her teacup. "He's upstairs with his nanny, no doubt begging for more cookies."

She patted the sofa beside her. "You must come here and sit and regale me with stories of your adventures on the high seas. It will be such an enjoyment after days of chasing Warren, and I do so yearn for adult conversation!"

We adjourned from the parlor to the formal dining room for a meal of fresh, grilled grouper cooked with garlic, oregano, and sour orange; skewered shrimp, pineapple, and mango; and *moros y cristianos*, a mixture of black beans and rice. We finished with flan and caramel sauce.

By now, my host knew I didn't drink and offered me mint- or lemon-flavored tea.

Mrs. Weld's questions about my life were gentle, yet inquisitive, and I found myself talking about fishing contests on the bayou, Morgani's Imports, and shooting at Morgan's Camp at the Rigolets. As I described my mother's Italian cooking and the scents of sausage, garlic, and tomato sauce, Mrs. Weld asked if I had any of those family recipes. I was a bit ashamed to admit that I had no recipes except what I remembered.

"But you can shoot the big guns," her father interjected, "and you have done well enough to be the first enlisted man promoted to officer."

"Yes, sir, that's true," I answered. "And I would lead the same life I have had in the Navy if I were given the same choices in 1882 again."

"What made the Navy your choice?" he asked.

"Well, I needed to make a living," I said. "Times were hard. For me, it has always been the view of the sea, the sound of the waves, the green fire of the sun leaving a treasure to remind us she'll shine again tomorrow. There is nothing finer than seeing the Navy fleet cutting through the sea at full speed, the froth sweeping against the prow, or watching a man running up a mast as a gale comes in and securing the sails. That time is gone now, for the most part, but the memories remain."

"And yet it is not all pleasant," Warren added.

"No, it is not," I said quietly. "I have watched men die and seen bodies torn apart, sometimes by accident at sea, sometimes by the enemy. The Navy serves our country well. And I have been honored to serve our commander in chief."

Over the next few days, we traveled to the various offices of the businessmen who still planned to ship with Flagler. They were getting impatient.

Gelford Hampton, who represented The Hershey Company, asked if we had any idea when the railroad would be finished.

"We are working hard, Mr. Hampton," I assured him. "We have 300 men laying in dirt and marl, building bases for the bridges. It is a huge process, and the work continues."

Warren, Mrs. Weld, and I dined on the terrace sometimes. We talked of my sailing with the Navy.

"I don't discuss the *Maine*," I said. "It's a tragic story that would greatly diminish the evening's pleasantness."

I added casually, "I've been promoted to foreman on the Key West extension. The Navy gave me a year to be off."

"Good news!" Jerry smiled.

"Wonderful!" Mrs. Weld added, her hazel eyes alight.

Once or twice, I walked on the beach with Mrs. Weld. Her son and his nanny came along so young Warren could play in the sand. Mrs. Weld always treated me with such kind respect. Her husband was back in the United States. I wondered why he would stay there and not with her, but it was none of my business. Since Mr. Warren never mentioned him, I wondered what differences might lie between them.

I had enough to worry about as a railway foreman. We had so much to overcome. We brought in homeless people from New York to work. Many only wanted a drink and a smoke. They discovered how miserable the heat and mosquitoes could be. Eventually, we shipped some of them back.

"We have a plenitude of military veterans who desperately need jobs," I told Parrott.

"Send them," he said.

We also brought in some workers from Grand Cayman and Spain who knew how to work and understood heat and mosquitoes. We had improved the worker camps so the barracks and porches were screened against the mosquitoes. The men woke at five, ate at five thirty, worked from six to eleven in the morning, had lunch, worked until five in the evening, and ate again. They had Sundays off.

The main problem was getting fresh water. The company had to bring in 700 train carloads of fresh water from the mainland every month to meet the needs of the locomotives, stationary steam engines, cooking, and our workers.

Every so often, some gamester in Key West or Miami would ask: What are the chances the extension will be hit by another hurricane in 1910?

"I never bet on the weather," I told Fogarty as he read a similar question in the *Key West Citizen*. "When you've ridden on ships and looked at monster waves, you know Mother Nature is a capricious wench who enjoys tossing men into the sea. Two days before the previous storm, the sun was out, the waves were gently rolling, and the men were listening to a harmonica at sunset."

So, no, I don't bet on the weather.

Assistant Chief Engineer William Krome had determined that we would work in the late summer and fall to make up time. On

October 10, the Knights Key viaduct was nearly completed, and Flagler was discussing printing timetables to Key West.

The US Weather Bureau reported a hurricane had hit western Cuba and was approaching the Keys. On the morning of October 17, a telegraph operator raced into Krome's office in Marathon with the news from Miami that a hurricane would hit the Keys that night.

By noon, winds of 125 miles per hour were slashing Sand Key. Krome sent out an alert for the foremen and camps. We battened down as best we could, but this devil of a hurricane was slow. Thirteen men died on the tugboat *Sybill*. The men who had come on land to our shelters were safe.

The hurricane took her time hammering at the roadbed, the track, and the bridge. The bridge's massive steel girders were torn into the sea. More than forty miles of roadbed and track were washed away in the Upper Keys.

I surveyed the damage with Krome and our other foremen.

"Not sure what we did to anger Mother Nature quite so much," I said quietly.

Silence fell. We walked back to our launch. "Get me figures on the damages," Krome said. "Have your estimates on my desk at seven in the morning."

Mr. Flagler claimed that he estimated damages were no more than $200,000. The newspaper experts raved about those figures.

At least the piers and viaduct supports for the Seven Mile Bridge and the Long Key span were still there. Meanwhile, Mr. Flagler demanded that we push ahead, and by November 8, we had passenger service to Knights Key.

Invited back by Jerry Warren, I went to Cuba to tell the businessmen we were on track to finish.

I met Warren first at the Vedado Tennis Club, where the men had gathered to play tennis and drink Cuban rum.

"It's always better to make your pitch when they're a bit tired and have a good glass of rum in their hands," Jerry opined, with what I have come to call to myself "the Warren gleam" in his eye.

"I like that you don't drink," he said. "You need a clear head to do business."

And he turned that look on me. "Vivian is divorced. She was so unhappy, and I put an end to it. We'll go to the house, and perhaps she can tell you a little about it."

My heart thundered and my ears filled with the pulse of it. My hand trembled slightly with my glass of water.

What would she see as I walked in? A forty-two-year-old man in good physical form dressed in a white linen suit. Did I still have those "melting Italian brown eyes" that my shipmates had teased me about using with women? There were no women, but still. Had hard life experiences changed the "melt?" I never took time to admire myself in a mirror. Just got up and went to it. Made the day happen.

We sat on the terrace that night under a full moon, drinking tea and enjoying a Cuban cake roll. Jerry had excused himself for bed earlier, after mentioning that he wanted me to represent him in some real estate investments in Miami and Key West.

Vivian laughed quietly after he left. "My father likes you a lot," she said. "I like you as well. Do you think we may spend some time learning more about each other?"

"Yes," I smiled, looking over the flickering candles. "I think we can."

On January 22, 1912, the first scheduled train crossed the Key West extension from Miami. I received a major promotion for my work, and I stayed until July 1912.

Then I began working for Warren Investments and left for New York to join my future father-in-law to explore business prospects. We had barely unpacked our bags at his grand New York City townhome at 235 Central Park West and settled in to enjoy a light supper with Jerry and his bride, Clarissa, before the police arrived at the front door asking to see Mr. Jerry Warren.

Marriage has its pitfalls. More than one marriage at a time could be a deep mess.

Illustration by Wanda Stanfill

Vivian was an elegant bride on her wedding day in Washington, DC.

"By all means, marry. If you get a good wife, you'll become happy; if you get a bad one, you'll become a philosopher."
Socrates

Chapter Twelve

Wedding Bells Toll

The news of Jerry J. Warren's August 1, 1912, marriage to Clarissa Prescott of Shreveport, Louisiana, before Judge Boyle in Fairfield, Connecticut, had been in the newspapers. His former wife—at least, I thought she was former—saw an article in the Key West newspaper and appeared in New York along with her son Rudolph, age twenty-five, and her attorney, Mr. H. M. Holds from Nassau, to file a warrant.

Late in the day on August 1, the family's longtime butler, James Cross, announced Sheriff Hezekiah Elwood and Detective Mike Quinn of the West 100th Street station as we finished tea in the parlor while Jerry enjoyed his customary snifter of brandy.

"Ladies and gentlemen," Cross intoned. "I apologize for the interruption. We have two officers here desiring a conversation."

Vivian and I were seated in two red velvet Chippendale wing chairs with our teacups and a plate of shortbread teacakes on the mahogany table between us. We'd barely had time to freshen ourselves upstairs before the dinner bell rang. Jerry, still dressed in a splendid suit from his wedding, and Clarissa, quite elegant in her midnight blue silk gown for dinner, sat on the loveseat across from us, while the late afternoon sun reflected on the light traffic below, the noise barely audible indoors.

"Show them in," Jerry said calmly, with a hint of boredom in his voice.

"I wonder if we have trouble at one of our businesses," I mused, shifting back in my seat, teacup in hand.

Cross ushered in a stocky man in a tweed suit, bowler hat in his hand, black hair slicked back, and dark eyes assessing the room and us.

"This is Detective Quinn," Cross said, and gestured to his right, "and Sheriff Elwood."

Elwood was a lanky man in light gray trousers, a vest, long-sleeved white shirt, bow tie, and light gray pinstriped suit jacket.

I suspected that they had dressed differently before coming to the luxurious home of the Sugar King of Havana, which was a wise move on their parts, showing a bit of respect. Their clothes were neither stained from the day's heat nor rumpled.

"Gentlemen," Cross said. "Would you care for coffee or tea?"

"No, thank you," Detective Quinn said politely, and turned to Jerry. "Mr. Warren, we have a warrant for your arrest."

"On what charges?" Jerry asked, just as politely, as he crossed one leg over the other.

"The charge is bigamy, sir," said Sheriff Elwood. "You need to come with us."

Clarissa gasped, and Vivian's eyes widened. Her teacup clattered a bit in the saucer. I reached for her hand and squeezed it gently.

"Charles, if you don't mind, finish your tea with the ladies," Jerry said. "James, please call Mr. Marshall, my attorney. Ask Henry to meet me."

With perfect aplomb, as though he was leaving for lunch at the club, my future father-in-law rose, took his hat, and left with the officers behind him.

In the echoing silence, I sighed. "Clarissa, this will be settled shortly. I will not speak for Jerry regarding any charges. I know that he cherishes you. His ex-wife has been highly upset about the divorce. I'm sure he'll get this settled and be home for breakfast."

Having shot me a worried glance, Vivian told Clarissa with admirable calm, "My father will take care of this, and all will be well by tomorrow."

As we parted at our bedroom doors upstairs, Vivian turned back to me briefly. "I hope I told Clarissa the truth. She is trying hard to hide her fear, I think."

"Vivian, I can assure you that your father is one of the most indomitable men I've ever met," I said quietly. "He'll be home tomorrow, and this situation will be resolved."

Actually, he was home before midnight. I thought his attorney got the city judge out of an opera performance.

"No," Jerry laughed. "He was at Riley's Bar around the corner from the courthouse, clearly into his sixth beer, seeking wisdom in the foam, and finding he could froth over being told he had to go back to work!"

Jerry told his butler, "Cross, you can leave us after you pour a brandy for me and hot tea for Gunner."

As I expected, his ex-wife claimed they were not divorced and that he had not paid anything to her.

"Jerry, you owe me no explanation," I said.

"But I do. You intend to marry my daughter, and I want you to know that I am not as bad a scoundrel as my ex-wife says. I don't really care what the rest of the world thinks. What I'm telling you now will be in the newspaper tomorrow anyway."

"All right then." I settled into my chair.

"My marriage to this woman was dissolved by the courts of Cuba last June. There are no divorce laws in Cuba," Jerry said, tapping one finger on the mahogany chair arm. "I got a divorce from her in this country—my attorney can give you the exact date—and then remarried her at Rudolph's request in Cuba. I felt his anguish over his mother, and I should not have done it, but I did. This was dissolved on the grounds of fraud.

"I gave her $50,000 just before the marriage was annulled in Havana, and I gave Rudolph enough land to help establish him in business and sell it profitably. You've seen it—a large plot near the Vedado Tennis Club."

Jerry paused. "Of course, my ex-wife is now at the Hotel Astor with Rudolph and holding forth to anyone who will listen about what happened. I hear she has a society reporter from the *New York Sun* who is drinking in every word. Meanwhile, I'm sure she is sipping champagne."

I knew he had married well back in 1886. His ex-wife was a Bouligny whose grandfather had been governor of Louisiana at one time, and her uncle was in Congress. She described Jerry in the *New York Sun* the next day as nothing but a "struggling drug clerk when we married."

Later that day, when Clarissa had gone shopping with Jerry, I sat on the sun porch with Vivian enjoying lunch and we read the latest newspaper, which gave some inches of space to the story. Money, scandal, and bigamy are always big sellers.

Yet the world was still reeling after the *Titanic* sank in April. A foundation had been established to help the affected families, and many of us had donated. I thought with great sadness of the 1,517 who died when the *Titanic* sank, many freezing in the water. The wreck inquiries had claimed headlines for months.

When I focused on lightening my thoughts, I found the sports pages. Fenway Park had opened with the first official game on April 20. Boston Mayor John "Honey Fitz" Fitzgerald threw the first pitch, and the Red Sox defeated the New York Highlanders 7–6 in extra innings.

Jerry wanted to take us to a baseball game, and I'd managed to get Vivian as excited about the game as I was.

Even as we prepared to enjoy some weeks in the States, Jerry and I felt concerned over the situation in Cuba, where the president, General Jose Miguel Gomez, had brutally suppressed the Cuban rebels. We sent in US Marines, and 3,000 rebels were killed. Our Marines took control of the Cuban government to protect American interests—such as our own. President William Howard Taft had assured the American public that this act did not constitute "intervention."

There is an old saying that my fellow Navy men and I have shared many times. "When is a dolphin fin not a dolphin? When it's a shark." And you'd better know the difference. I didn't want to believe the American public thought we were swimming with dolphins in Cuba.

America's intervention was intended to protect and save the sugar and tobacco plantations.

One man and his ex-wife seemed not to warrant the newspaper space allotted. I said so to Vivian.

"There will always be those who love to read of the peccadilloes of millionaires, dearest," she said.

Vivian smoothed her portion of the paper and glanced at me as she read, brushing a wisp of hair back into the bun at the base of her neck.

"As his ex-wife, she's doing quite a job of smashing my father's reputation," Vivian commented wryly. "She says they quarreled in 1896—the cook said their anger curdled the milk. Father tried to get a divorce then. The Cuban laws did not permit divorce; he got around that. I don't know exactly how. It was none of my business, and I haven't asked."

She continued reading: " 'We found a way to solve our troubles, and we remarried in 1901 in Havana. We repeated our vows. Last January, he gave up his home in Havana. He told me it was because of business, that he was making important deals in New York and that I encumbered him.

" 'I was willing to go to Europe. Of course, after that insult, I couldn't have anything more to do with him. The annulment was granted July 23.' "

Vivian continued, "And here she claims that my father didn't give her $50,000. She says her mother deeded him the house worth $86,000 in New Orleans when they married, and he sold the house for a mere $28,000. That doesn't sound like my father.

I've never known him to accept a loss on anything. And she says the $50,000—that he didn't give her, mind you—was money due her from the house and that he owed her mother even more."

Vivian sighed and sipped her tea, and nibbled on a cranberry and cream scone. "Here, you read the rest of it."

According to the *Sun*, Rudolph said in court, "My father didn't put me into business through his generosity!"

"I'm somewhat surprised that Rudolph would deny Jerry's gift," I said grimly. "Your brother lacks some level of common sense. Jerry is developing more business in America and Cuba that could someday involve Rudolph. I suppose he felt he had to stand by his mother."

Jerry had plans to bring fresh pineapple to the American market as a drink. We loved fresh, cool pineapple juice in Cuba, and our guests raved about it. The first US transcontinental flight from San Francisco had landed in Jacksonville, Florida, in February, and Jerry was looking at Jacksonville as our potential factory location. He saw the West Coast as a potential market, since he was considering pineapple from the Hawaiian Islands.

We sat quietly for a few more moments, and I laid the newspaper aside and stood. "Enough of this drama today. Let's go to Central Park or go to Luger's for steaks. It's a beautiful day, and there's a city beckoning us to join in the liveliness!"

"You're right, of course." Vivian tapped my cheek lightly. "I'll get my hat. The newlyweds certainly don't need us here!"

After dinner, we returned to the house and joined Jerry and Clarissa for sweetbreads and coffee. They seemed to have resolved any concerns from the day's turmoil.

The next day, we went to Washington. Jerry had been called to a private meeting of sugar plantation owners, others with businesses in Cuba, and Secretary of State Philander Chase Knox. We checked into The Willard Hotel, and Vivian and Clarissa planned to play tennis and shop.

The first two days of our trip, Jerry and I spent several hours in meetings with other American and Cuban business owners.

Knox had met with Cuba's President Gomez and Secretary of State Manuel Sanguily on April 16. Next to nothing had appeared in the news because the *Titanic* had sunk the day before.

We knew Knox's policies from reading his speech to Congress in January. We needed to hear how the United States would bolster the Central and South American governments and keep the peace so money could flow both ways. Then there was the continuing instability in Cuba.

Among those at the table were representatives from the Cuban-American Sugar Company, which controlled thousands of acres of sugar plantations; Milton Hershey's sugar factory; Standard Fruit Company; Cuyamel Fruit Company; the Havana Sugar Company; and others.

"Gentlemen," Jerry said. "As we are aware, money talks. You are here, and your message is clear to the secretary of state and to the president."

I listened as I sat at the oval conference table with men who talked in quiet tones and wielded power and money like a sharp-edged sword, carefully disguised. Most were brilliant; a few had inherited wealth and business but not common sense. They wanted anyone opposing their companies swept into the ocean for the sharks' dinner. The companies had British, American, or Spanish names; there were investors behind those names from many other countries.

Jerry and I knew President Taft's simple analysis of social unrest didn't remotely take into account the complex issues. It was easy to say America would keep a region financially stable and, at the same time, protect our commercial and financial interests if you didn't have an in-depth knowledge of what needed to be done.

Knox baldly said that these countries looked to the prosperous and powerful United States for aid and guidance. I knew some of the rebels in Cuba, and so did Jerry. They wanted us gone.

"In 1909, the total foreign trade of the Central American states, including Panama, amounted to approximately $60 million, of which about one half was with the United States," Knox said.

One of the treaties that Taft and Knox favored would make certain American officials were in the customhouses. They said that would ensure an end to corruption or bribes. Knox said that trade with the Dominican Republic, for instance, had more than doubled since American officials took over.

Jerry did not even glance my way. I knew what he was thinking. Yes, there are American men of integrity who don't take bribes; there are men who would and do.

When we ended the meeting, I looked at Jerry. "You have done well to maintain your strength with this group."

Jerry grinned like a cat finishing a fresh minnow. "Yes, I have."

The business owners left satisfied that the United States military, if necessary, would make certain the import-export business continued to thrive.

After spending a day listening to men pontificate, Jerry and I were ready for a more casual dinner, and we took Vivian and Clarissa to The Occidental at 1411 Pennsylvania Avenue, where Gustav Buchholz, the former headwaiter at The Willard, was in charge of the restaurant. It was an easy walk from The Willard at 1401 Pennsylvania, just down the street.

"You have to try one of his pork chops marinated and grilled in oranges and bourbon," Jerry said. "Gustav knows a thing or two about fine food."

The next morning, we had tea and pastries delivered, opened the windows over the small balcony, and enjoyed a breeze while we read the *Washington Post*.

Vivian peeked around her newspaper. "I'd like to be married in Washington. Many of my friends are here."

There's no denying the irresistible sparkle in your woman's eyes. My heart leapt into a tango. "Yes. May we keep the list small? We're not a young couple at thirty-one and forty-seven."

On August 5, 1912, I married Vivian in Washington, DC. Let me tell you how that went.

A number of my friends would be in the city for the opening of the new Army-Navy Club downtown on August 9. President

Taft would attend the dedication. Jerry had been invited, and so had I.

We talked with hotel staff about marrying at The Willard. That didn't happen.

Jerry invited Edward McLean, heir to the *Washington Post* and the *Cincinnati Enquirer* fortune, to dine with us at The Willard.

"Edward wants to know about our meetings with Secretary Knox," he said. "I'm willing to share some information that might help our long-term goals to keep the peace in Cuba and the economy steady."

At dinner with the McLeans, we mentioned that we planned to marry quietly, with only a few friends, somewhere in Washington.

Evalyn McLean clattered her fork on her plate and waved her hand in the air. "You'll marry at our home. We have lovely gardens. Please say you will. It will keep our staff on their toes!"

Edward joined in her excitement, and the deal was done.

Evalyn, Vivian, and Clarissa began discussing a July *Good Housekeeping* article, "An Introduction and Dissertation on Marriage," about the favorite colors of weddings, pink and blue, that the society fashion writer had described as "the simple colors of La France roses and of a summer sky that our mothers and our grandmothers loved."

They grinned at each other and said, "Orange blossoms!"

"And my champagne silk gown with turquoise ribbons!" Vivian laughed.

The three began creating a design for her hat to protect her from the summer heat.

"Oh, our archway of purple clematis is just beautiful for a wedding," Evalyn exclaimed. "Why not purple ribbons, the color of royalty? They would be lovely on champagne silk."

"You are so right! That would be beautiful," Vivian said. "Thank you for thinking of it!"

Clarissa added, "What did you think about the butterflies Evelyn Schley had embroidered on her gown for her wedding to Max Behr, Evalyn?"

"I know the butterfly is considered the symbol of immortal love," Evalyn said, "yet butterflies have a short life. Oh, well, we can't understand everyone's perspectives. Indeed, that's such a bother that I try not to do so!"

They smiled companionably and lingered over their chocolate cake, drizzled with whipped cream and topped with cherries.

Vivian saw me watching her scoop another bite and waved her spoon at me. "I'm playing tennis in the morning, dear heart. I'll work it off!"

"I'm just relishing your enjoyment," I laughed. "You might want to order that cake for our wedding, too."

Although I had continued painting in Cuba, and I'd never stopped carving my ships, this wedding setting was not my cup of tea. Edward and Jerry, deep into a discussion of the import business, glanced at me over their coffees.

"Jerry, let's take poor Gunner to the gentlemen's bar and pool room," Edward chuckled. "Evalyn, Clarissa, and Vivian don't need our male viewpoints right now. Ladies, join us on the terrace in an hour. Would that allow you enough time for planning?"

At the chorused "Yes!" we escaped to play pool.

My goal was to be married to the love of my life with a Bible in our hands in hopes we'd have a blessing. We would marry August 5, 1912, at the Walsh mansion, at 2020 Massachusetts Avenue.

Evalyn Walsh McLean was five years younger than Vivian, yet they had become friends, perhaps because of their backgrounds. Evalyn's wealth came from her father's mines in Colorado and Vivian's from sugar plantations in Cuba. They were both world travelers who met at a yachting race in Boston, yet they enjoyed the friendship of people from many walks of life.

I was grateful for their outlook, after starting life poor in New Orleans and making my way in the US Navy, rich in patriotism and a world education, though not deep in funds.

Skip and Valerie Beveridge were coming from Jacksonville. I had called my friend Henry Tresselt; however, he couldn't attend because he was directing a street project for the city of Oakland,

California. He wished us well. As for my New Orleans family, Vivian and I decided to travel there and hold a reception at the Hotel Monteleone later.

My sister, Louise Depew, had called to offer her congratulations. "Gunner, you are marrying well. You've always landed on your feet like a cat!" She laughed a bit into the phone, adding, "She's a lucky woman to have a man like you who can seize the world in two hands and shake it out to create a fine life."

"When we come to see you in New Orleans, Louise, your sworn duty is not to tell any tales of my misspent youth!" I laughed with her. We hung up with me promising to give her plenty of warning on the reception date.

I was perfectly fine with only Skip and Valerie. Vivian asked four more friends and their husbands. Jerry, Clarissa, and the McLeans were there. We had about twenty people, counting staff and the violinist and pianist.

Clarissa, as matron of honor, walked down the aisle wearing a deep purple silk gown and carrying a lavender rose bouquet with ribbons. I craned my neck to see my beautiful Vivian walking gracefully toward me, wearing her draped champagne silk gown with its long lace panels and deep purple satin ribbons flowing with each step. She carried orange blossoms and lavender roses in her bouquet, and matching roses adorned her wide-brimmed hat with chiffon draped around and down her back.

I memorized every detail to share with my sister, as she had made me pledge to do.

Skip stood with me as best man.

As Jerry stepped back, I stepped forward to meet my bride under the arch of purple clematis, and I pledged to honor and cherish Vivian forever.

I have to confess that Jerry had told me what Vivian hoped for in Washington.

"I believe that you are in harmony with her?" he asked.

"Yes." So in a black velvet pouch, I had brought her ring and wedding gift.

"With this ring, we are wedded." I slipped a band of Brazilian emeralds with a pure white pearl onto her finger. Later, I would give her a three-strand pearl necklace with an emerald clasp. My vow wasn't traditional. We didn't care.

I kissed her gently, then murmured, "I will carry you away before long."

Turning to face our guests, I slid my arm carefully under my bride's chiffon drape so as not to jerk her hat off, like I was a young seaman reefing a sail under gale conditions.

We walked forward toward our friends as the violinist turned to light music.

Skip clapped me on the shoulder and whispered in my ear, "You're a lucky sod, old man."

"Yes, I certainly am, lucky that is. Not old. That would be you!" I laughed. "Look at that gray showing in that red hair at your temples!"

"Yes, well, I always knew your Italian brown hair and eyes would be everlasting to charm the ladies." Skip lowered his voice and looked at Vivian as he did so, with a twinkle in his bright blue eyes.

We'd seen too much, the two of us, in war, and we knew to celebrate that we had so much more to enjoy in life.

I took Valerie's hand. She was a blonde whose curls were hard to contain around her sweetly dimpled cheeks. I could see in my mind's eye Skip's children with wild, curly hair, and it made me happy for him.

"Skip is really fortunate that he married you. I hear you have a little one coming next year?"

She blushed a bright red due to her fair skin. "Yes, we do. I hope it's a little boy to drive Skip crazy chasing him!"

As we went in for champagne and cake, Vivian removed her broad-brimmed hat, pinning one small bouquet of orange blossoms at the back of her head. Edward and Jerry took over a corner table. Evalyn had the women talking about a fashion show the next day at The Willard. Skip and I took over another corner table and regaled each other with tales of our past. Finally, I looked over at Vivian, and Skip nudged me.

"Get out of here, old man, with your bride," he grinned.

I walked over to Vivian and the women parted like waves.

"About time you came to get her," Evalyn laughed. "Ladies, we're about to enjoy the most delicious ice cream ever! Vivian, you're going to miss it, not that you'll care, my dear."

We escaped to the Pierce-Arrow waiting outside with our driver. Within a half hour, we were at The Willard and entered to find that Jerry had given orders to move us and our clothes and luggage to the penthouse suite for the next two evenings. The windows looked out toward the White House.

We walked in to find staff waiting on us with more champagne, chocolates, and bouquets of white roses. Candles were lit at a small table by the balcony.

The valet and two maids offered their well wishes for our marriage, then closed the door quietly behind them as they left.

I placed my hands gently on Vivian's shoulders.

"Well, my lovely Vivian, you are now Mrs. Charles Morgan. You've promised to love and to cherish. We're about to begin our life together."

"Yes, we are," she smiled with a mischievous twinkle. "And it will be an adventure, I promise you."

"I don't have to have adventures every day." I leaned forward, seeking a kiss. "A quiet harbor and peace in our souls would be really exceptional, though."

Illustration by Wanda Stanfill

Rudolph Warren was killed in a duel with Hannibal Mesa on April 5, 1913.

“I don’t pity any man who does hard work worth doing. I admire him. I pity the creature who does not work, at whichever end of the social scale he may regard himself as being.”
Theodore Roosevelt

Chapter Thirteen

Death by Duel

What can I say about my brother-in-law, Rudolph Warren? Young, spoiled, charming, sulky, entitled. Each day I thought about how the Navy could straighten him up.

He’d run his hand through his curling hair, look at a woman, and off they’d go. Then he’d run his hand through his curling hair, toss off a glass of Cuban rum, and off he’d go to the clubs of Havana. Then he’d come dragging in about dawn.

Vivian sighed over her brother. "Rudolph, you look like you’ve fallen into the harbor," she laughed one morning when, still dressed in his linen suit, he strolled in to slump into a chair on the terrace, begging Carmela, the housekeeper, for fresh pineapple juice and eggs.

He lifted his bloodshot gaze to Vivian. “Perhaps I did," he muttered and reached for bread.

She waved one admonishing hand at him. “There’s no reason not to be polite."

“I don’t feel like being polite this morning," he mumbled around a mouthful.

Add boorish to my list. I stood and touched Vivian's shoulder. "You're especially lovely today in your new outfit," I said as she smiled at me, only a little cloud behind her eyes due to her bothersome brother. "Is that from the new seamstress?"

"Yes, it is," she said. "I'm thinking about investing in her little shop. She does such lovely work, and she'll be doing quite well before long."

I paused as Carmela cleared away my plate and glass.

"I'll be back for lunch a little late. I have a meeting at ten regarding some shipments going to Key West," I said.

Following up on Jerry's discussion with me the previous week, I added, "Rudolph, some of these gentlemen might be interested in your property and getting your export business going, if you'd like to meet me at the office."

He shot me a look and flicked back that irritating lock of hair.

"I have my own meetings to attend," he scowled.

"That's good news," I said calmly. "If you need any help . . ."

"I handle my own affairs, thank you," he said, and stuffed a big forkful of eggs into his mouth.

I'm not an eye-roller. Never have been. But it took some determination to keep my smile in place and move on.

Since Jerry's divorce from Rudolph's mother two years earlier, Rudolph had done nothing to show he deserved the considerable property Jerry had given him and invited him to develop and sell at a profit.

Instead, he traveled abroad on his father's good name, then came home and partied. He had just returned from France, his valet's patience worn from trying to keep his employer, Jerry, happy while keeping an eye on the young man of the world.

Sometimes the wealthy never drop in on the staff; I have always found it's the best way to test the temperature of the household.

Jerry told me the previous week that he was at his wit's end.

"I've come to the conclusion that I will have to tell him he has six months to show he can run a business or he will have no further help from me, nor will he be welcome in my house," Jerry said. "My son needs reforming. I'm going to do it, though I know it's late to try. Hell and damnation, he's twenty-six!

"After that time, I will cut him off from my funds, my clubs, everything he takes so cavalierly," Jerry continued, his tone colder and more even. "I've had enough."

Young Rudolph was making a serious mistake in assuming he would be forgiven everything.

Vivian and I had spent about ten months in Havana at the home in Vedado, not far from the tennis club. I ferried back and forth to Miami and Key West to develop Warren Investments' holdings in real estate. Jerry could see that people would always want to leave the snow of New York and Boston to come south for the winter, and they would need comfortable homes and resort hotels. Jerry was right, as he usually was.

I considered telling my father-in-law some months earlier that he should ship Rudolph to military training. Then Jerry looked at me one night at the Havana Yacht Club and said, "I wish Rudolph could be more like you. Military service would help. I think it's too late. He hasn't paid enough attention to his studies. He has little discipline due to his mother's coddling. I know that I bear some fault myself, being too busy developing our plantation and sugar mill business. A young boy needs a man beside him not only when it's convenient but most of the time. Remember that with your children, Gunner."

Jerry did bear some fault. Rudolph was immersed in the Havana party scene when he wasn't traveling to Paris or London. His father gave him the money and sent him off to travel. That's one way of not being reminded daily that you haven't been the father you could have been.

I had the benefit of a father and uncle who had made certain I'd become a gentleman, although we weren't wealthy. The Navy shaped me into a stronger man.

Sometimes Rudolph invited me to go with him; however, I was forty-eight, married, working, and didn't drink. He did it as a courtesy, I'm sure. I had no interest unless I was going to a society event with the money men who would be interested in our business enterprises, and that was not Rudolph's métier. To be perfectly clear, the businessmen weren't interested in a sulky, rich, twenty-six-year-old man who had done nothing to give himself credit for an intelligent life well lived. They might take a bet with him on a baseball game or the horse races because he was, after all, the Sugar King of Havana's son.

I can see how that life would erode any man's soul. There is nothing better as the sun sets than to know you have made a change in the world that day.

Vivian wanted to help her brother, but she had Warren to raise and our baby on the way. She chose to focus on the young mothers of Havana and the elderly, and used her funds to have a free medical clinic built with a small school next door in the stucco building.

Jerry Warren took good care of the household staff as well. We were working to get American citizenship for one of our Chinese staff, Eng.

I knew this kindness had some effect when the town saw unrest as locals fought over whether their president was taking care of his people or giving us Americans control over the economy. Nothing happened in our neighborhood or on our street.

Vivian appealed to me as I finished a cup of tea and a bowl of mangoes and pineapple with sweetbreads for breakfast.

"Gunner, darling, I know Rudolph is irritating; however, he does admire you," she said, as she cut red roses for a crystal vase. "He wishes he could be more like you. He doesn't know how."

I paid close attention to the way the sun stroked her hair, bringing out the light in it. She stood there clipping flowers, dressed in a simple, white pleated blouse and split skirt for riding, with her hair pinned up from the heat.

"He must be trying to keep it a secret," I smiled, as I stood and reached for my Panama hat. "Because he avoids me every morning when I head out to work. Maybe he's afraid I'll invite him yet one more time to join me at the office."

"Well, I heard him say he might stop by this morning," she said, cocking her head to the side and nibbling her lip in that way she had when she was concerned. "If he does, please encourage him to stay. Perhaps he'll find that dealing in business is not boring."

I sighed. "I'll try again. You know, dear, I'd help him market that land and develop it properly. I offered once before, and he brushed me off."

She finished her flowers and turned to me, straightening my collar. "Thank you for trying," she smiled and patted my chest.

She heard Warren's laughter and turned to go upstairs. "Madelena," she called. "Let's take Warren to the park before I ride today."

Anything I said to Rudolph would be a waste of time. She asked, so I would try.

I decided to bypass taking the Model T to work and walk instead. I could go by the newsstand on my way, stop for a moment for a quick haircut, and then get to the office. My new assistant, Henry Parsons, would have efficiently straightened the papers on my desk. Jerry had brought him back from the last trip to New York.

Parsons was a business school graduate, well lettered, and needed a job. I never wanted an assistant. I'm perfectly capable of doing my own bookwork and letters. Jerry assured me that employing Parsons would elevate my prominence in the business world. I decided to look upon it as having a first mate.

The sugar mills had been repaired after the war, and under treaty terms, Cuban sugar received a 20 percent tariff reduction in the United States in exchange for reductions of 20–40 percent for US goods entering Cuba.

"Good morning, sir," Parsons said as I walked in from the back terrace. "The reports on our shipments are on your desk."

"Good morning, Parsons. Do you have time now to take some notes on what we're sending out next week?" I asked, surveying his neat linen suit and bow tie. The young man never looked wilted in the heat.

"How do you do that?" I grinned.

"Do what, sir?"

"Keep yourself looking cool and unwrinkled," I laughed.

He was still so fresh off the ship that he blushed a bit at the compliment.

"My mother preached many sermons to me on dressing well," he smiled.

"Ah, that's it, then," I nodded solemnly. "My mother did, too. Mothers rule the world, and aren't we glad they do!"

We settled in as I pulled out his reports. Business was growing so fast that we were loading trains and ships every day. It was a bountiful time. The Cuba Company built a 350-mile railroad connecting the eastern port of Santiago to the existing railways in central Cuba. Sugar was everything.

Our troops had left in 1909, after over three years in Cuba. When President Palma's regime collapsed in 1906, our commander in chief, President Roosevelt, sent troops partly to stop the fighting among the Cubans and mainly to protect American businesses and hold free elections. In these peaceful times, money was pouring into our Cuban sugar mill operation.

Then we began building homes and hotels in Havana, Key West, and Miami. Jerry already had homes in New York, Key West, and Havana. His business with the Cuban Sugar Manufacturing Co. had quadrupled in a short time.

By the time we finished going over the shipping costs for the week and planned our exports for the following week, two Cuban gentlemen representing a consortium of wealthy families were waiting in the reception area to discuss investments in America.

Eduardo Gato Sr. planned to build a large cigar factory in Key West, using tobacco from Cuba for his hand-rolled and boxed cigars. We had visited his home at 1327 Duval Street in Key West to talk about Señor Gato importing tobacco from Cuba to Key West for his factory.

Jerry had made certain I met Señor Gato and his son, Eduardo Gato Jr., when we were in Key West. Before our first meeting,

Jerry told me, "You can appreciate that he is a fine Cuban patriot. He bankrolled many attempts to overturn the Spanish. He also began buying real estate in Key West long ago, and he owns the Key West Street Car Company. He's a wise man who foresees opportunities."

I stretched out my hand to Gato Sr. and Gato Jr. "*Señores, buenos días*."

Then I switched to English, knowing both men were proficient speakers of our language.

"You honor us by stopping in when you have such extensive business to transact. We're glad you plan to entrust our company with your tobacco shipments."

"We do have much to accomplish," said Gato Sr., "but we combined a little family visit with checking our tobacco harvest."

"We are beginning construction on our plant in the spring, and we intend to create our own workers' cottages near the plant," added Gato Jr. "We talked to certain of our workers here about coming to Key West."

"I would imagine they were pleased," I said. "Because we know that Key West is an attractive gem, a great place to live with a glowing future."

By the time they left, thousands of dollars were to be transferred from Gato Sr.'s Key West bank to ours.

That night, Jerry decided to send me to Miami immediately to purchase land and work with his construction crews to plan neighborhoods with more homes for Cuban families aiming to develop their import businesses—Cuban rum and cigars, plus pineapple shipments.

One of the families indicating an interest in real estate was the Mesas, whose eldest son, Hannibal, was a particular friend of Rudolph's. Hannibal Mesa was training with his father to take over the import business someday. When I had met him some months earlier, I was impressed by his knowledge of the business and the intensity in his dark eyes, which missed nothing of the conversation.

Rudolph and Hannibal often went to dinner or out on the town together. Sometimes I wondered what young Hannibal's goal was. Rudolph, when drinking, could probably share too much about his father's business interests.

I had grown somewhat cynical after observing and participating in the business meetings in Havana. And I'd learned from watching Jerry, who always had a glass in his hand—of plain water or tea—whenever he was involved with other businessmen.

And then disaster struck. Rudolph got a young woman in trouble in town, and Jerry had to settle a large sum on the family.

"How could you be so stupid?" Jerry yelled. "You were brought up to know better!"

Their shouting that evening before dusk should have made the tiles slide off the roof. Vivian took Warren out to the harbor so he wouldn't hear it.

I sat on the terrace sipping a cold tea and stayed out of their way. I wasn't eavesdropping—not when the angry words echoed throughout the house.

"You can consider what I paid for that girl's upkeep and her child for the next several years to be the sum total of your allowance," Jerry growled, hitting his fist on the table. "You are officially cut off. You can live in this house, but not a penny will you get. Until you go out and work in business, you are done. You have a month to get a job since you won't work in my office and make an attempt—any attempt at all—to bring in some income for yourself!"

"Don't expect to run tabs at the clubs," he raged. "I've told them I won't honor your bills."

What I heard after that was Rudolph charging down the stairs, flinging open the front door, and striding angrily down the steps.

What happened afterward is conjecture based on what those involved had to say about it.

Rudolph sent a message by his valet to Hannibal Mesa asking Hannibal to meet for dinner Friday night at the Havana Yacht

Club, completely disregarding Jerry's last words. Hannibal accepted the invitation.

Rudolph ordered drinks and food and proceeded to party by himself. Hannibal didn't show. Rudolph was told that his friend was at the Vedado Tennis Club, ignoring him.

By that point drunk, Rudolph took a taxi to the Vedado Tennis Club, walked to Hannibal's table, and whaled at his friend's shoulder with a walking cane. Hannibal came out of his seat and issued a challenge to a duel. Rudolph, the young fool, accepted, although he knew nothing about pistols and was nearsighted. Seconds were chosen.

They traveled to the riding fields out past Morro Castle Road early the next morning, and within a short period of time, Hannibal drew his pistol and shot Rudolph in the abdomen at twenty-five paces. Rudolph died later that day with Jerry and Vivian by his side. I leaned against the wall near the window, listened to his last labored breathing, looked at the brilliant sky, and said little.

Call it whatever you will—I called it committing suicide by duel on April 5, 1913.

Dr. Orestes Ferrara, former speaker of the Cuban House of Representatives and a major in the Cuban Army, wrote a letter to the *Havana Times* in defense. The *Times* had condemned the duel, saying that the seconds should have stopped it.

"I was Mesa's second," Dr. Ferrara said, "and my name, as well as my companion's and those of the distinguished seconds of his adversary, is a guarantee of the complete correctness and honor of the affair. In view of the gossip which has reached the newspapers, we have decided to tell the judge everything. Why should we not do this, when we are being denounced as felons, though all we did was to take the trouble to assist two gentlemen?

"The evil is in our social organization. You oppose the duel, but please defend our attitude, which, I assure you, could not have been more correct nor more gentlemanly, and bear in mind that next to the afflicted parents, our sorrow is greater than that of anyone else. It is not right that any friend should be less generous than Mr. Warren, who, while dying, pardoned his adversary."

The duel was not fought over a woman, as first reported. Rudolph invited Mesa to dine with him. Mesa accepted but did not appear and gave no explanation. He also refused to explain why Rudolph had caned him. Both drew their pistols and were separated. The duel followed with its tragic ending.

Young Mesa boarded the Ward liner *Havana* and left immediately for New York, checking in under his valet's name, William Hourant. The Cuban government said it would have him arrested; that didn't happen.

Mesa told the New York police that Rudolph Warren insulted him, and he killed Rudolph in a fair fight after being challenged.

Was the girl the source of this trouble between Rudolph and Hannibal? We never knew.

We draped the front door in black. Vivian sat upstairs with Warren nestled next to her on the sofa, and I shut the door softly as she cried and ran her hand over her swelling belly carrying our child.

Jerry shut the door to his library and drank.

I walked to the harbor and inhaled the fresh breeze off the sea. What a waste of a life.

I promised our child, not yet born, that he or she would be loved and taught that living is a gift.

Two months later, I held our son in my arms and told him he would play baseball, serve in the military, and be a good man with high moral standards.

"Really, Charles?" Vivian smiled at me from her lounge chair on the terrace. "Serve in the military?"

"Oh, yes," I said. "The military will teach him more of the world than you and I can. And it will be a good stepping-off point for his future ventures."

"What about tennis?" she teased me as she breakfasted on fresh bread, fruit, and a poached egg. "Can he play tennis? Or ride horses? Or go fishing?"

"He can do all of that," I said, smoothing back his soft baby hair. "And now, he's going back to you before he wets the front of my suit!"

She laughed, her eyes alight with the love of her baby son, and me, too, even after several years of my business travels. She knew I loved to board a ship or a train, going somewhere. And she loved, equally, the peace of home life.

"I've traveled the world with my father," she always said. "I've lived on enough ships for my lifetime. But we can go to New York before long!"

Vivian recovered well from the birth, thank God. I said prayers for that.

While she always felt the loss of her brother in her heart, she rarely mentioned him in conversation, knowing that the memories were not sweet or pleasant to Jerry. He had erected a large monument in the Colon Cemetery for Rudolph. He gave orders for the staff to keep it clean and furnished with flowers for the next year.

If Jerry visited the grave after the funeral, I never knew it. Each man grieves in his own fashion.

Hannibal Mesa was sentenced on May 27, 1914, to a year and eight months' imprisonment on the Isle of Pines for dueling.

The *New York Times* report read: "Mesa tried to avoid the duel because he is an expert pistol shot, but Warren insisted, and under the Cuban code, Mesa had no other honorable course than to accept. He escaped to New York after the fatal encounter, but recently returned to stand trial. He pleaded guilty and received the minimum penalty."

Jerry continued handling shipments for the Mesa organization.

"Rudolph's dead. That's a fact," he said. "Can't be undone. The business continues now for you, Vivian, and my grandsons."

"From the Land of Sunshine"

—COMES—

"The Sunshine Drink"

Pin-Ap-Ola

No Secret About Its Formula

Made of Pure Pineapple Juice, Refined Cane Sugar; carbonated; pasteurized.

It's a Food and Drink Combined

Like sunshine, Pin-ap-ola brings happiness into homes. Enjoyed alike by well and sick people. The "kiddies" love it.

Try it—you will like it and want more. Get the habit. It's a good habit.

5c THE BOTTLE

Photo courtesy of Library of Congress

An ad for Jerry Warren's new company, Pin-Ap-Ola, ran in the newspaper in Jacksonville, Florida, where the first office was located. Havana's Sunshine Drink promised fresh pineapple juice and refined cane sugar.

"If you want to succeed, you should strike out on new paths, rather than travel the worn paths of accepted success."
John D. Rockefeller (1839–1937),
co-founder of the Standard Oil Company

Chapter Fourteen

Taking Pineapple to the Bank

War came again in 1914. It was only a matter of time. Men live, and therefore there is war. Britain declared war on Germany in early August.

I won't go into the long list of reasons. When a young, hotheaded, Bosnian nationalist shot and killed Austrian Archduke Franz Ferdinand and his wife, Sophie, while they were riding in their open car in Sarajevo, that was the match that lit the fire. Austria-Hungary had annexed the Balkan provinces of Bosnia and Herzegovina in 1908, angering the Serbs and Russians. The Russians and French joined the Brits in the war against Germany, Austria-Hungary, and Turkey.

President Wilson had promised neutrality, and the US clung to that like a barnacle on a rusted ship, sinking at the stern.

Jerry and I knew it was a matter of time before we joined the war. Meanwhile, business must continue. We had to eat and so did our families, as well as the families of those we hired.

We planned a great product—fresh pineapple juice for Americans. Go to any hotel in Havana, Cuba, and you'd see

Americans sipping their pineapple juice, nodding their heads to each other about its taste.

A street vendor named Roberto in Havana assured me that pineapple was what kept him young.

"Really, Roberto? You feel younger?" I grinned.

"¡Sí, soy joven porque bebo jugo de piña!" He flexed his arm, showing his muscles, and ran a hand through his thick, dark hair as his friends catcalled.

That memorable day, I walked the rest of the way to our home in Vedado and strolled onto the terrace. Jerry sat on a lounge chair, taking his afternoon siesta. He opened one eye, then the other, and abruptly sat up, fully energized, as he always did. He would have been good in a ship's emergency.

When I mentioned my conversation with Roberto to Jerry, he grabbed that image like solid gold. He hunted for a chemist who would say, "Pineapple juice is the elixir of youth!" Needless to say, Jerry found one.

The *Tampa Tribune* reported: "Dr. Davis T. Day, the well-known scientist of the United States, says: 'The juice of the pineapple contains the natural ferment of a healthy digestion to a remarkable degree, and I believe that if we adopted the pineapple juice as a national beverage, the Americans would be the healthiest people on the face of the earth.' "

Our *Jugo de Pina* was described as the Cubans' national nonalcoholic drink, "absolutely pure," with not "a particle of artificial flavoring, coloring matter, or preservatives."

I had quietly visited Jacksonville off and on since summer 1913, looking at buildings and warehouses. Jerry sent me back in September to look at the top five sites for our new Pin-Ap-Ola Company, which we planned to open in spring 1915. I narrowed our options to the top three by November and went back to Key West for the holidays. Sipping his Christmas brandy, Jerry selected our plant location.

By January 1914, I had a plant operator and a team of engineers to design the operations floor and pick the equipment we needed, and we'd settled on the number of employees required to keep the plant and equipment operating. Then I stepped back. My job for Jerry was to keep an eye on the operations and help with hiring the early staff; then I was done with that project. He kept me moving.

By mid-summer, we had the plant coming along, and I had been busy ordering our future fruit shipments. We expected to be operational soon after the new year.

Jerry and I were staying in the Hotel Duval and drove over to Jacksonville City Hall to meet Mayor Van Swearingen and talk about our business.

Swearingen was running for re-election in a hot race between three other Democrats—Rudolph Grunthal, a local businessman; Dr. Charles Johnson, a physician; and J. E. T. Bowden, a former mayor. The first primary was January 26, 1915. The *Times-Union* and the *Metropolis* were packed with election news and candidates' advertisements.

The mayor walked around his mahogany desk to greet us. Neat stacks of paperwork shared space on his green felt desk blotter. I like a man who is organized.

"We're glad to have you opening in our city," Swearingen smiled as we shook hands. "Mr. Warren, your reputation, and that of Gunner Morgan, has preceded you. I'm glad to make your acquaintance. Please, gentlemen, have a seat."

His assistant, introduced as Adam Darnell, offered us drinks. The niceties over, the mayor launched into his chamber of commerce speech.

"Jacksonville is developing into a major port city," he said. "There are rumors we may become the New York of the South. Carl Fisher's Dixie Highway will be constructed through Jacksonville on the way to Miami. In short, we are the perfect location for your bottling company."

"Mayor, we are delighted to be here," Jerry said. "And I agree with you that Jacksonville is set to become a major port city. It is perfect for our shipments to come in from Cuba and South America, and for our shipments across the United States. You also have a good class of working men we are pleased to hire."

The mayor, an attorney-at-law, was a member of the Freemasons and Knights of Pythias, and invited me to visit both organizations with him.

"Thank you so much, Mr. Mayor," I said. "I appreciate the opportunity."

"I'm making great inroads against the vice in our town," Swearingen said. "We intend to grow our economy without the other element."

"You refer to the sixty bordellos frequented by seamen and railroad travelers," I said. "What the hotel bartender mentions as 'other entertainment.' "

"Yes, that entertainment," he said. "We don't need it here."

"Are you concerned about the upcoming March election?" Jerry inquired politely.

"No," Swearingen said. "I have a strong support base, and the ladies of the city support me in driving out the criminal element. After all, it is a moral stance, and who wants to stand against what is good and right?"

Once in the car, I turned to Jerry. "I have found sometimes that a politician's moral stance is as deep as a rain puddle."

"That deep?" Jerry grinned.

During the day, the Pin-Ap-Ola third-floor suite was filled with staff handling phone calls to potential distributors. Jerry had plants opening in Atlanta, New York, and elsewhere.

In truth, I grew tired of pineapple juice before it was over. We handed out Pin-Ap-Ola at every business meeting, reception, party by the pool, and fishing excursion. We hired lovely ladies to offer cool, refreshing tastes of our pineapple soda at tables set in nearly every hotel lobby in the city. Our assistants promoted it for the railway restaurant cars: "Pin-Ap-Ola, the Elixir of Youth."

I traveled to the Panama-Pacific Exposition in San Francisco with Pin-Ap-Ola. With sodas delivered, I called Henry Tresselt.

"Old man, do you know what they have docked at Mare Island? Let's go stir things up!"

"Gunner!" he laughed. "What are you doing here?"

Turned out he couldn't get free as he was expected in the city mayor's office in two hours. One hour of tale-telling later, I smiled on my way back to the exposition and received first place for the best soda.

When I returned to Jacksonville, Jerry was so pleased, he clapped me on the back and named me plant manager.

Jerry and I walked downtown the Saturday before the primary. Bowden, one of the mayoral candidates, hired the Aerial Howards to perform their high-wire bicycle trapeze act on a cable between the Florida Life Building and the fifteen-story Heard National Bank building, the tallest skyscraper in Florida at the time.

Thousands gathered in the city to watch the fireworks, and we were among them.

There is a reason that reporters describe politics as a circus. We saw it in action—free—from seven to ten thirty in the evening on January 23.

The day of the primary, the *Metropolis* estimated a crowd of seven or eight thousand stood outside its offices watching the returns as they came in on the stereopticon on a large screen.

The results were Swearingen, 1,541; Bowden, 1,366; Johnson, 1,103; and Grunthal, 258. There would be a runoff between the top two candidates.

At lunch, over a lobster cooked in a light wine and buttery cream sauce, Jerry said, "We need to meet the former mayor, Bowden, who's running against Swearingen. I hear Bowden has major support to keep the bordellos operating.

"Jacksonville suffered after the 1901 fire that nearly destroyed the town. J. E. T. Bowden did a fine job in pulling the city back together. I heard he was exhausted from the struggle, which is why he didn't run again."

"And here he is now deciding he's what the city needs," I said.

"He may be, and we'll attempt to make friends with both men," Jerry replied.

The following day, we contacted J. E. T. Bowden and invited

him to lunch. We chose a private meal in our third-floor suite.

Bowden was an interesting man, bluff and jovial, who lit his Cuban cigar, puffed, and said, "My initials stand for my platform, Just Easy Times Bowden.

"I'm a businessman," he said, "and I understand that we can't let the social evil be everywhere in our city. I believe that we should keep the unfortunate women in these female boardinghouses segregated in one area. Prostitution is like death and taxes—it will exist until the end of time. The best we can do is control it."

"Do you believe the economy of Jacksonville is improving?" Jerry asked, looking up as he buttered a yeast roll. "We are making quite a significant investment here."

"Oh, yes," Bowden answered, sniffing the bouquet of one of Jerry's red wines. "We've made a heroic comeback from the terrible 1901 fire. We lost more than two thousand buildings that day. Fourteen years later, we have rebuilt. Our port is developing daily. We're adding docks and ship berths. It may be a bit before we get the area cleaned; sometimes progress is like constructing a house. You have to build it well before you paint and plaster."

"When the war comes to America—and it will, we know that—Jacksonville will be a major port of call," Jerry said.

"And we'll be ready for it," Bowden smiled.

Later in the evening, Jerry sipped his favorite brandy, mulled over the day's visit, and said, "I'll contribute to both men for the election. I predict Bowden to win. Cora Crane, owner of the best-known bordello, has been dead five years. There are other madams who invest heavily in the city, based on advice from the men they service. Cora was a remarkable woman. She never married Stephen Crane. I met them both when he came to Cuba as a war correspondent long ago. He was a brilliant writer. Even then, I could see he was not well with that hacking cough. It's a pity he didn't live past age twenty-eight."

In the years I had grown to know my father-in-law, I had ceased being surprised at the people he knew.

Our Pin-Ap-Ola building edged toward the finish line on

construction despite some weather delays. We had added to the distribution warehouse. We'd be ready to open soon.

Buying property always waves a flag for reporters. Anyone worth his salt would go check the deeds at the clerk's office.

A business reporter from the *Florida Times-Union* newspaper, Ted Denby, came to interview me.

"You're opening Pin-Ap-Ola, your first plant, here in Jacksonville next month. What do you think about our city?" he asked.

How should I answer that? The mayoral race between the incumbent, Van Swearingen, and the former mayor, J. E. T. Bowden, was broiling.

Our research showed that the city had far too many unpaid tax bills. The silent film industry was booming in Jacksonville, boosting the faltering economy, yet the conservative locals didn't like sudden car chases on city streets, or fake bank robberies, or impromptu fires—especially due to memories of the one that nearly destroyed the city.

I've lived in many towns, and I know what it is to go to Washington and promote the naval base in Key West, or the Key West Amusement Company.

I kept my answer simple. "Mr. Warren and I believe this is the perfect climate to establish our new business," I said. "Pin-Ap-Ola will add to your industrial base. The town looks good. I find it interesting that silent movies are filmed here. I can turn a corner and see a film crew shooting a scene!"

Then I turned the tables. "Mr. Denby, who do you think will win the mayor's race?"

He paused, pencil over his reporter's pad. "I'm not willing to predict the outcome, Gunner Morgan. Too many variables."

I smiled and let him off the hook. That seemed to satisfy him.

The usual candidate bashing continued. There were "unconfirmed reports" from "anonymous sources" that Swearingen was a member of the Guardians of Liberty, who were anti-Catholic and anti-Semitic. Bowden emphasized throughout the race that he wanted to be mayor "for all of Jacksonville."

The night of the primary runoff, Jerry and I made our way through the crowded hotel lobby to meet my friend Skip, and then we joined the flood of people on the sidewalks. We headed to Hemming Park, across from the St. James Building at 117 West Duval Street, where we found twice the number of people we'd seen there on election night in January.

Swearingen spoke from his touring car, a Cadillac Touring 30, and drove around the park to talk to the masses. Bowden had several men speaking on a stage inside the park. Both proclaimed the polls said they were going to win. Now there was a surprise.

Several women rode around the park on horseback with red lanterns and carried placards for J. E. T. Bowden. These ladies were polite enough not to point fingers at the well-dressed men whom they knew only too well from visits to the New York Inn, the House of Spanish Marie, and the Turkish Harem—the Ward Street bordellos. There were catcalls from their audience. Some men pretended they had no idea who the women were. Those, I figured, had regular appointments.

"I wouldn't wonder if the men here won't be voting for Swearingen," Jerry said under his breath to me.

"I wouldn't wonder long," I replied quietly, smothering a grin.

Skip chuckled. "I can assure you many men don't want Swearingen to win. And," he paused, grinning at me, "I have NOT visited the ladies with red lanterns, Gunner. I saw you glancing my way."

"I never thought a thing about it," I claimed.

At ten thirty, the band stopped playing "It's a Long Way to Tipperary" and left.

We headed back to the Hotel Duval to a crowd of revelers who were celebrating. Skip shook our hands and headed home. "You won't get much sleep tonight," he laughed.

The final tally: Bowden, 2,655; Swearingen, 1,888.

The *Florida Times-Union* headline read: "Bowden Swept City in Second Primary; Mayor Swearingen Defeated by Largest Margin in History of Jacksonville."

The June election would be a formality against a socialist candidate who didn't have a prayer of winning.

Jerry and I opened the first Pin-Ap-Ola plant on April 25, 1915, at 34-40 West Beaver Street. I served as the Florida state agent for the company. I coordinated the contract for the raw pineapple juice from J. G. Husenkamph, the manufacturer at the Cuba Fruit Juice Company of Havana. We would finish and carbonate the product in Jacksonville.

I appointed Charles Davis, one of my friends from Key West, as city agent. He was known as "Get the Habit" Charlie, always boosting the image of Key West. If he said the gray sky was blue, you'd believe it because Charlie was so likeable.

Yet the grandest moment was when I stood in the Florida Country Club and saw Skip Beveridge waiting for me across the dining room. He stood as I approached the table, a grin stretched across his broad, handsome face.

"And here he comes! He of the 'Eyetalian' gunner's eyes," he exclaimed.

I reached him in time to slap him on the shoulders, which didn't move him an inch.

"I hear your ship has come in, Skip," I said. "Despite your hard Scotsman's head."

"Many ships, my good man," he murmured. "Not to put too fine a point on it."

We sat down to order baked flounder and oysters, and savored hot dinner rolls and Gruyere cheese.

I watched Skip slather garlic butter on his rolls and said, "You remember those hard rolls we used to eat with salted fish, Skip?"

"Yes, my teeth remember them, too," he grimaced. "Fresh food in port was great. The last dregs left before reaching port were not too good. And here we are now, enjoying a country club dinner!"

Skip waved his hand expansively as a waiter refilled our water glasses.

"Who would have thought?" I laughed quietly.

"Gunner, we have come up in the world!" Skip said, sipping from his water goblet.

We locked eyes, and it was like we were back on the ship's deck, telling jokes about what the next young seaman could bungle in a big way.

We settled back into our meal. I glanced around us, making certain there were no avid ears perked our way. There was plenty of room between the tables, and we were in a corner near the French doors opening to the gardens.

Skip was a primary owner in Beveridge & Milburn, a transport business with his partner, Edgar Milburn, as a middle man brokering deals for companies on various shipping means—could be ships, trains, or trucks. He made a commission from the freight lines for getting them the deals.

"I have some business for you from our new company, Pin-Ap-Ola, bringing in pineapple from Cuba to our plants and shipping carbonated pineapple drinks across the country," I said. "I can't think of anyone I'd trust more with our business, Skip.

"Jerry has built a new plant in Brooklyn, New York, and with E. G. Ashe as manager, Jerry's installing an Atlanta plant, Pinapa Bottling Works, that can complete 120 bottles per minute or 3,000 cases of twenty-four bottles each daily. It is pure pineapple juice with no preservatives. The local distributor is Atlanta Mineral Waters Co. People love this drink, and it's going to sell exceptionally well."

"We'll be able to ship by truck, railway, ships, and eventually planes," Skip said. "Have you kept up with the Dixie Highway development? Carl Fisher is a genius. He's not investing cash himself. He organized the Dixie Highway Association so that the states will be responsible for constructing and maintaining the highway from Chicago to Miami. Everybody wants to be located off the new highway."

"Oh, it will work," I said. "I've watched Henry Flagler for too long with the Florida East Coast Railway and all of his hotel projects in Florida. People want to come south to vacation and buy homes. The businessmen want a route for their product. Yes, this is a major development, not only for Jacksonville, but throughout Florida."

By the time I left, we knew we would hit this business partnership out of the ballpark.

A year later, President Woodrow Wilson signed the Bankhead Act, offering $75 million in federal funds to create federal highways across America.

I spent much time in Cuba overseeing the operations harvesting pineapple and getting the shipments to our Jacksonville plant. It was not hard work, certainly not when I was able to stay with Vivian and the boys at our home.

Jerry was a busy two-year-old, always running and often splashing in the terrace fountain.

Vivian looked beautiful, with a light tan on her face and a radiant smile that lightened my heart. She was as slim as the day we married.

"Are you done traveling, my love?" she asked, wrapping her arm around mine as we walked upstairs to see the boys. The ceiling fans stirred a few tendrils of her soft hair on her neck.

"At least for now."

We opened the boys' bedroom door to find them crouched over their electric train as it whistled around the tracks. Then Jerry kicked one of the cars, causing the train to turn over, and Warren jumped up, yelling, "Stop that! Stop it! Stop it!"

"Welcome home, sweetheart," Vivian laughed.

"Boys!" I said quietly. "Daddy's home."

"Daddy!" they whooped, leaving the train on its side and running for a hug.

They slammed against my legs. "Oof! You are so strong I may fall over!"

They giggled, and the brewing fight was over.

"Read me a story, Daddy!" Jerry begged as I lifted him into my arms.

I wish every day was that easy when raising two boys.

Later, Vivian and I lay quietly in bed together, the wind lightly blowing the curtains and the smell of the sea drifting over us as the ceiling fans turned lazily.

I confessed, "Vivian, war is coming, and I've let the Navy know I'm available if they need me."

I heard a quick intake of breath and braced for her reaction.

"Charles," she drew out slowly. "You are fifty years old. You have a good job working for my father. He likes you and appreciates your skills. We have a good life. What do you want?"

How could I tell her? The sea called me as it always has. When I went to sleep wherever I was, I heard the waves in my head as I drifted off. But it was more than that.

"Do you want to be killed in war? Is that it?" Vivian asked me softly.

"Oh, no, Vivian. I'm too old to go on a battleship. When war comes, they will need men my age to help on base. I am a patriot. I believe in serving my country."

She sighed and turned on her side away from me.

"You just got home. Let's talk about this tomorrow. I'm tired."

My answer was the same the following day.

I'd never lost my Navy habit of waking at sunrise, and Vivian always joined me when I was at home. We sat on the terrace watching the sun rise over the trees while I drank cold tea, not Pin-Ap-Ola.

"You don't know if they'll call you back," she said as she snipped a rose for a crystal vase.

She had dressed to ride that morning and wore a pale blue, tailored shirt and riding pants.

"No, I don't," I said. "I wanted you to be prepared for the possibility."

"Well, I'm prepared now," she said with a quick smile that didn't reach her eyes. "I'm heading out to ride first and then for some shopping. I'll see you at dinner?"

"Yes. I'll be at the office today."

For two more years, I worked behind the scenes for Jerry,

handling contacts and personnel, and passing the information to his plant managers.

Jerry's investments in transportation, such as the Cardenas Railroad & Terminal Company in Havana, continued to pay off. The railroad linked the north coast and Punto Gordo on the south coast, running through large sugar estates. He also invested in the Dixie Highway in Jacksonville.

I never worried about Jerry, who always anticipated the trends, made his profits, and moved on.

Vivian stayed in Havana most of the time with Warren and little Jerry, but she came to Key West when the Navy called me back to duty.

Then came the fateful day when the famous Thomas Edison arrived in Key West.

I was ordered to help him develop a secret lab working on defensive weapons for the Navy. He wanted to help the US win the war. The first time I shook his hand, I knew Mr. Edison would make naval history.

List of War Subjects upon which Mr. Edison worked in
1917 and 1918 - Experiments still being continued on some items.

1. Extension observation points for battleships (ladder)
2. Low visibility (sighting of periscopes)
3. Smudging periscopes
4. Turbine head for projectile
5. Smoke smudge
6. Phonographic range finder
7. Preserving submarine guns
8. Systems of protecting coast from submarines
9. Ship telephones
10. Searchlights
11. Sailing lights for convoys
12. Extinguishing fires on vessels
13. Absorption of light by seawater
14. Power for torpedoes
15. Mirror reflection system for vessels
16. Devices for observing splash
17. Underwater searchlight
18. Special projectile for direct water-penetration and to hit target
19. Freeing range finder from spray
20. Aeroplane bomb
21. Induction balance
22. Protecting observers from smoke stack gas
23. Submarine buoy for coast patrol
24. Stability of submarines
25. Mercury column for wireless
26. Special projectile for smudging periscopes
27. Nitrogen from the air
28. Night glass
29. Observing periscope in silhouette
30. Obstructing torpedoes with net
31. Searchlight shutter
32. Aeroplane detector
33. Oleum bombs
34. Mining Zeebrugge harbor
35. Camouflaging ships (Cunard) and burning anthracite
36. Water brake - Hearing torpedoes, etc.
37. Rapid turning of ships
38. Hydrogen detector
39. Zigzagging
40. Destroying periscopes with machine guns
41. Reducing rolling of warships
42. Reacting shell
43. Detecting submarines by sound from moving vessels
44. Strategic plans and maps for avoiding submarines - Gt. Brit., etc.
45. " " " " " " " - United States
46. Detecting torpedoes and cargo boat listening apparatus
47. Taking merchant ships out of mined Harbors
48. Collision mats

New York Public Library/Collection of Charles Hummel

Thomas Edison kept a list of his work for the US Navy.

"When you have exhausted all possibilities,
remember this–you haven't."
Thomas Edison

Chapter Fifteen

Surviving Thomas Edison

The Navy needed me even in my fifties—I was experienced at sea, a master diver, and chief gunner. Plus, I could shoot the big guns well.

"You are too old to go to war," Vivian said with a snap. "You have two boys at home. Warren and Jerry need their father." The plates clattered a bit on the kitchen counter.

My lovely Vivian was an elegant lady who knew how to give orders quietly and with steel in her voice. I smiled, at which she huffed, and her heels did a little rat-a-tat as she swept by me to the parlor.

Vivian left her first husband, John Gardner Weld of the Boston Welds, because he was "difficult," Jerry told me.

How fortunate I am that we met when we did, and that when I saw her a few years later, it seemed as though we had known each other forever. Vivian loved me, even though I was ready to go to war.

Commandant Edward Hayden had written to the secretary of the Navy on February 7, 1914. I was grateful for it.

Refer to No.: 758-1914 Date: February 7, 1914
From: Commandant.
To: Secretary of the Navy.
Subject: Requests detail of Chief Gunner Charles Morgan, U.S.N., Retired, to duty at Key West Naval Station.

"Referring to the application made to the Department under date of January 28, 1914, by Chief Gunner Charles Morgan, U.S.N., Retired, for assignment to active duty at this Station: I beg to urge that said application be granted, in view of his previous good record here, his experience in ordnance work and with destroyers and submarine and the present shortage of officers at this Station.

Such detail will assist materially in carrying out the Department's announced intentions of building up an effective torpedo-boat base at Key West, and I should like very much to have the detail made, if the Department approve, before the expected arrival of the Atlantic Torpedo Flotilla at Key West.

This Station is at present without an Engineer Officer, Public Works Officer, Medical Officer, and Inspection Officer, and a Carpenter is Acting Construction Officer. Chief Gunner Morgan, if detailed to duty here, would be of great assistance, not only in connection with ordnance stores (kept at Fort Taylor, about a mile away) but in many other ways."

Having decided that I probably wouldn't qualify for at least two of those descriptions, I took the examinations to become a master and pilot on September 11, 1914, and proudly hung my license in my office. I could captain "steam vessels of not over 250 gross tons upon waters of the Florida Coast and also act as a First Class Pilot on the waters around Key West and inside Route to Knights Key, Fla." I delivered a copy of the license to the commandant with due haste. It turned out to be a perfect choice.

Meanwhile, I worked on Pin-Ap-Ola with my father-in-law. We stayed at the Warren house in Havana and kept a house on White Street in Key West, and I had a second home in Jacksonville and made regular trips. Jerry had me involved in some Key West real estate deals.

At first, Vivian tutored Warren at home in Key West, but she had her hands full with the two boys. "We need a tutor," she told me at supper late one evening, looking up from a tasty bite of red snapper with the Cuban flair of fresh lime juice, onion, garlic, Spanish oil, and peppers. "Warren is restive when I have to take a break with Jerry. Amalie is good at keeping Jerry, but sometimes he just won't quiet down if I don't check on him. Warren's smart, and we need to keep his mind occupied."

Warren and Jerry were already upstairs in bed asleep. I had checked on them earlier, clean from their baths, faces looking cherubic, though I knew well they could be scamps with little encouragement. Amalie, our nanny, helped with their baths before she left every day. Vivian liked to be a part of bath time, too.

"Bath time with our boys is a grand time to get soaked and laugh and laugh," she said, her sweet eyes twinkling. "You could come get water thrown on you, too!"

"I've had so much water thrown on me on board ship that I'm half merman now. No need for me to experience the splash and dash of it. I know it all too well!"

Thinking about Warren and his intelligence, I wondered where we'd send him to university, and Jerry as well. We had a public school, but Vivian wanted to teach Warren at home for a while.

"Do you have someone in mind to hire?"

"Yes, several mothers have recommended Miss Samantha Eason. I've checked her teaching credentials, which are impressive. The main thing is the mothers say she maintains discipline, yet is kind and encouraging," Vivian said, waving her fork at me. "Besides, if Warren was enrolled in regular school, I'd have more issues taking him with me to Cuba."

"I think it's a good idea," I said. "And you will have a little more time to meet with the Woman's Club and your book club."

I was not usually home for dinner. When I was, we had tea on the back porch late in the evening. Too many nights Vivian put the boys to bed without my help. I'd get home from a meeting and find her reading to them in their bedroom. She enjoyed taking the boys to Cuba, where she had more household help and the social life with her old friends.

Our Havana house at 15th and C streets in Vedado was wrapped in porches and gardens with fountains in the center, and had cool marble tile floors. Vivian often took the boys there when I was working and traveling. I missed our quiet times on the terrace, but I was in Cuba often for Pin-Ap-Ola, so it worked.

The Navy played with paperwork until September 25, 1915; then I was slated for duty at the Key West Navy Yard. The Atlantic Torpedo Flotilla was expected to arrive.

I reported to Commandant Hayden, who looked at me in front of his desk and smiled. "Sometimes prayers to the US Navy are answered, even with a salty dog like you. Welcome back."

The United States entered the war in 1917. German submarines were sailing in our waters around Key West with impunity, taking out ships one after another.

Jerry couldn't get pineapples shipped and sold the plant. "We can't fight a war with pineapple soda."

On May 5, I was ordered on secret duty to go to Tallahassee and take over the armed state fish patrol vessel *Roamer*. I met with the governor and some state legislators in secret to get the *Roamer*'s loan approved. The US Navy promised to return the vessel to the state of Florida in the same condition as when she was delivered. My job was to sail her to Key West, where she would be used to patrol. I was to report daily on my negotiations with the state officers and return with the *Roamer* as soon as possible.

On July 13, 1917, the Navy leased land from the Florida East Coast Railroad Company on the basis of my advice and began constructing a coastal air patrol station. We managed dredging and built station offices, three seaplane ramps, a dirigible hangar, and temporary barracks.

I watched Coast Guard Lieutenant Stanley Parker take off in a Curtis N-9 seaplane on September 22, the first naval flight from Key West. In December, Naval Air Base Key West was commissioned as a primary seaplane training station.

Our Naval Air Base pilots, armed with machine guns and hand grenades, searched for German submarines resting on the surface to recharge their batteries. The biplanes flew so low over the surfaced submarines that our gunners dropped grenades into the subs' open conning towers.

This was just the beginning. Hundreds of pilots headed to the base to train.

Vivian returned to Key West, knowing I would have my hands full at the base. She volunteered to become a counselor to the young wives who chose to live off base and be near their husbands.

"You've given some good help to the young wives, talking to them about their men being on duty overseas," I said late one evening as we dressed for bed.

The daughter of Jerry Warren, the Sugar King of Havana, had a social cachet. Vivian was a world traveler, and it helped that she could talk to the younger women, many of whom had never left home until they came to Key West and knew little of what was expected. She was able to calm them down for the most part, although I do recall once when she gently told a homesick young wife, "Your husband can't come home just because you want him here. They'll put him in jail. You don't want him to be locked up in jail, do you?"

In the middle of building Naval Air Base Key West, we received a coded telegram from Washington explaining that Thomas Edison would arrive soon in Key West to work for the Navy.

He came by train, and we sent a driver and car to bring him to the base. When he unfolded his long frame from the car, I stepped forward to introduce myself.

"Mr. Edison, we are honored to have you here," I said smartly. I was ordered to help him set up a secret lab working on weapons for the Navy. I'd been warned about his deafness, so I spoke directly to him.

With a pleasant smile, Mr. Edison extended his hand. "Chief

Gunner Morgan, my pleasure," he said in a high-pitched voice that I didn't expect for his height.

"Get me a decent-sized building and men to help, and then let's get busy," he said.

He was already famous for his inventions, yet he was not arrogant. I wanted to be in his lab whenever I could.

Mr. Edison worked in his laboratory on smoke bombs, depth charges, and many other inventions that would help the Navy. He had a list of approximately forty-eight items, although we had only part of the list; some were at his other labs up north.

That summer, Mr. Edison experimented with his depth charge bomb. The volunteers in the lab included Marine Major Henry W. Carpenter, Seamen Will Meadows and Jefferson Bright, and me. Mr. Edison didn't want too large a team in the lab.

"Are you sure you want to do this?" I asked.

"Yes, sir!" they chorused.

Then the cylinder of the smoke box leaked, and the Edison experimental shell exploded. Seamen Meadows and Bright were killed. Major Carpenter wasn't hurt; he was across the room working behind a counter when the explosion occurred. My clothes were in tatters, and Major Carpenter beat out the flames in my hair with his jacket.

I took the base car home to get another uniform. I raced to our house on White Street with my Navy whites torn and burned, the fabric hanging in shreds, and blood on the little white that was left. My chest hair was burned and the hair on my head was singed. I could feel the heat from the burns, but I was alive, thank God.

Warren stood on the porch with a book satchel in his hand, his eyes widening in shock when he saw me.

"Mama!" he yelled. "Come quick! Come quick!"

I brushed past him and rushed into the house as Vivian came running from the back yard.

"Oh, no!" she said, racing to me.

I headed straight to our bedroom and bath, trying to tear

off the remaining pieces of my uniform and wishing I could rid myself of the thick stench of blood and burned hair.

"Seaman Will Meadows was in front of me," I panted, out of breath and beginning to feel shocked.

"He took the brunt of the blast, he and Jefferson Bright," I said. "They're both dead."

Vivian saw Warren poking his head around the door.

"Warren, go to the kitchen and get your milk and cookies," she snapped. "Stay there until I come into the kitchen. Do you understand?"

Vivian turned back to me quickly. "Let's get what's left of your clothes off. Let me call Ned Benedict. He can be here in a few minutes from the hospital."

By the time she had gently removed my clothes and given me a sponge bath to clean off the blood and gore, Dr. Benedict was tapping at the front screen door. I was sitting on a stool with a towel over my lap. I shivered in the heat with my small burns bright red in the sunlight.

Vivian rushed to the door and let him in. "Thank you for coming so quickly, Ned. Charles is in the bathroom down the hall on the left," she said. "Let me check on Warren, and I'll be right there."

I looked up when our friend Ned stepped in beside me.

"Gunner," he said quietly. "Why didn't you come straight to the hospital?"

"Ned, all I could think about was coming home," I said, tired, bruised, and burning in spots. "I could tell nothing was broken. I had two seamen in front of me who took the brunt of the blast. And the weapons development is top secret."

Ned looked me over carefully, pulling out a salve for the burns and checking my head, eyes, and ears. He took a fresh washcloth and wiped away a little more blood behind my ear.

"Are your ears still ringing now or has your hearing cleared?" Ned asked.

"I can hear much better now. It's slowly come back to normal," I replied.

Vivian came to the door. "How is he, Ned?"

"He's going to be fine, but he's not going to feel good from these burns for several days. You should have gone straight to the naval hospital," he said.

"I want to stay off the sick list so I can continue to help Mr. Edison in the final experimental work on the shell and smoke bomb. If I report, they'll put me on mandatory sick leave," I said.

"They certainly know that the two seamen are dead," he pointed out.

"If I can put on a clean uniform and get back to the base, I'll be first-rate," I said.

Ned sighed. "Okay. I'm going to bandage these burns. You need to keep them clean so there's no infection. This salve has a soother in it that will help. None of these burns are serious; you have some bad bruises. You are a lucky man. I'll come back and check you over in three days."

He fixed me up, and I rested for about an hour, and then went back to the base. Mr. Edison had left the lab for the day because it had to be cleaned and the building repaired. I wrote a brief report for the commandant and sat quietly in my office with my feet propped in the chair.

Within a week, the lab was open and operating.

Mr. Edison sat down with me in his office. "I'm so sorry for the loss of two good men," he said. "What we're doing is dangerous work. Are you willing to continue?"

"Yes, sir," I said. "We have a job to do."

I wrote letters to the families of Seamen Meadows and Bright, who would receive medals posthumously. I knew that nothing would be enough to ease the families' grief. So many young men were dying in this war. At least these two would have a proper military burial with honors.

The rest of my work with this great man, Thomas Edison, a hero for our country, was uneventful.

After he left the following spring, he wrote me a letter that I placed into my scrapbook.

FROM THE LABORATORY OF
THOMAS A. EDISON
Orange, N.J.
May 1, 1918
Chief Gunner Charles Morgan,
U.S. Naval Station,
Key West, Fla.
Dear Sir,

Having returned to my laboratory here at Orange, I look back upon my recent sojourn in Key West with pleasant recollections of the many courtesies that were extended to me by you and other persons connected with the U.S. Naval Station. Let me assure you of my appreciation of the attention you showed to me and to the members of my staff during the period of our stay in Key West.

Yours very truly,
Thoms. A. Edison

On the base, I continued overseeing the construction of more barracks and other buildings, with ground-leveling work needed for foundations as the base grew and more men arrived.

I served as relief for other officers and worked as a liaison with the city of Key West when our sailors grew a little too rowdy or we received complaints about some of the bars and bordellos. Occasionally, Key West was declared off limits to our sailors, and that always caused discontent, but it had to be done. We needed men able to fight, not down with the clap.

Due to the German subs, Vivian stayed home more with the boys. We worried from daybreak to sundown about the Spanish flu pandemic, and Vivian tried to keep the boys away from public events as much as possible. A few blocks from us, an entire family died from the flu. Newspaper ads promised a cure if only we ate more onions. Some quacks prescribed a few drops of kerosene on a cube of sugar, or quinine, or morphine. I preferred Vicks VapoRub for the boys, though fortunately, neither one needed it.

Soldiers coming home and an influx of war refugees exacerbated the Spanish flu pandemic, which spread to some cities, such as New Orleans, in September 1918.

The armistice of November 11, 1918, ended the war on the Western Front. I could see joy and relief on so many faces as the troop ships arrived. It was as though I could stand on my porch, look to the sea, and feel the peace at last.

Yet the flu claimed another victim, my father, Gaetano Morgani. He died December 29, 1918, and was buried a day later in Greenwood Cemetery in a rushed funeral because of the flu.

When my sister Louise called, I was stunned.

"I know he was old, Louise, but he's been in good physical shape. You've taken such good care of him." I fought a sudden catch of tears in my throat.

"People are dying everywhere here," Louise said. "He's been sniffling like he had a cold, and suddenly, overnight, he was really, really sick. Your being here won't bring Father back. And it's dangerous for you to travel. You could catch the flu and take it home to your family. I'll handle everything."

I clutched the telephone in a tight grip, then sighed. "I know you're right, Louise. But not to be there to honor him is hard."

"You can honor him when it's safe, brother," she said softly. "He worried about you every day of your life in the Navy. If he thought you'd endangered yourself coming here, he wouldn't be able to rest peacefully at last. He knows you honor him in your heart. You can come later."

I sat with Vivian and the boys in the living room and told them their grandfather had died. They had only seen him once on a brief trip to New Orleans. No, I didn't go often. I left it to Louise to take care of my father. I had let time and distance keep me away. Now I would know that regret forever.

We spent a quiet New Year's holiday at home, sending the boys to bed early, reading books together, and lighting a fire for the first time in quite a while. The weather had been unusually cold, even in Florida. We agreed that 1919 would be better and toasted with our warmed cider to good things to come.

I'd heard that Theodore Roosevelt, my president, was going to run again. But on January 5, 1919, he had trouble breathing; his doctor checked him; and around four in the morning on January 6, he died in his sleep. What a shock! I could not believe he was gone.

The US Navy grieved its champion. I sat quietly on the back porch in Key West for several hours, remembering my conversations with him and thinking about his devotion to the military man—indeed, to every man, no matter his beginnings.

In 1919, I was still on duty as captain of the Navy Yard at Key West when we had a hurricane strike in September. Afterward, the local newspaper sent a reporter to interview me.

I was sent to investigate any damage the hurricane had done to installations on the Dry Tortugas as well as lights and markers on the way. The morning of September 15, we were returning to Key West, some twenty miles east of Fort Jefferson, when I noticed two spars rising from the water, too far apart to be a sailing ship.

"A merchant ship had been blown onto the quicksands not far from Rebecca Light," I told the reporter. "When we arrived at Key West, word had come to be on the lookout for the *Valbanera*, a Spanish merchant ship that was unreported following the storm.

"We returned to where we had seen the spars and identified the ship. There wasn't a trace of lifeboats or survivors. No bodies were found, and the cargo had disappeared."

The *Valbanera* may have been blown from its course by the forces of wind and tide. The lighthouses at Morro Castle and at Rebecca had blown out, so the captain may have been confused.

I expect that sharks got the men as they sank in the waves. We called off the search after several days.

Working for the Navy fulfilled me, and I found it hard to leave the sea when I was needed. My sister Louise told me I wasn't really a good husband, that I was married to the sea. Vivian and I reached an understanding before we married that the sea was my mistress.

"As long as you are not with other women, I forgive you,"

Vivian said. "The sea is demanding. You must promise always to come home to me."

Absent though I may have been half the time, I kept my promise and always found safe harbor when I returned home.

My father-in-law hadn't really forgiven me for choosing the Navy—again—over him, and I understood that sentiment. We remained friends.

Vivian and I saw Jerry whenever he came to Miami. His pockets were flush. Due to the war in Europe, the price of sugar in the world market jumped from a few cents a pound to about twenty cents a pound. The plantation owners and sugar mill owners prospered, as well as anyone who supplied workers and materials. Jerry brought in cash right and left, and he had increased his investments in transportation and the oil industry. He knew sugar would crash when the Europeans made a comeback.

In 1920, I leaned back in my wicker chair on the veranda and looked at Vivian. "I'm fifty-five. I want my pension from the Navy, and I want to stay home."

"You're tired, Charles. I understand," was all she said—yet with kindness and love.

For some years now, I'd had the Navy and other work. I'd put enough aside that I felt we could live a good life in Key West.

"I'm going to teach my boys the art of playing baseball," I added. "Some days I want to go to the beach with you. Some days I'm going to the ballpark to hear someone yell, 'Play ball.' "

"That's good, Charles." She reached for my hand and held it briefly. "You have done everything that's ever been asked of you and more."

"So many men I've known will never come home from the sea, from war. I'm one of the lucky ones. When I see their faces in my dreams, I know I'm tired."

"We will be fine. When have we ever not had a good life together?"

At daybreak, I lifted my eyes to the heavens, thankful that I'd shared in one more sunrise as Vivian slept peacefully beside me.

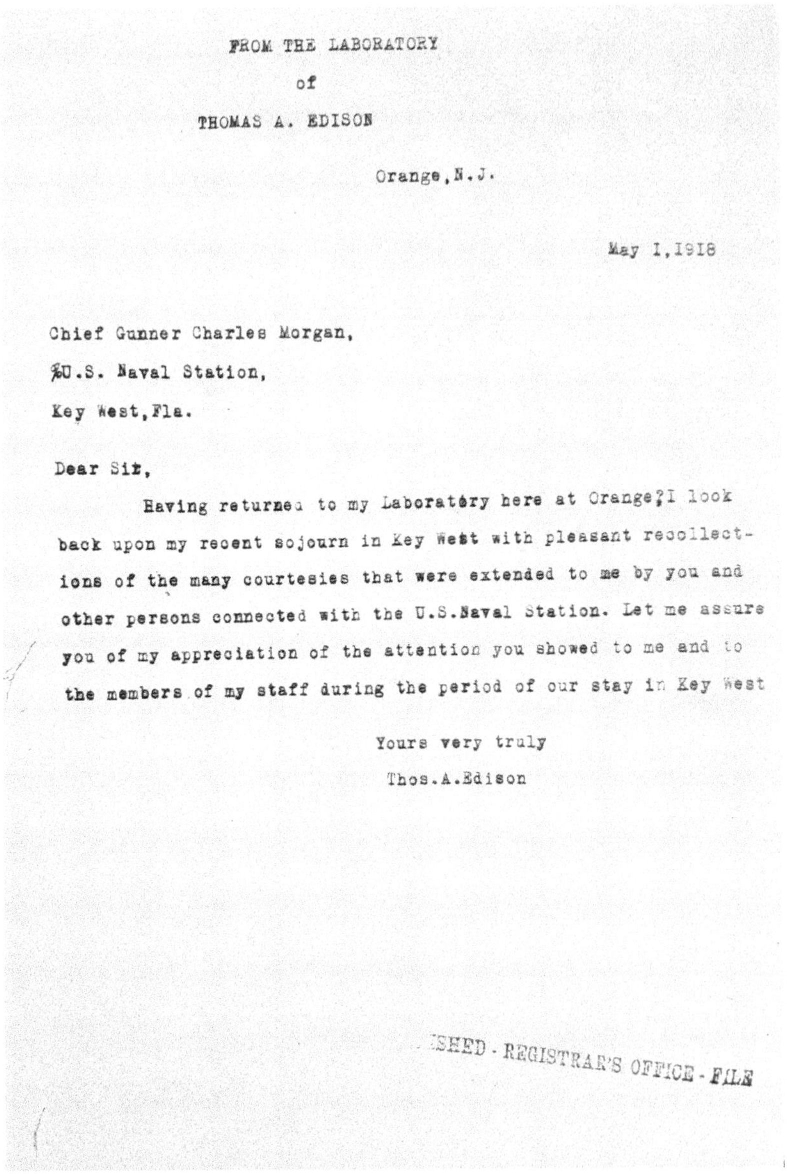

FROM THE LABORATORY

of

THOMAS A. EDISON

Orange, N.J.

May I, 1918

Chief Gunner Charles Morgan,

℅U.S. Naval Station,

Key West, Fla.

Dear Sir,

Having returned to my Laboratory here at Orange, I look back upon my recent sojourn in Key West with pleasant recollections of the many courtesies that were extended to me by you and other persons connected with the U.S. Naval Station. Let me assure you of my appreciation of the attention you showed to me and to the members of my staff during the period of our stay in Key West

Yours very truly

Thos. A. Edison

Photo courtesy of the Morgan family

Gunner Morgan kept the original and a photocopy of a letter from Thomas Edison in his files. The original was kept in the family safe deposit box but vanished after some years.

IN REPLY REFER TO
NO.

UNITED STATES NAVAL STATION
KEY WEST, FLORIDA

February 15, 1919.

MEMORANDUM.

From: Lieutenant Charles Morgan, USN, (Ret.)
To: Major Henry W. Carpenter, USMC. (Ret).

SUBJECT: Accident received by me while on duty; assisting Mr. Edison in his experiments on Smoke Bombs.

1. You will recall the explosion of a 3" shell, known as an Edison experimental shell, wherein I was hurt, and all others, with the exception, yourself, who was one of the party at this experiment.

2. The report of my case has been forwarded by the Medical Officer at this Station to the Medical Department at Washington, D.C., on the 1st of January 1919. I was authorized by the Commanding Officer, this Station, to use my best efforts in helping Mr. Edison in his experiments on Smoke Bombs.

3. The accident was due to a leakage in the cylinder of the smoke box.

4. My reason for not staying on the sick list and receiving treatment from the Medical Officer, this Station, was that I wanted to keep up and help Mr. Edison and my Country in the final experimental work, to complete his shell and smoke bomb.

5. My other accident occurred while loading depth charges on the Isle of Cuba.

6. I am enclosing a letter from Mr. Edison, which will explain itself.

CHAS. MORGAN.

Photo courtesy of the Morgan family

Gunner Morgan sent this letter to the Navy about his injuries on duty.

38 Lincoln Terrace
Yonkers, New York

Dear Jerry and Mary Lee,

I never know what to say when someone is taken away but believe me, my thoughts have been with you this past week and reflecting on the many, many colorful and jaunty things that made Daddy Morgan the personality that he really was. Having the edge on you by a few years, I remember so well those early years in Key West, particularly during World War 1 when you and I would ride around town and the Naval Station in a spanking shiny black carriage with white fringe on the top and driven by one of the minions of the station and also, the never to be forgotten day when I came home from school for lunch and Daddy Morgan rushed into the house on White Street like a volcano- all his Navy whites had been completely torn off him - he was in tatters and all his hair singed - that was the famous day when the only Thomas Alva Edison had experimented with his famous depth charge bomb and no one but three sailors would volunteer and they needed another volunteer and Dady Morgan stepped in the breach - its a miracle he wasnt killed as two of the sailors were. These and myriad memories too long to enumerate keep rushing back - I do hope you kept all the wonderful newspaper accounts of his fight with Sampson as they are quite historical data by now. I sent three of the New York Tribune clippings to Tia Sibyl and told her to forward them to you. Am so glad the New York papers remembered him at the end as they certainly had a field day over the case for nearly two years at the turn of the century. Bless him.

I am so happy Tia Sibyl is going to see you. She looks so old but she is still the same endearing person - she will tell you all the news. Your young hopefuls must be quite the sprouts by now. Do give Tia Sibyl a snap so I can see. Good luck always and

The Best,

Warren
Warren

May 15, 1959.

Photo courtesy of the Morgan family

Warren Weld wrote to his half-brother, Jerry Morgan, on May 15, 1959, recalling the day that Gunner came home with his white uniform in tatters from the smoke bomb explosion in Thomas Edison's lab.

PAN AM HISTORICAL FOUNDATION

Photo courtesy of the Pan Am Historical Foundation

General Machado flew the Fokker FVII, the first Pan Am Airways mail flight from Key West to Havana, on October 28, 1927. Fifth from left above is Gunner Morgan.

"The human bird shall take his first flight, filling the world with amazement, all writings with his fame, and bringing eternal glory to the nest whence he sprang."
Leonardo da Vinci

Chapter Sixteen

Pan Am Airways Takes Off

I've never claimed that US Navy bureaucrats are the brightest. They closed the Key West base after the war ended. So much time was expended to build the base, and then it was gone, along with a lot of paychecks for the people of Key West.

I knew the base would reopen someday because the location was so well suited for ships and planes to monitor the seas. But for the time being, many small businesses closed.

Not Sloppy Joe's Bar, though. Joe "Josie" Russell, the owner, kept the men in line most of the time. In tough times, men find solace in drink with friends. I understood the interest in playing pool and enjoying alcoholic beverages, although the trouble I saw this create for young sailors had convinced me years ago not to drink.

With my boys and my beautiful Vivian, my idea of a good time was walking on the dock, piloting a boat, taking Warren and Jerry to a ballgame, and having a quiet dinner at home.

Yet events around us influence our lives in ways that may go unnoticed at the time, rippling under the surface. Not so with the ratification of the Nineteenth Amendment on August 18, 1920, in the Tennessee General Assembly.

I said to Vivian, "My dear, you now have the right to vote. How do you feel about that?"

"It's about time," she laughed, placing her sunhat firmly on her head as she left for a walk with the boys. "Women deserve that right! I'll go to the polls with you and listen to you men pontificating outside about how the world will be reshaped."

"If my mother was living, she'd beat you there," I grinned at her. "Some papers claim the morality of the South will perish. They claim you women won't stay home with the children, and families will fail."

She tossed her head and winked at me. "I've managed this family while you've been off gadding about the world. Failure hasn't happened yet!"

"It certainly hasn't," I agreed, pecking her on the cheek as Warren and Jerry raced outside, happily talking about catching tadpoles in the ditch.

I wasn't rich on my Navy pension; we did all right. Our home in Key West was full of light from the tall windows and the laughter of our boys. I could sit on the wraparound balcony and watch the sea in the distance as her waves danced in the sunlight, or the angry whirl on stormy days.

Although I was less involved in the chamber of commerce once my friend Dr. Fogarty was no longer the mayor, I was still called in for meetings to discuss the Navy's future role in Key West.

Then our world turned topsy-turvy in a moment, and fear blossomed for our boys' lives.

We had a new fight on our hands in America.

I strolled in downtown Key West, enjoying the blue tropical sky on a warm, late September day, when I heard the newspaper boys hawking the headlines at the corner. I went over to my favorite little guy, Gordie Tetchford, who was always eager and smiling, with a missing front tooth that caused him to lisp. He wasn't smiling much today.

"It's terrible news, Mr. Gunner!" he said as he pocketed my two cents. "All these people were blowed up! Flames went everywhere!"

On September 16, 1920, a bomb carried in a horse-drawn cart exploded on Wall Street's busiest corner, killing thirty-eight people and injuring hundreds more. I snapped open the paper to read that witnesses said two sheets of flame seared the width of Wall Street. Was the explosion an attempt to assassinate J. P. Morgan Jr.? An attack on our American institution? Or an attempted robbery?

The papers claimed this horrendous attack was the evil work of anarchists and communists.

Those people were calmly going to work or shopping, and suddenly they knew this world no longer, or they suffered severe injuries, and their lives would never be the same again. The brilliant sky above my head became as brittle as a china plate with a crack. Would it hold? Or would the sky come crashing down on our heads?

I said as much to Vivian when I got home.

She laid her hand on my sleeve. "Gunner, you have seen the worst that happens in wartime. It's natural that you feel this way about this horrendous explosion on Wall Street. We are far away from it. We are safe, and so are our boys."

Yet that night, I awakened drenched in sweat, fighting the covers as the arms of the dead reached for me. My heartbeat slowed as I felt the breeze fluttering through the lace curtains. The moonlight filtered across gleaming, wide plank floors.

Vivian touched my arm and spoke to me gently. "Gunner, you are home. You had a nightmare. I'll fix you some hot tea."

I followed her to the dining room, and we sat quietly in the dark since the moon shone so brightly.

"Thank you for your patience with me," I said, my voice sapped by the nightmare.

"Charles, you are not the only man who came home from war with nightmares. I think we're blessed that you handle it better than most, and what matters is that you survived and have a good life now and in the future."

I drank in her smile as she reached her hand for mine. "You are my world. You keep the darkness away."

About a week later, Jerry called me. "Gunner, I have so much business right now that I hope you'll consider coming back to the Havana office. My assistant quit. He simply wasn't capable of doing the job. I need you keeping an eye on my best interests. You're a man of integrity. You can operate in Havana and Miami or Key West. Vivian and the boys can stay here. I hope you'll consider this an opportunity and not a burden."

I wasn't about to tell him it was a burden because it wasn't. He knew that. We had an easy camaraderie. Jerry began as a wholesale druggist in Key West, and he came to Cuba in 1898 to furnish drugs for the US Army Medical Corps in its island sanitation drive. He had arrived in Havana when I did with the Navy. He didn't come from money. He understood how to manage, and how to take funds and triple or quadruple his investment.

When Jerry became director general of the Mutual Life Insurance Co., he took his salary and invested in the fast-growing sugar industry. He built Central Jagueyal into the most modern and best-equipped mill of its time. After he sold the mill to the Cuban Cane Co., he financed the building of Central La Francia in Pinar del Rio province. He always kept his money churning and creating new investments. I had learned so much from watching him operate.

Vivian and I both loved Havana, and while working for Jerry was a little like balancing on deck during an incoming squall, he paid me well.

"Jerry, working with you is always interesting," I said. "If I can help, I'll be glad to do so."

And so I jumped into the middle of Jerry's business interests. Vivian settled into the house in Vedado at the corner of 15th and C streets, perfectly happy to be there.

On my first day back in the Havana office, I settled behind

my old mahogany desk again as the ceiling fan lazily stirred the air, shifting the newspaper pages. Herve Aquino, Jerry's new secretary, brought in a tray of hot Earl Grey tea with lemon and orange slices and a small jar of fresh honey from the household's beekeepers.

We settled into our morning ritual and went over the business operations—what needed attention most quickly.

"I know you're involved in various organizations in Key West, and I have no issue with you traveling back and forth if you need to be present there," Jerry said. "I hope you will continue. Your connections have also helped me with my businesses."

He was being kind. Jerry was a founder of the Island Masonic Lodge and a member of the American Club, the country club, and more private societies than I could name. Still, that meant I could remain active as a thirty-second-degree Mason. I could visit with my veteran friends at the American Legion and occasionally hand-carve a sailing ship. I gave one to the *Key West Citizen* newspaper for a contest for the paper delivery boys.

My good friend Dr. Fogarty kept a hand in everything going on in Key West, so I meant to pay him a visit.

"Now to the tasks at hand, I want freight cars on our new railroad to be full going and coming. Let's get a report on what our customers will need end to end," Jerry said.

My days were packed, as I expected they would be.

In November, Vivian and I went to the polls in Key West to vote for either Republican Sen. Warren G. Harding of Ohio or Democratic Gov. James M. Cox of Ohio. Harding won. I didn't ask Vivian for whom she voted and she didn't ask me.

What was amazing was that KDKA in Pittsburgh, Pennsylvania, broadcast live results of the presidential election. Only those involved in this great experiment called radio heard the results; 99.5 percent of the American public didn't.

"Vivian," I said as I tossed my hat onto the hook at the front door, "the radio is going to change America more than any president ever could."

"That's what Daddy said. He wants to buy one right away. Can we buy one?"

"Certainly we will. Not sure who's rolling them off the factory line yet, but we will get one when they're for sale. And when there is a station close enough for us to pick up the broadcast."

Meanwhile, Jerry shipped sugar and made millions; he diversified into railroads and freight trucks, and he kept the dollars flowing. Since the war was over, construction projects were booming. We hauled concrete, steel, barrels of nails, and tools to building sites.

I went to Key West on Jerry's behalf to see if he could buy into the Casa Marina Hotel project. Now that the FEC Railway was complete, Key West needed a full-service hotel.

"Come with me to the New Year's Eve ball at the hotel," I asked Vivian. "We can dance our way into 1921!"

"Of course!"

I held her in my arms, enjoying the fragrant scent of jasmine she wore. "You are the loveliest woman here," I said. "Isn't this ice blue silk and satin gown new? The pearl necklace is perfect." Yes, I am a romantic Italian, and I whirled her away.

I held her close as we waltzed to one of my favorites, "Three O'Clock in the Morning."

Seated again at our rattan and glass-topped table, she sipped a glass of champagne, and I balanced a teacup on my knee. We started with a plate of cheeses, nuts, and Belgian chocolate. Later, we had larger plates of shrimp crepes with garlic butter cream sauce and thinly sliced beef Burgundy on toast points.

Truly, the developers had done an exceptional job with the hotel, built in Spanish Renaissance style with loggias and designed so the rooms had access to the outside. It was advertised as the perfect place to relax before continuing to Cuba, with the average temperature in Key West never below sixty degrees or above eighty degrees. A single room cost nine dollars a night with three meals a day.

Vivian and I sat on our private porch and watched the sunset over the gulf. Jerry wanted the largest suite so he could sample the best they offered.

The next day, he made his approach as an investor. Vivian and I surely enjoyed staying there for a week while Jerry worked on the details.

By the second week of January, Vivian was ready to return to Havana and the boys.

"I know the boys are fine," she said. "Probably don't miss us a bit. But I miss them."

"I'm enjoying too much of the good life," I grinned. "I don't believe in wearing it around my waist! More walking, more baseball practice with the boys, and more swimming are certainly in order."

I stayed behind in our house on White Street. Time with the boys had to wait. I set myself a regular walking course in Key West. I had plenty to do, booking shipments going and coming on the FEC Railway and our Cuban railway. I worked with the Gato family getting tobacco shipped for their cigar factory. I sent some business to Skip in Jacksonville.

Vivian had thrown herself wholeheartedly into helping two young women, Angelina and Heather, who had created a dress and accessories boutique in Havana. Over the past few years, she had helped them branch out into handcrafted leather goods. She'd invested in the business and helped them market their goods to the wealthy American tourists.

"I do have a good eye for excellent handiwork," she pointed out one morning in Havana. "I spend three days a week helping out at the shop. On Mondays, we have people lined up showing us their beadwork, lace, and leatherwork for sale."

"And I think you've arranged well for the boys' schooling while you work," I said. "The boys' tutor is doing a good job, and I'm glad they're learning tennis and swimming. I'll be here every other weekend to teach them to play baseball and the art and science of sailing."

As Christmas drew closer, the boys dropped hints.

"I could play baseball better if I had a new bat, glove, and ball, Daddy," Jerry grinned, grabbing a pastry one early December morning as I reached for a fresh orange.

"You're too easy," Warren chortled. "I'm getting a new saddle for Thunder! I'm riding in the parade, aren't I?"

"Hush, boys," Vivian scolded. "Let us eat in peace. Go entertain yourselves."

Both boys got what they wanted under the Christmas tree.

One February day in 1922, I opened the mail at the Warren Enterprises Key West office to find a letter from W. S. Meriwether. I hadn't corresponded with W. S. in some time, so I was surprised to see his name on the envelope.

Inside, I discovered a column he had written in his newspaper, the *Mississippi Sun*. W. S. had become known as "The Skipper" in Charleston, Mississippi, because he'd written so much about the US Navy. He was also the reporter who broke the story of the Navy's board of inquiry blaming Spain for the sinking of the USS *Maine* in Havana Harbor.

He had written a Sunday column, his "now it can be told" story of why the USS *Maine* had been sent to Cuba. W. S. claimed in his column that the ship had steamed to Havana because an assistant cable editor at the old *New York Herald* couldn't properly decode a telegram from one of their correspondents in Havana.

W. S. said a fellow reporter had sent this message: "Camera received but no plates, please hurry by next steamer." This indicated he had received a revolver in a parcel from New York but no cartridges. The correspondent wanted the weapon to protect himself because the Cuban capital was in turmoil.

The assistant cable editor on duty in New York translated the coded telegram to mean that the American consulate in Havana had been attacked. Within a few hours, Washington officials had learned of the message and ordered the USS *Maine* to sail.

Then on that fateful February 15 in 1898, the ship exploded. W. S. said the editor's error could be called the cause of the Spanish-American War.

My old friend included a short note to me: "Gunner, I discovered this a few years after the *Maine* was sunk. But even if I had known then, I probably wouldn't have said anything. All those poor men dead, you so fatigued and heart heavy—knowing wouldn't have accomplished anything. Anyway, I hope this finds you well. Thank you, my friend, for those good years of friendship when we were young."

I wrote him a return note: "W. S., old friend, I'm glad you didn't know then to tell me about the USS *Maine*. I'll always remember you as the reporter who dashed off to Labrador wearing a Palm Beach suit to meet Robert Peary on his return from the North Pole! Have you stopped shivering yet? Maybe someday we can take a break and meet again. If I make it to New Orleans to see my sister Louise, I'll let you know. Regards, Gunner."

Pausing, I turned my office chair around to stare at the framed photo that included my dive team at the scene of the *Maine* wreck in Havana Harbor. The dreams of the dead floating around me didn't come as frequently as before.

I took the column, opened the back of the picture frame, and placed the folded copy inside. Someday, maybe one of my family would find it.

Then I went back to the ship inventory reports. That didn't last long. I returned to the house, dressed casually, and went down to the dock where I kept my small sailboat, the *Ariel*. It was a beautiful day to let the lines sing in the wind and the sails snap their salute. The sea, fickle mistress though she may be, cleanses the spirit and leaves us whole again.

I didn't talk about it with Vivian, deciding that bringing such a tragic event into our lives again simply clouded the day. No amount of talking would bring any of the USS *Maine* crew back.

Fine times at Yankee Stadium

We spent at least half of the year planning our family trip in 1923. Yankee Stadium opened on April 18, and in the grand first game, the New York Yankees defeated the Boston Red Sox 4–1.

We were in Jerry Warren's Windsor box seats on the lower level and had the best hot dogs we ever ate.

"George Cornell," Jerry confided, waving his hand toward the upper levels, "was paid fifty cents per seat to install these 57,898 seats. Made a nice amount. Nearly $29,000."

I just grinned. Jerry always "had the scoop," as W. S. liked to say, down to the penny.

Warren and young Jerry were beside themselves with excitement. Warren tried to act more adult but twisted in his seat trying to see everything at once. Young Jerry like a jack-in-the-box until I touched his arm. I was just as excited. Vivian was in the middle of us with our wicker picnic basket, passing along Nathan's hot dogs, Coca-Colas, and Cracker Jack.

We stood at three o'clock when John Philip Sousa led the Seventh Regiment Band in playing "The Star-Spangled Banner." The players and dignitaries paraded around, and Babe Ruth was given a case with a big bat. New York Gov. Al Smith threw the first pitch.

Ruth hit a three-run homer into the right-field stands. And we were there to see it!

Nothing much in life can beat that day we had together.

Then Jerry and I did the business we had come to do. We had brought a letter of credit for $1 million for Jerry to invest in a New York property.

The world kept on turning

Our lives went on from day to day. Skip and I talked about a German named Adolf Hitler who attempted an insurrection against the Weimar Republic in November 1923. He failed. Even so, we speculated about Europe's stability.

The freight kept coming in, and we kept the money rolling in for Warren Enterprises.

The days rocked by with good business, the boys doing well in school, and Vivian enjoying the fashion industry. My boy Jerry was quite an athlete; even at age ten, he had good moves running to catch the ball, light on his feet and fast. He said he wanted to be like me and join the Navy.

"I think I see more Navy insignia in our future," Vivian smiled, rolling her eyes.

"It never left, my dear. I can still wear my uniforms."

"And you look wonderful in them!" she said promptly. "I'm just not ready to see Jerry wearing a uniform. Thankfully, he has some years to go, so I'm not going to worry about it now!"

Warren, our fifteen-year-old math genius, wanted to run a business. His grandfather was delighted. He wanted Warren to attend the best university for business, probably Harvard. My stepson also looked outstanding riding on horseback and competing in polo. Vivian wasn't certain she wanted Warren that far away at a northern school.

My goal was to work on what I could control in our lives. Jerry and I agreed that we could see the bottom dropping out of the sugar industry in the next year or so—too much competition, too many mills, and the price of sugar was falling. His eagle eye was on freight shipments and resorts. With a home in Havana and two in New York, he sold one to use the cash for other prospects.

President Calvin Coolidge gave the first presidential radio broadcast from the White House in December 1923. National news was on the airwaves.

"Coolidge is as dry as dust," Jerry opined, "but he believes in lowering taxes on wealthy Americans and regulating business and industry as little as possible. He's gold dust to us, Gunner!" And he laughed and poured a brandy.

The dock strikes in February 1924 proved to Jerry and to me, if we needed any proof, that we needed to keep our sails up and the wind behind us in our business decisions.

Prohibition wasn't significant in Havana or Miami, which is why Miami had become a boomtown. The population had doubled in three years because gambling and booze were easy to find.

We shipped load after load of construction materials, until

the transportation company owners met and agreed they had to embargo incoming goods except food to keep the grocery stores open and people fed.

Sometimes Mother Nature watches over us puny humans and decides to direct walls of wind and water to destroy our grandiose plans. That was the hurricane of 1926.

"The boom is over," Jerry said.

Jerry took a hard hit, and I was restive. I heard that an investor wanted to start an airline for mail and passengers and sought someone with connections in Cuba and South America. I went to find out about it and came back at age sixty-two with a job offer and a grand salary, plus a chair and office in the Pan American Airways building in Key West. Not that I was ever in it for long.

Wings over Cuba

My job was to secure airfields in Cuba and South America and to help get airmail and passenger service operating between Key West and Havana for Pan American Airways. We started with a small team.

In 1927, I had been building airports for two years for Pan American and the Cubans. My official title was marine inspector, but I did pretty much anything that needed doing. We had twenty-four airports on the island, and now my job was to improve the one in Key West.

When I flew back to Miami, I was transferred to Key West to get the operation up and going, along with my team. We had located a flat spot of sandy brush on the city's outskirts to create a landing field. On October 3, 1927, construction engineer F. J. Gelhaus and Captain J. E. Whitbeck watched over the crews as they set to work.

"We've got two weeks before we're scheduled to make the first airmail flight between Key West and Havana," I said to Shorty Palmer, one of the crew. "Anthony Fokker's tri-motor plane is going to land with US mail. We've got to work harder and faster."

We had a contract with the United States Post Office to fly the mail to Havana, and we had put up a bond to guarantee that we'd start on or before October 19, 1927.

The bond decision had been made above my pay grade. I knew from listening to Gelhaus and Whitbeck that Ed Musick kept coming up with reasons he couldn't get there in a plane from the Fokker factory in New Jersey.

When a reporter from the *Key West Citizen* appeared to talk to me, it was obvious we were up against it.

We met our deadline, and here's how we did it. We made a deal with Cy Caldwell, who was flying a little single-engine Fairchild on pontoons—the *Nina*—for the West Indies Aerial Express, to take the mail over to Havana. He was on his way down to the West Indies Company.

On the morning of October 19, we got the mail from the railroad station, and I had a US Coast Guard boat ready to take the mail to the *Nina* in the harbor. My friend Robert Boy of the post office was having a fit.

"You lose this mail, and I could lose my job, Gunner!" he said, almost choking.

"Calm down, Robert," I said. "Nothing's going to happen to the mail."

That evening, I had dinner with Vivian and Jerry and told them Cy took off from Key West at six thirty in the morning and traveled the ninety miles to Havana in two hours and forty-two minutes. That saved the contract.

"You won't do, Gunner," Jerry laughed. "I'll always want you on my side! Whatever it is!"

Then we got the next mail over nine days later, on October 28. Musick came in from New York with the Fokker F-7, the *General Machado*, on October 26. I had my photo taken next to the plane with some of our crew. I wish I'd kept a copy of that notable photo, but I didn't.

I decided to write my notes and put them in my scrapbook.

Musick made the first regular flight for a Pan American plane two days later, on October 28, 1927, and did it regularly for thirty days. Then he and flight mechanic Johnnie Donahue went north to get another plane, so Hughie Wells, a grand guy, flew for about a month.

We would have about 1,700 pounds of mail, and we'd make room for one passenger to squeeze in among the mail sacks. We tried to get somebody to go on most flights.

"Gosh, we are carrying a lot of mail!" I told Hughie. The post office gave us the first-class mail when it came in on the railroad, and the Cuba mail.

They wanted to add a radio to the plane; the dang thing weighed 172 pounds. I thought you could figure that wouldn't work. They had to build a new radio that was lighter.

Then Andre Priester, Pan Am's chief engineer, and Vic Chenea, the traffic manager, were there. Sometimes Chenea had to take the train to Miami, or to Jacksonville, to find some fellow going to Havana, then try to get him to fly over with us. We had to show we were carrying passengers!

Among the others down there were mechanics Stephen Whalton and Angel Alfonso. Well, we got everything running along smoothly, and she's been running along pretty well ever since then.

In 1930, I got the nicest letter from Colonel Sanguily. I placed it in my folder.

From: Cuban Army Air Corps
To: Chief of Bureau of Navigation
Subject: Lieutenant Charles Morgan, USN, retired; official record of.

1. Lieutenant Chas. Morgan, USN has been for the past three years employed by the Pan American Airways, Inc. During this period, he had done valuable work on the building of landing fields throughout the country which has been of considerable assistance to the development of aviation in Cuba and to his organization.

2. It is considered that (by) these activities Lieut Morgan indicates commendable initiative and cooperation and it is requested that a copy of this letter be attached to his official record.

J. R. Sanguily
Col. Chief of Air Corps

The day the stock market crashed

On October 24, 1929, the stock market collapse devastated families we knew. Rockefeller remained optimistic, saying he'd seen downturns throughout his ninety-three years and the economy always rebounded. Yet prices dropped; people held onto their money so they weren't buying products. Factories closed. Banks failed. Construction stopped. Farms went under.

People wouldn't invest or buy. I understood that. And I was darned glad I had gone with Pan American because even though global trade was down, we knew that the airports would be needed on the rebound.

President Franklin D. Roosevelt set up the Civilian Conservation Corps to provide jobs for men who had no money, no food, and no way to support their families. He tried farm subsidies, but many farms went under despite that effort. Slowly, the economy began to improve, maybe not because of what the economists said. People had to believe life would get better. Optimism will make a man reach into his pocket for five cents to buy a hot dog. That means the hot dog stand owner makes money. The cook makes more money. He moves out of his parents' house and rents a room. The landlord makes money.

I'm no economist; however, even I understand that.

A year of firsts came in 1930. Our son Jerry became a football star as a running back at Oak Ridge Military Academy in North Carolina. He graduated early at age nineteen in 1932. He wasn't big at five feet six inches tall and 120 pounds, but I can tell you he was lightning fast!

We attended many of his ballgames from 1930 through 1932.

It worked out okay with my Pan Am schedule because the worst storm weather was usually in the fall. You can't lay out airports in the mud. That meant I could take off work and ride the train to Oak Ridge for Jerry's football games, or I could catch a ride on a mail plane.

Warren worked in Havana with his grandfather, which was good. Jerry Warren wasn't quite as spry as he had been. He looked good, albeit a bit thin, and his dark hair was barely streaked with gray. He continued his evening brandy and cigar on the terrace in good weather, and in his study otherwise.

Jerry spent most of his time in Havana, and Clarissa stayed in New York. They seemed perfectly happy seeing each other every three months or so.

I certainly had nothing to say about them living apart since I was on the road for Pan Am half the year myself. Sometimes Vivian took the train to New York to join Clarissa at the townhouse. They'd go window-shopping, go out for tea, and walk in Central Park. Thanks to Jerry's caution with investments, even though Vivian's portfolio had lost some money, it was not anything like the other poor folks we knew with stock portfolios.

Well, I stuck with Pan American until 1937. I was seventy-two, and I was ready to sit on my front porch. We'd had great success getting the airports laid out, and it was time for someone else with a different set of skills to run the show.

There was another influence. A few months later in 1938, Jerry died suddenly of a heart attack. His valet found him on the bedroom floor.

"I can't believe it," Vivian cried into my shoulder.

"Me either, dearest." I stroked her head softly. "Maybe he didn't know he was ill, sweetheart."

We buried him with full Masonic honors at Colon Cemetery with the funeral procession beginning at our house.

Warren assumed the helm of Warren Enterprises and discussed moving to New York. He was twenty-nine, well trained, and perfectly capable.

I really felt my life was changing, and it was time for something different. Can you feel a shift in the universe sometimes? Like doors are opening or closing? Or a misalignment in the stars? I always have. Maybe it came from watching the horizon and feeling the shift in the wind at sea.

Vivian and I laid plans to travel together and see some of the states we hadn't visited before. We talked about another visit to New York to Yankee Stadium.

The universe and Mother Nature had different plans.

On a beautiful day, February 27, 1939, my sweet Vivian and I enjoyed a delightful dinner of fresh fish and fruit on the terrace, then went walking on the beach in Havana. That night, she became terribly sick. I knew it had to be the fish, even though I was not ill. The next day, I took her to the Anglo-American Hospital. She was so wan and weak by March 1; the doctors said to give it time, that she'd recover. She rallied, felt better, ate clear broth, and laughed a bit at the boys.

"You'll be home in no time," I promised her, kissing her hand.

Then suddenly, her fever spiked and her gut pain increased. The doctors thought surgery might be her only hope; they were concerned because she was so weak. I called her sister Sibyl in New York.

"Sibyl, I'm sorry to tell you, but Vivian is terribly sick. I think you'd better come down immediately." I hung up the phone and blinked away tears.

On March 12, the doctors operated on Vivian and found peritonitis from a pierced intestine, caused by a tiny fish bone. Vivian never awakened The next day, my beautiful wife took her last breath as I held her hand. Warren and Jerry stood at her right side, their hands lightly touching her arm, and Sibyl held her other hand. She was gone. Only fifty-seven, my sweet girl. This was not supposed to happen. So many years we had before us. How many sunrises and sunsets should we have had yet together?

I could not hear for the pounding tide in my soul, sweeping

my peace out to sea to sink into the cold depths. Warren and Jerry came to stand beside me as their Aunt Sibyl sank into the bedside chair and wept. Their hands on my shoulders helped.

Gently I laid Vivian's still-warm, frail hand on the bed. I felt my heart break as surely as a ship's great mast cracking in a storm.

I tried to plan her funeral. I couldn't think.

Sibyl said, "Let me do this, Gunner." She and Vivian's many friends took over the arrangements in our home.

We buried my Vivian at Colon Cemetery in the Masonic Mausoleum. I recall few of the details even today.

What more could happen? Ah, but you ask Fate, and she'll quickly answer.

Germany invaded Poland on September 1, 1939. War was coming. Again.

Jerry joined the US Navy Reserves. In a short time, he would be on active duty, fighting another war. The first day I saw him in his uniform, I squeezed my eyes shut.

"The sun is blinding me!" I said, blinking away tears I didn't intend to shed.

"I do look good, don't I, Daddy?" Jerry grinned.

Even though we'd talked long hours about what he would face, I knew that none of it would seem real until the day he saw the dead bodies of his friends and enemies. War is a terrible thing. Those who describe the glory of battle have never been in one.

I could not stand being at home when my son was fighting.

Photo courtesy of the Morgan family

Gunner Morgan was still dashing in his Navy uniform when he and his friend Henry Tresselt went to Washington, DC, to ask to serve during World War II. They were turned down by the Navy board, much to their disgust.

Photo courtesy of the Morgan family

Henry Tresselt and Gunner Morgan were both trained as gunners and served together before moving on to other duty assignments. They remained fast friends long after their military service was over. This photo of Henry Tresselt was in Gunner's sea chest and is dated 1885, Nagasaki, Japan.

"I must go down to the seas again, to the lonely sea and the sky,
And all I ask is a tall ship and a star to steer her by;
And the wheel's kick and the wind's song and the white sail's shaking,
And a grey mist on the sea's face, and a grey dawn breaking."
John Masefield, "Sea Fever," 1902

Chapter Seventeen

Old Sea Dogs

Henry Tresselt and I looked at each other as we sat on the park bench, watching young naval officers strutting by with their coats unbuttoned in the June heat in downtown Washington, DC.

"That just wasn't done at any of our stations," Henry said, rubbing his chin as he glanced my way.

"Because we knew what would happen if we looked that sloppy," I replied.

The newspapers had small communiqués the previous day, June 5, 1942, from Admiral Chester W. Nimitz, commander of the Pacific Fleet, that Japanese planes had attacked Midway Island and its Marine Corps garrison. On June 6, the newspapers' giant headlines proclaimed a victory "for US forces of apparent major proportions in defense of Midway and the whole, vital Allied supply lanes in the Pacific."

How many of our ships were lost that day? How many men sank below the waves to become shark fodder?

Our nation was at war, and we needed real military men to stand up to fight. Henry and I knew we could do it. There weren't many Navy gunners better than the two of us, even though Henry was eighty-two and I was seventy-six. We were in better shape than most of those young officers on parade.

I had sent a telegram to my friend Tyler Page, clerk to the minority in the US House of Representatives, asking him to please try to have me ordered to duty. Page wrote to Admiral Stark, US Navy chief of operations, on December 10, 1941, but I had heard nothing from it.

Henry and I were in Washington to ask the secretary of the Navy to let us back in to fight in the war. I knew I could lead a patrol off the coast of Florida.

Civilians were shocked back in April when people on the Jacksonville Beach pier saw a huge explosion out in the water. Then a German submarine surfaced between the pier and the burning ship, and the Germans used their deck gun to finish off the *Gulfamerica*, an 8,000-ton steam tanker loaded with furnace oil, en route to New York City. Until then, Americans felt safe; the war was in Europe, not here. The US Navy began convoys with attack planes overhead and fast ships running guard.

The German submarines were still out there lurking, waiting for freighters to come into view.

I had retired from Pan American Airways in 1937, and Henry had been deputy superintendent of the Oakland Street Department in California for many years. We'd done well, even though it would never compare to standing on the deck of a ship as the wind catches the sails or the great engines rumble to life.

Henry had brought his records showing that he enlisted in the Navy on October 10, 1876, when he was not quite sixteen years old. He got paid $9.50 a month and had to buy his own uniform. It was a long time, too, since I had enlisted in January 1882 in New Orleans to begin my life with the Navy.

We had some young reporter wanting to talk to us, the old salts. We could tell him a thing or two, like about the time I was honored to fire the first gun on the USS *New York*, Admiral Sampson's flagship, at the Battle of Santiago. The return Spanish fire blew my cap off my head and killed seven good men close by.

Henry had his own stories to tell. He survived the hurricane that hit Samoa in March 1889. We'd sailed in nearly every ocean and lived to tell about it. Many old friends weren't with us to tell their tales. They were buried at sea or on land with great monuments in their honor, or small stones in their hometown cemeteries.

"Congress is going to raise the pay to forty-six dollars a month, Gunner," Henry grinned. "We could get rich!"

"It's an election year," I said. "They won't want to take the youngest boys, even though they can be trained to be the best soldiers. They need us, Henry."

He nodded. "We used to send boys twelve years old to sea to learn to become midshipmen. Now we worry if they're eighteen or nineteen."

"The US Navy is getting soft," I said, tossing a few breadcrumbs from my sandwich to the birds that swooped down from the cherry trees.

We each had our ghosts. Henry was a gunner on the USS *Trenton*, a frigate that sailed into the harbor of Samoa fifty-three years earlier when the Germans wanted to take over the islands, and our American squadron and one British squadron sailed into harbor to stop them. Then on March 16, 1889, a hurricane hit Samoa. The *Trenton*, the *Corvette Van Dalia*, and other British and German ships were lost. So many men died that day in the storm. Henry made it to shore along with some other friends. They spent days pulling bodies out of the surf.

Henry and I met in 1891 when I was on the USS *Chicago*, one of the White Squadron warships. Some friendships are meant to be. Henry and I could finish each other's thoughts, and all it took was a little glimmer in his eyes or mine to know that we were chuckling at the world together. We had a signal when the heat was on; he'd point his finger at me and I'd point at him. It meant, "Shoot well and stay safe, brother."

Henry had retired as a warrant officer in 1895. He came back to help fight Cervera's fleet in the Spanish-American War. Henry was as good a gunner as I was—and we knew it. When you're good, you just are. You don't have to point it out. Every time we entered a Navy "big guns" contest, we won the match.

We both went back into the Navy for duty in 1917. I was captain of the Naval Yard at Key West. That was when I served in Thomas Edison's lab, working on smoke bombs, and had my clothes burned in a blast in 1918.

Now we were both lieutenants on the retired list, and Henry was a little upset with the Navy.

"Gunner, they asked me when I had my last checkup," Henry said. "I told them 1895, which they knew anyway—or should have known from my records. Then they said I wasn't in good enough shape. I told them any man who could fight his way across Constitution Avenue into the Navy Department was in good shape for active duty and didn't need a checkup."

"I know, Henry," I sighed. "They said the exact same thing to me. I sat there looking at that pasty-faced board of flabby bureaucrats and thought that none of them had ever climbed a ship's rigging in a gale or fought to bring a big gun into target range as the ship plunges through heavy swells. What do those bureaucrats know?"

"We can jump into this war like the others. As for the Japanese, I know how they think and how they react. I taught them how to shoot the big guns at the Russians," I said. "People are still talking about how the Japanese surprised the Russians in 1905. Why, it was the thirty-five US gunners who taught the Japs! We made the difference."

"I'm almost sorry I missed that little adventure," Henry laughed. "But not quite."

After serving in the American military for as long as Henry and I had, we knew that there was always a war somewhere, and our allies from yesterday could be our enemies tomorrow. That's the way of it.

Vivian had always loved it when Henry visited, even though

the times were spaced far apart with him in California and us in Havana and Key West. Some days I woke up thinking Vivian would be in our house singing somewhere, or out in the garden. She had been gone for three years, and I had moved to a smaller place at 126 Mendoza Avenue in Coral Gables. It was a nice apartment right off Ponce de Leon Boulevard.

Henry and I had a good time that day in Washington. He was lonely, as his sweet wife, Cora Marie, had died six years before.

You know, the Navy wouldn't let us back in. They kept those sloppy-looking young guys who needed to be taught to climb the riggings.

I took the train back home to Key West, and Henry caught a military flight back to Los Angeles. We wrote occasionally or called. That was my last meeting with one of my best friends, Skip being the other.

On the way home, I stopped by Skip's house in Jacksonville, Florida. He had done well for himself in his shipping firm and built a two-story house a lot like those in Key West, not far from the beach. From the second story, he could see the sunlight dancing on the curling waves.

We sat on the porch facing the beach and sipped cold tea that his daughter Cornelia brought to us. Skip's wife, Valerie, had died back in an influenza outbreak. He had raised seven children by himself. Three boys were serving overseas, and one, James, was a lawyer managing Skip's businesses.

"James couldn't go military after he broke a leg riding a horse and it didn't set right," Skip said. "I'll never forgive that surgeon for it. We had better ones in the Navy."

"You must be worried about the other boys," I said. "I worry about Jerry every day."

"Yes. It doesn't help, though. Robert is flying with the Air Force, and Samuel and Edmond went into the Navy. They'd hoped to stay together, but Samuel is on the USS *New York*—get this, as a gunner!" Skip grinned. "And Edmond is on the USS *Tennessee* as a navigation officer. Of the three girls, two have married and given me four grandchildren between them. Cornelia stayed with me. She's never married, said there aren't any men left here to marry. She keeps my house and hosts my business events.

"We watch the mail every damn day for letters from the boys, but the letters don't come often."

"No, they don't," I agreed. "I keep the few I've had from Jerry in my top drawer. Sometimes I read them again. It reminds me that he's still out there fighting, and until I know any better, I need to believe he's doing well."

I paused, and we watched a ship far out at sea on the horizon.

"Did you ever think we'd last this long?" Skip laughed, his red hair threaded with gray.

"Skip, I had my doubts," I smiled. "We were young and full of ourselves."

"Yet we weren't foolish," he added.

"No, we'd already seen rather much of life and death and the journey between one and the other," I said.

"You want to drop by the Solomon Lodge?" Skip asked.

"Not really," I said. "Half the men I knew are probably gone. If you don't mind staying here and watching the sea, I think this is the best entertainment."

"We're going to win the war," Skip said, musing into the sunset. "We have to win it."

"Oh, yes, we will," I agreed. "Yet we have lost so many men and ships already. Every day I open the pages of the *Miami Herald*, I see another list. Even though the Battle of Midway has been a turning point."

"Oh, yes. The Japanese lost four aircraft carriers and a heavy cruiser," Skip added. "The Navy's building ships so fast, the Japs can't keep up. The tides always turn."

We mused briefly over the ships we'd read about, and the battles near ports of call we'd docked in many times. We talked of the men sinking beneath the waves and offered a brief prayer for them.

Cornelia brought us rum cake and more tea as we sat at the

bamboo table. "Dad, you two are looking far too solemn to be sitting here together. Be glad you are both not on a ship! I certainly am!"

She looked stern as she placed her hands on her hips, and lovely in her light linen day dress with her curly red hair, her father's gift, pulled up on her head with Italian gold combs inlaid with coral and turquoise. Then she smiled at both of us, that smile I knew so well from Skip that encourages everyone around to feel better. I knew someday she would find the man she sought.

Cornelia patted Skip's shoulder. "I have correspondence to attend to today with my ladies' club. I'll leave you two to talk. Don't get too hot, Father." She left us to our reminiscences.

Skip chuckled. "She worries over me."

"Of course she does."

We turned our thoughts to Jacksonville in 1915, and the parade of the ladies of the evening at the park on that memorable March day of the mayoral primary runoff.

"There were some fine lassies there that evening," Skip guffawed, slipping into his Scots vernacular.

"There were indeed," I smiled. "Not that we looked!"

Skip laughed so hard he had tears in his eyes recalling our instructions not to look at native women's attributes when we were eighteen and nineteen years old sailing with the US Navy.

It was a great day together.

The war wore on. I went to Yank's Newsstand and the American Legion meetings as often as I felt like it.

The German subs roved up and down the Atlantic coast. The July 19, 1942, edition of the *St. Petersburg Times* proclaimed, "Ship Toll Passes 400-Mark."

At night, we could see ships burning at sea. The Nazi submarines had their torpedoes ever ready to sink ships loaded with oil and supplies. Bodies of seamen washed up on shore, most with terrible burns.

I decided when the injured arrived at the naval hospital that I would put in some time helping wherever I could, sometimes working in the hospital office with military records. Sometimes I just sat by the bedside of an injured, lonely seaman and talked to him for a while.

Finally, the war ended. Thousands of sailors were coming home to Key West. The American Legion welcomed as many as possible. The ladies planned Christmas trees for the hospital and a contest for the best one on the wards.

I felt sorry for the boys left stranded by Atlantic storms, trying to get home to their families. At least they were on ships headed for home. The ships were bringing about 50,000 military men a day into our seaports. I heard there were about sixty ships that couldn't be used to ferry men home because there were not enough crews. If they would just take a chance on us old men, we could bring those boys home.

So many war stories kept coming out, even though by that time the *Miami Herald*'s big headlines were given to the horse races. There was a young Navy pilot who was shot down, presumed dead, ended up in a Japanese prison camp, and came home to find out his wife had married again. She'd had their baby son and then married an Army sergeant. The pilot wanted his wife back. The sergeant had the marriage annulled. Life can be a mess at the best of times, and then toss in a war.

I celebrated Christmas Day at the American Legion; then I went home for a nap.

I'm not complaining about my life in Key West. It tickled me that people wanted me to do shows in art galleries of my ship carvings and paintings. I took some of my works to the antique shop, along with a few of the collectible Navy relics I'd saved.

About four days a week, I took the bus to Miami to Yank's Newsstand at the corner of Flagler and First Avenue.

"What?" Yank always demanded. "Are you back here again? Didn't I see enough of you last week?"

To which I always answered: "No, you didn't, and you know it. You'd miss me."

"Like I'd miss a bayou rat on my back porch!"

He poured me some coffee, snorted at his own humor, and sat on his stool.

Yank and I had a good time visiting. Sometimes I waited on a customer, and we discussed the latest gossip about town.

I snapped the newspaper out on my lap to read the day's headlines. My Panama hat kept my head from getting sunburned. My thick head of hair wasn't so thick anymore.

Still, sweat pooled at my temple on that day, June 24, 1948, and I whipped out my cotton handkerchief as I read the headlines. The Soviets had blockaded West Berlin, and the German people were desperate.

"And here we are today, Yank, with talk about how we'll put our Air Force to work airlifting food and supplies," I said. "Great Britain, France, and the Germans plan on joining the action."

"Of course we will," Yank replied. "We're not going to let the Soviets starve those people."

"It's better than another war," I said.

"Oh yeah," he said. "By the way, the Red Sox beat the White Sox 8–5."

I snapped open the sports page. "Yeah, well, the White Sox also beat the Red Sox 3–1. Look at those Dodgers—beat the Pirates in both games of the doubleheader.

"I still think of Christy Mathewson, Yank. That was a hard death, dying of TB the way he did, after the mustard gas got his lungs. It's been a long time, more than twenty years. He was a good man. He wouldn't still be playing now, but it would be good to call him up," I said.

"Ever thought about going over to the new NASCAR races in Daytona Beach?" Yank asked.

"Not really. I'd rather see a great baseball game."

I was long done with bringing entertainment to Key West. I could go to the baseball field, buy a hot dog, and watch the young stars on the field.

Sometimes I caught the next bus over to the movie theater. *On the Waterfront* was one of my favorites, with a cast that couldn't be beat: Marlon Brando, Karl Malden, Lee J. Cobb, and Rod Steiger. And the story was true. I had talked to more than one young sailor who started on the docks and got out because of the racketeering on the waterfront. It's easier to serve in the Navy than to be coshed because you wouldn't take a bribe to look the other way so a shipment could be stolen.

The Port Authority Police Department in New York and New Jersey was formed in 1928, and that cut down on some of the mob thefts. I suspected there was still plenty of chicanery going on. There will always be human wharf rats somewhere.

Times changed. I can remember a woman in Detroit making the sailors get off the boat so they wouldn't see her legs when she embarked. Short hair and cigarettes changed things. There's nothing less attractive than cigarette smoke perfuming a woman's clothes and hair.

I started making regular trips to check on my sister, Louise, in New Orleans, and took a plane to Memphis to visit my son Jerry, his wife Mary, and my two grandsons, Jerry and Charles. Love those boys! Mary had her hands full chasing them.

My friend Cecelia Knotts sometimes was my "date" to events at the park on sunlit days. We both had white hair that we didn't worry about. She laughed at me and said my eyes were still melting Italian.

"I'm glad you like my eyes, Ceci, and I'm glad I can still see with them," I said.

"Gunner, I wish I'd known you at age twenty-five! I'd have pursued you," she declared.

"No, Ceci, you wouldn't. Back then I was young, yes, but not the man you know now. Life has polished up my rough edges." I patted her knee and draped my arm across her shoulders as we listened to the band play John Philip Sousa for July 4. As twilight fell, the band played "How High the Moon," a new piece by Les Paul and Mary Ford. Young couples walked over to the concrete by the bandstand and danced with more energy than we had. We stayed on our bench and watched.

"Time was we could have danced that jig all night, Gunner," Ceci smiled.

"Time was," I agreed.

So many Fourth of July celebrations. And the bands play on.

I began having more trouble remembering things. Jerry wanted me to move to Somerville, Tennessee, a little town east of Memphis. His family lived in a house with white siding on a nice, tree-lined street with good neighbors. I'd have to consider moving someday. Meanwhile, I enjoyed my pineapple juice in the sunshine on my patio. I could still smell the sea air there and get a lift to the docks to watch the fishing boats come in at twilight.

Photo courtesy of the Morgan family

Gunner Morgan, in his nineties, sits in the sun in Somerville, Tennessee.

"A graceful and honorable old age
is the childhood of immortality."
Pindar

Chapter Eighteen

Going Home

"Mary," I said. "May I have more iced tea?"

"Of course you can!" She smiled at me and busied herself at the kitchen counter.

I thought back to my Vivian, who always had the teakettle on the stove, ready for me, and enjoyed sitting on the terrace at night looking at the moon. She might be directing Amalie or Carmela, yet Vivian made certain I had whatever I needed. So did Mary. I was a blessed man.

I had no regrets about coming to Somerville, Tennessee, to live. The view was different from my window. Jerry and Mary added onto the house for me so I'd have my own room and sitting area. I could sit in the shaded backyard or move to the front and lift my face to the sun. I felt like an old ship's cat sometimes, creaky in my joints and seeking warm sunshine.

The silly doctor in Miami assumed I was dying because I was ninety-one and older than swamp cypress. He told my family so they'd rush down to be with me. The news of my death was greatly exaggerated, to paraphrase Mark Twain.

With my son Jerry's attention and Mary's care, I could be here through the next war, though I wouldn't want to go to another one without Skip and Henry.

Each day I put on my white linen suit and Panama hat to walk to town. Sometimes I carried a cane to keep Mary happy because she worried about those spells where I was a bit lightheaded, but mostly I would swing it in my hand. Exercise is the key to a good life, and no alcohol or cigarettes.

I walked five blocks to the Reliable Furniture Store and commandeered one of the rockers. Usually there would be someone there to join me, also as old as cypress knees in bayou water. We'd shake out our newspapers, sharing pages, and generally find some tales to tell.

That Eldon Roark, a reporter with the *Memphis Press-Scimitar*, liked to talk to me about my life in the Navy.

"Are you ever going to get tired of my tales?" I grinned at him one day.

"No, sir," he assured me. "You keep telling them, and I'll keep sharing them. You are a legend."

"Old legends never die," I quipped. "You might have to start charging me ad space."

Sometimes I wondered if I was confusing dates. So every now and then, I'd pull out my scrapbooks that I had started in 1881 to remind myself.

Louise came up from New Orleans to see me. We sat in Jerry's living room while Mary brought us cookies and iced tea.

"When did your hair turn gray, Louise?" I grinned. "You've turned older overnight!"

Louise laughed and patted my hand. "At least it's gray," she said. "You have such a thatch of white hair, brother!"

She smiled gently at me. "Charles, I'm not sure how much time we have left. Are you okay with that? Are you ready to meet our Maker?"

"Sister, I couldn't ask for a better life," I said. "Who would have thought that I would do what I have done? I have no regrets, only an old man's dreams at night. I hope when I cross over that my old pals are standing on the ship's deck waiting for me to sail into that good night. I believe there will be blue skies and fair seas, with a light ripple chasing along the waves."

Louise smiled as her eyes glistened.

"We all die, sister. I have attended too many funerals of my friends. I've prayed over them, sung the hymns, saluted when the rifles are fired. Sometimes I wonder why I got left here. It would be good if we could choose the method of our going. In my journeys on the seas, I escaped death so many times. I won't get to choose, any more than any one of my friends chose theirs. It is enough to know that I have lived a good life. I'll be ready when it's time.

"Meanwhile," I grinned, "I have grandsons to talk to and tales yet to tell."

I held her hand briefly. "It is enough."

When Louise left, my grandsons, Charles and Jerry, sat beside me while Mary cooked supper.

"One day there was a young boy who wanted to go to sea," I began. "Overhead, the seabirds swooped and called. The smell of the sea swept over him, and in the hot, bright sun, he signed his name and walked on board, staring up at the tall masts. When the tide turned, his ship would set sail. Truly, he knew he was about to have an adventure."

Photo by Jacque Hillman

Charles Morgan found his grandfather's scrapbooks, lucky rabbit's foot, and other memorabilia in an old sea chest.

Photo courtesy of the Morgan family

Gunner Morgan went to live with Jerry and Mary Morgan in Somerville, Tennessee, in 1955. Here he is playing with his two-year-old grandson Gary in February 1959. Charles 'Gunner' Morgan died on May 14, 1959.

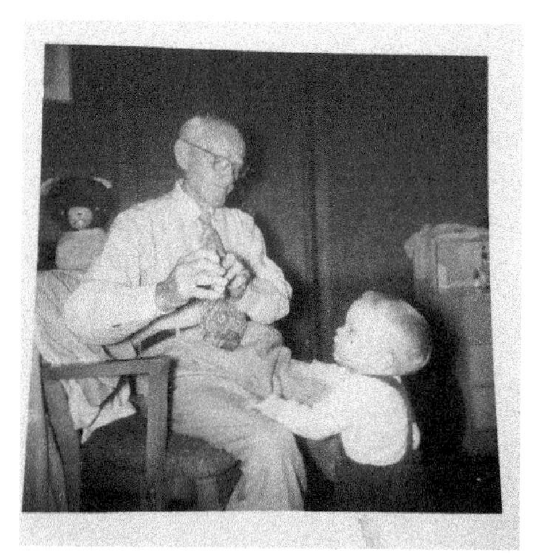

Epilogue

Written by Charles D. Morgan, his grandson

"Cap" placed a nickel and dime beside my brother's dinner plate and mine every evening. He had come to live with us at age ninety-one. My memories of Cap are those of a nine-year-old. Even then, I felt there was so much more to the old man, my grandfather. My curiosity was only beginning at age eleven, when he died just short of his ninety-fourth birthday. In the late 1890s, he was Gunner Morgan, "The Man Behind the Gun" and "The Man Who Started the Spanish-American War," highlighted in newspapers across the United States.

Most of what we learned through extensive research for this book had been forgotten or lost, and we uncovered some secrets. I had become the family keeper of his massive scrapbook of newspaper articles, gold pocket watch, and ruby ring. His home city of New Orleans presented him with a ceremonial sword that is now lost. At one time, my mother's lockbox held a signed letter from Thomas Edison thanking Cap for his assistance working on Edison's naval inventions. That letter disappeared, although we have a copy.

The newspaper articles were over 100 years old and fragile. I would carefully read through them, amazed at the historical content and thinking that his story should be told.

Then in 2009, I discovered that the upper tray to his old sea chest had fallen in and created a false bottom. Under it was another scrapbook filled with more exciting historical information, certificates from two presidents, a personal letter from Edison, and my grandfather's thirty-second-degree Mason certification.

At the height of the Vietnam War, I was on a long waiting list to join the US Naval Air Reserve. There was little chance of getting in until my father talked to the commander of the naval station, no doubt providing the Navy history of Gunner Morgan. I joined the next week. The stories passed down in my family that seemed too amazing to be true . . . were real.

CPSIA information can be obtained
at www.ICGtesting.com
Printed in the USA
FSHW020218050121
77376FS